POWDER

by

Leopold Borstinski

##

LOS ANGELES, SUNDAY JUNE 29, 1968

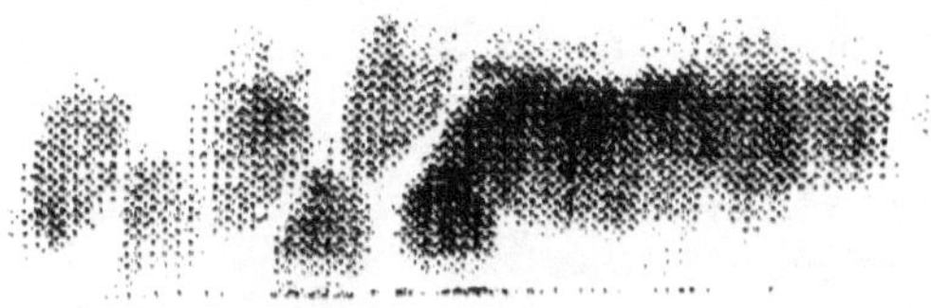

1

MARY LOU LAGOTTI drove at five miles an hour below the speed limit away from Burbank Airport. The first time since 1962 she felt alone, certain there was nobody on this planet who she could rely on for anything.

Always checking in the rearview mirror for signs of trouble, she headed to the Clements Fitzrovia Hotel. Occasionally, she'd glance down at her bloody skirt and glimpse the red ovals on her arms—the small globules of her husband's blood which had splattered over her while he was shot twice as he kneeled beside her.

Tears still dribbled down her cheeks as the shock and torment of those few moments juddered across her mind. No matter how much she concentrated on the road ahead, Mary Lou couldn't shake off the image of Frank bleeding out in her arms. Of her shooting the Fed before he arrested her. Of her zigzag escape from the parking lot that brought her to within three blocks of her current location.

She drove the green saloon to the back of the hotel and grabbed the two holdalls she'd stashed in the front passenger footwell. Mary Lou looked around, saw nobody and bent down to open the lighter bag and move its contents to its heavier twin. Then she zipped it shut and dragged it out the vehicle. She fingered every cent of the one hundred and forty thousand dollars contained inside. Laundered money from the robbery at the Lansdowne branch of the First Bank of Baltimore. And she was the sole survivor of the entire gang now that her Frank was no more.

Into a side door, Mary Lou hoped to find a service elevator but somehow she headed straight for the main reception area. She spotted the bellboy, Tom who strode over to her.

"Jeez, miss. What happened?"

"No time to explain, but I need your help."

"I'm not surprised. Housekeeping will be hard pushed to take those stains out."

Mary Lou looked down at herself and realized how blood-drenched she appeared. Never mind.

"Has anyone else been asking about us since we left this morning?"

"No, none."

"Good. I'll come down in ten minutes and I want you to call a cab and have him wait at the side of the hotel. Got that?"

"Sure, miss."

Mary Lou laid a clean Jackson on Tom who nodded, smiled and went off to find that taxi. Meantime, she hauled straight up the stairs to the second floor and then ran all the way to their room. She fumbled with the door key but after a lifetime the lock pinged open.

In front of the bathroom mirror, Mary Lou stripped out of her bloody clothes and stared at herself. Her legs and arms were splattered with too much blood. She used the shower attachment to wash away the red from her limbs but she still felt dirty inside. Unclean.

That unfathomable sense of disgust clung to her skin as she put on fresh underwear, a shirt, a pair of jeans and sunglasses. A walk around the suite enabled her to gather every ounce of possessions they'd scattered round the place since their arrival in LA. She stuffed all her clothes on top of the cash and shoved all Frank's things into the empty holdall. Mary Lou checked her revolver and filled the chambers with slugs.

One final trip around and by the time she returned to the bed, she knew it was clear. Another image flashed in her head as she recalled Anthony flying through the air with the force of the bullet slamming through his body. His death meant nothing to her—he was one of the thugs Uncle Frankie hired to hunt them down, kill them and return the money. The Shylock had played fast and loose and was left with bupkis. Not even his life.

Mary Lou reckoned the hit she'd arranged on Uncle Frankie must have been executed by now. All that stood between her and some kind of future was the New York mob and the Feds. Her best hope was to leave the country soonest and wait for the heat to die down.

One last check of herself in the mirror, Mary Lou grabbed the holdall and left the room. Down the stairs and into the lobby where Tom hustled over to her.

"The cab is waiting like you asked."

"Thanks."

"Is there anything more I can do for you?"

"No, you've been great."

She placed another Jackson in his palm.

"If anyone else comes wandering past asking questions…"

"…I know nothing."

"You said it. You keep your mouth shut. Even if it's the cops."

"Especially if it's the pigs."

She gave him a peck on the cheek to seal the deal. There's no way that sixteen-year-old boy would spill his guts even to a G-man.

Without turning her head backwards, Mary Lou strode out the Clements and into the back of the cab. It was less than thirty minutes since Frank drew his last breath. She sank into the rear as the taxi dredged its way to the depot.

She bought a ticket for the first vehicle leaving town. After only a quarter hour, she stepped onto a bus, shoved her bag in the overhead shelf and slumped into the aisle seat so no one could grab it without her taking direct action against them.

Ten hours later, she reached San Francisco where she laid overnight in a fleapit near the station. Her time in the city was uneventful but unpleasant. She picked her way past the hookers plying their trade as she entered the hotel.

The following morning, Mary Lou returned to the depot and purchased another ticket—with Vancouver as her destination. There was a two hour wait, so she trooped over to a diner to fill up on food. Her appetite was still shot to hell from the previous day's violence but she ate, anyway.

Thirty hours later and Claudia Starr stepped out into the Canadian sun. She showed her fake ID to cross the border so once the Feds identified her, they'd not be able to trace her departure from the land of the free.

As the mob used intel from the Hoover boys, Mary Lou figured the trail of carnage around the city of Angels would stop at the Clements Fitzrovia. Even if someone worked out she had made it to San Francisco, they wouldn't be able to follow her any further.

As she walked on the foreign concrete sidewalk, Mary Lou removed her sunglasses and tried to breathe and act like a normal person. Only trouble was: she couldn't remember how to do it.

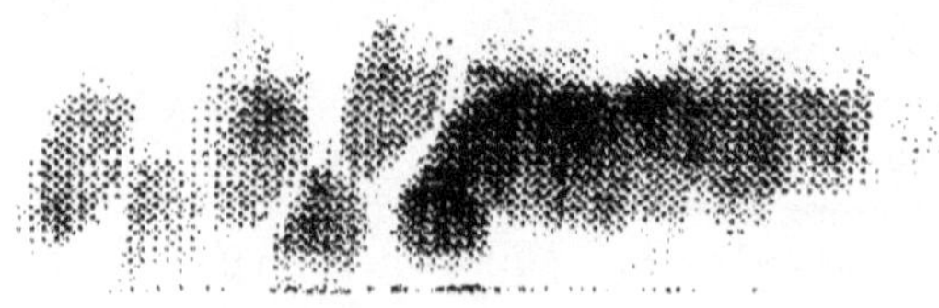

2

CHARLIE PENTANGELO ACCEPTED his mob money had floated into the wind. He was calm about not seeing the money ever again, but he continued to fume at the people who'd taken the proceeds of the heist from him.

As he never held the cash, he was no worse off than before the robbery was mentioned. The Shylock, Frank Lagotti Senior, felt differently. He had the money almost in his hand before his step nephew snatched it out of his grasp. The real issue for Charlie was that people shouldn't steal from him. Rob from a bank? Knock yourself out. Take from Pentangelo? Not if you want to see your next birthday.

Earlier in the day, word reached him about a gunfight in LA and how the Feds had done for his boys while they were trying to get the money back. Details were scant, but he knew the proceeds were gone and two of his own needed a funeral.

Now he sat on his own in his favorite chair contemplating his next move. Frank Senior had been wise to let his step nephew take the First Bank of Baltimore and its half a million even though the man himself was a parasite on the carcass of the world.

The phone rang.

"Hello?"

The voice on the other end of the line spoke flat, no intonation. Just the facts with no comment.

"The money has left Burbank Airport. Our two are deceased, the Shylock's men are offed."

"And?"

"Our FBI sources confirmed Frank Lagotti and one unknown guy are dead. The woman took the proceeds and ran. She is still at large."

"Any good news for me?"

"Nothing to put a smile on your face."

"Keep me informed."

Charlie heard the click of the receiver as the call ended. That girl, Mary Lou, held his cash and would need to pay for her mistakes. The phone rang again—a different voice on the line.

"Bad news, Charles."

"What now?"

"There's been a death."

"Who?"

"Frank Lagotti Senior."

"The Shylock? How?"

"Bullet through his face."

A professional hit.

"Any idea on the perpetrator?"

"Not yet but we're working on it."

"Where did the deed take place?"

"In his cathouse. No struggle. The hitman walked in, plugged Lagotti, did for the girl sat on his dick and strode out. Too much of a coincidence for Lagotti's murder to occur the same day as the fracas in LA. Make some enquiries. I want to know more details."

Pentangelo waited ten minutes and dialed a special number—it was never written but always memorized by those who used it. When serious men needed professional help to complete their murderous tasks, they contacted Murder Inc: the nickname for a unique group of killers who originally came out of Brooklyn. These fellas were the most dangerous the mob families knew. If anyone would take out a hit on someone outside their territory, these were the people to call.

Charlie booked a requisition on the head of Mary Lou and it was immediately sanctioned even with a specific request. He wanted the best man for this job: Arnold Roach. A killer's killer. An elite fiend with a knife or a gun. A relentless murdering machine. Once you hired him, he never gave up. Whoever he held a contract on always wound up demised.

As the sole survivor of the heist, Mary Lou must take responsibility for all that has happened: to the money, to the men and now to Frankie. Roach would track her down and slash her throat. Or cut her open from one side to the other. Whatever Charlie wanted.

Safe knowing Roach was on the case within a matter of hours, Pentangelo put on an aria on his record player and settled back down in his chair. Mary Lou was as good as dead.

MONDAY JULY 7, 1968

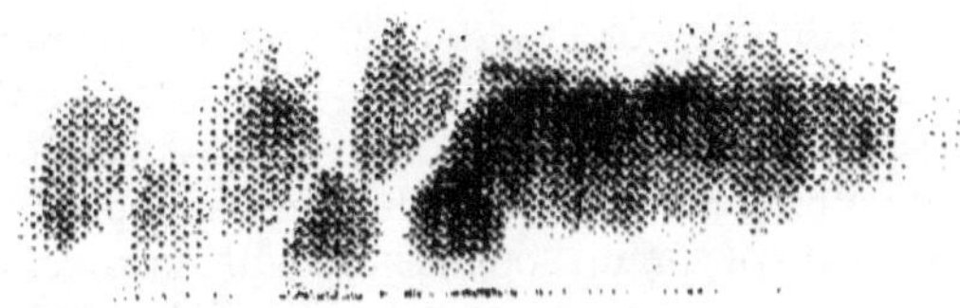

3

THERE HAD BEEN a Murder Incorporated since the day the Big Bankroll formed the Five Families back in the Thirties. Out of Brooklyn—and only Jewish—mobsters turned to these guys when violence between clans was required.

When not wreaking revenge on those they were paid to kill, the members spent their time playing penuckle and performing freelance assassinations instead. Arnold Roach was the best of the baddest and you could always rely on him to get the job done quickly, effectively and without leaving a trace of his passing through town.

As a result, he had little time to engage in extracurricular subversion but, and for the right price, he'd lend a hand to a stranger. A month ago Roach received a call from a woman seeking revenge on a moneylender. He never wanted to know the justification for his services being rendered. It was of no concern to him what the beef was about. He would happily kill anyone who moved, provided there was green in it for him.

The Shylock was based in Baltimore and the down payment arrived as requested. When the time was right, he drove down to the city, found the middle-aged man in his flophouse and shot him in the face.

Standard terms applied and Arnold waited a week for the second half of his money. He had learned to leave several days before getting the final payment as word needed to spread sufficiently far for his employer to hear the good news about the demise of their nemesis.

But the money didn't appear. One day late was of no concern to him as he was off on Murder Inc business and did not return home until a further two days. The absence of an envelope primed with cash caused consternation, but nothing more. Once a full week had lapsed, Roach was like a bear with a honeypot jammed on his nose with an angry bee inside.

Arnold sat in his armchair with one eye on the fire escape and the other on the door. The leather surface leaned him comfort, but he gritted his teeth every time he thought about Mary Lou and Frank Lagotti Senior.

The walls closed in so he grabbed his wallet, keys, checked his jacket holster and headed onto the street. Round the corner was a little cafe where everyone minded their own business and nobody listened too carefully to the conversation of adjacent customers.

Arnold strode to his usual location—at the back, half in shadow and an extra five inches from any other table in the joint. The owner ambled over and placed an espresso by Roach's elbow, who nodded and let the world pass him by.

He had been a fool: why take a job away from home and from a virtual stranger. Roach knew the answer before the thought had tripped out his head. Because the money was good and she was a woman aggrieved.

Something about her voice when they first spoke made him agree to the proposition she lay before him. Killing the moneylender didn't cause him a moment's lost sleep—before or after the event. There was an angry edge to her tone which screamed out how much she wanted the guy to suffer before he died.

Roach wasn't in that business. He was a murderer, not a torturer, and made that clear to her before they struck their deal. If Mary Lou was dissatisfied with the job he performed, she should tell him and they could discuss the matter but her absolute silence? That showed she'd flown in the wind.

And there was no way he could allow someone to fleece him. If word got out you could stiff Arnold Roach, his professional reputation would be over. Kaput.

He swigged down his coffee and headed back to his apartment. Arnold would have to find the woman and extract his money from her. If the cash was not forthcoming, he'd put a bullet between her eyes. Sometimes life can be as simple as that.

SATURDAY OCTOBER 20, 1962

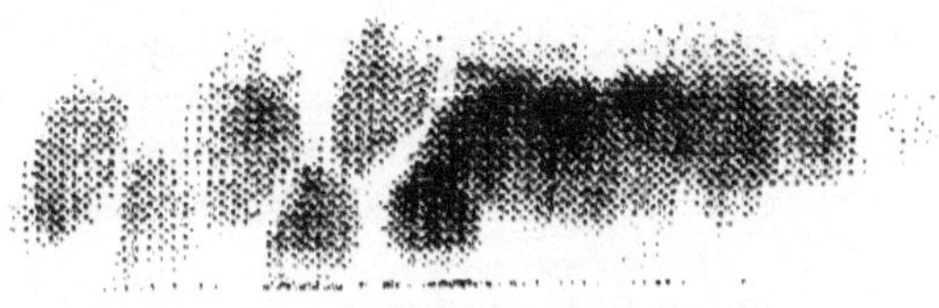

4

MARY LOU BELLE left home when she was fifteen and never looked back. Her mother, her sisters and her cold dead father ceased to feature in her existence from the moment she walked out the family bungalow and into the world. She headed straight for New York but never got there, instead alighting upon Atlantic City and, when the chips were down, over to Baltimore.

As a girl with no book learning, Mary Lou mixed with the wrong sorta guys because they were the only kind who'd give her the time of day. She paid no tax, and she surrounded herself with interesting characters from the dark side of town—a place she'd lived for six years.

One Saturday, her closest girlfriend suggested they go to a neighborhood party and Mary Lou agreed. What better excuse to drink too much and enjoy the laughs and indiscretions of youth?

She shared a fleapit apartment with Vicky Fischer. They'd met within a few days of her arrival in the city and split the rent for living quarters two weeks later when she grew tired of sleeping on strangers' floors and became disillusioned with sleeping in strangers' beds.

The party was one block from home—a neighborhood affair—and Vicky assured her there would be some fresh meat as well as the local boys. Mary Lou'd had her fill of the juvenile young men, who frequented the dive bars near the apartment. They never showed the level of seriousness nestling deep inside her own heart.

When she and Vicky arrived at around eleven, they discovered a full living room heaving with people and a kitchen rammed with liquor. The perfect combination. They remained a close partnership for the first thirty minutes to ensure no octopus hands got fresh while the night was still young.

After midnight, different rules applied and they split up. Vicky hunted for Jamie, a sweet kid with his own Harley. Mary Lou spent an hour chatting and dancing with a string of guys but none of them held her attention for longer than the record took to play.

One fella caught her eye. He sat on the edge of an armchair, laughing with another guy. The way he rested on the end of the furniture grabbed Mary Lou's attention. Self-assured but not arrogant. Grounded. She headed past the two of them, wending her path among the herd of twentysomethings congregating inside this single apartment.

The men were laughing about who knew what and she stopped as she sauntered by, clinked a glass with the brown-haired one and joined in the conversation.

"The thing is, you know…"

Calling it a conversation was generous: these were drunk musings and no more, but Mary Lou enjoyed hearing him talk and she enjoyed looking at his body, hidden under a skin-tight white tee shirt and a pair of jeans. Nothing special: like he was trying to appear as though he hadn't tried at all. His friend wandered off to get more drink.

"I'm Mary Lou."

"Frank."

A clink of glasses again.

"You from round here? I don't think I've seen you in the neighborhood."

"Lived here for years but I have been… away for a while."

She recognized that code. Jail, but the guy was an attractive felon. She liked the sparkle in his eyes and the muscles of his upper arms. And the small twitch in the corner of his mouth as he tried to smile but didn't know how. She understood that facial tic only too well.

"I moved here two weeks ago, so that explains it."

"Sure does."

Mary Lou was leaning on his shoulder: her heels were hurting and, besides, she wanted an excuse to touch him.

"You wanna dance?"

She nodded so he grabbed her hand and they walked a few feet to where the rest of the room was gyrating to the beat of the music. Mary Lou and Frank hopped from one foot to the other for over half an hour. Occasionally, she'd lean into him and say something in his ear and he would respond. Twice he did the same.

They smiled, laughed and danced. Like everyone the world over, each checked out the other to decide if they were attractive for more than a boogie with or without booze.

Some wise guy changed record to a slow number and half the people moved to the edge: either not drunk enough or not interested in getting that close to their current dance partner. But they stayed on. She took a step towards him and Frank placed an arm behind her back. She laid her head on his shoulder and she felt his chin on her hair.

Frank's thumb stroked her neck—slow, slow—until little tingles erupted from the point where he touched her. She nuzzled closer and he put his other hand on the lower portion of her spine.

Three-and-a-half minutes later the music stopped but Mary Lou and Frank remained stationary. She turned her head to look into his eyes and their mouths touched. All around them bodies jumped, hopped and wriggled to the fast tempo but they continued as they were: kissing and stroking, enveloped in the moment between them. She looked to find the world had moved on and she parted their lips and smiled at him.

"You wanna go somewhere quieter so we can talk?"

"Sure thing, babe."

Mary Lou stole some red wine from a nearby table, led Frank out the party and over to her apartment. She opened the bottle and poured two glasses but they never got to consume them. Instead, by the time Vicky came home three hours later, a spent condom lay on the floor and snoring emanated from the room.

SATURDAY OCTOBER 27, 1962

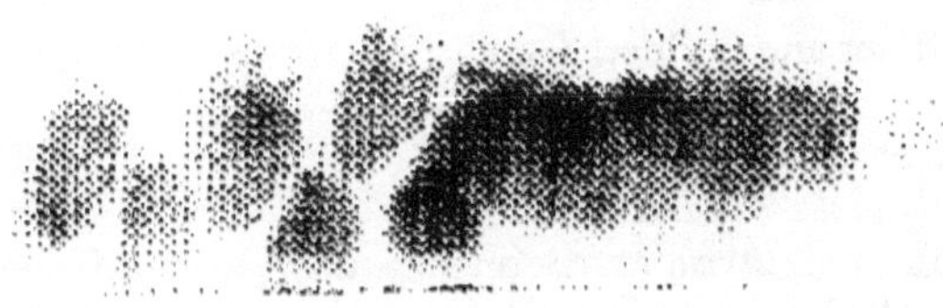

5

NEXT DAY, FRANK left early but not before he scribbled down an address for Mary Lou to find him if she wanted. Under any other circumstances, she'd have scrunched the piece of paper into a ball before going to the stove to make herself a morning coffee. But she had to admit this man was different.

Although she couldn't pin down what it was about him, he made her feel something: an emotion. Not that she'd hit the sack with him on the first night. Mary Lou had done that countless times before. What else was the point of going to a party? The difference with Frank: there was more to the experience than the thudding scream of an orgasm in her head spread across her entire body.

Despite only being with the guy for a few hours, she felt a strong affection for him. Crazy. And he fit so well inside her too.

On Monday she found the address he'd given and popped over. When she buzzed the apartment, a different male voice told her to wait. Then Frank appeared about thirty seconds later.

"Hi."

"Hiya, babe. You free for a coffee?"

She nodded and they headed to a place round the corner and chatted for an hour. The man explained how he wasn't getting on with his step-dad otherwise he'd have invited Mary Lou in.

"I understand. Families are strange beasts. Never trust a step-parent."

Frank eyed her and nodded. Conversation twisted and turned until his time was up.

"I gotta go or I will get shit at home."

"Sure. Why don't you move out?"

"It's complicated. If you're free on Saturday, we could have a bite to eat and I'll tell you all about it."

She thought for less than half a second.

"Yes. I'd like that a lot."

TO SAY MARY Lou thought about nothing else until the weekend would be an obvious lie. The woman had a job to hold down and weekdays were filled with the dullness of life. But to say she pushed the date to the back of her mind would not be true either.

By the time Saturday arrived, Mary Lou knew exactly what she would wear: dress, panties with matching bra and heels. She'd considered hair styles and nail polish. The whole enchilada.

Frank chose a local pasta joint for their rendezvous and they settled into a corner table, sitting on adjacent sides of the square surface. He ordered a bottle of red and she suggested a glass of water on the side. First order of business was to scan the menus for something worth eating.

"I'd recommend everything. There are no bad dishes here."

"Come here often with your lady friends?"

"Don't be like that. The food's good is all."

She squeezed his nearest hand while it held the menu.

"Only teasing, Frank."

He emitted another of his trademark side-of-mouth tics and she knew all was fine. Food ordered and drink delivered, they began the serious business of conversation.

"So where are you from?"

"Away from here. There's nothing to tell."

"Really? What about family?"

"I'm an orphan."

"Wow."

"Joking. My family's dead—or at least dead to me. Papa died when I was in diapers and he really is deceased. I have no idea about my mama and anyone else. Left home when I was fifteen and never looked back."

"What made you leave so young?"

"God and his minions."

She laughed, aware this trail of conversation could only lead into a dark, cold place she didn't want to enter.

"Jeez."

"Fuck him too."

Frank let go her hand and pulled a quizzical face.

"I didn't mean to touch a raw nerve. Sorry."

"Don't be. Not your fault, but some stuff will never be right."

"Say that again."

"And what's the deal with your step-dad?"

"The usual story, I guess. Mom remarried after my dad died. Mysterious circumstances they said, but he was with the mob so you join the dots."

"Fuck."

"Yep. And mom found herself a loser and I don't mind reminding them of that every opportunity I find. Means I'm not popular at home."

"So where do you spend most of your time because it ain't going to be in the bosom of your family? Do you seek out other bosoms instead?"

She tittered and squeezed his hand again. The comment was a joke although she was intrigued to know how much he slept around. Vicky said he was a small-time crook fresh out of jail but she didn't mind. To her, Frank had some oomph. More than most of the schmucks she bedded with since she arrived in Baltimore.

"Nothing wrong with seeking solace in a bosom, Mary Lou."

Another twitch at the side of his mouth.

"And what you get up to when you don't have your head nestled in a bosom?"

He laughed.

"There haven't been too many bosoms in my life. Some, but not many."

"We'll come back to that."

"Sure. I'm between jobs right now but I am cooking up an interesting project with a friend of mine."

"Oh?"

"Yeah. Me and Louis think we can make ourselves some easy money at a drug store or two."

"Is that how you see yourself making a living. In drug stores?"

"God no. I've got plans. Build some seed capital and invest it wisely in a convenience store. Then who knows?"

"I'm sitting beside the next Rockefeller?"

"Next Dillinger, babe. There's a difference. I won't rob from poor people. That's not right."

"I love a man with principles."

Mary Lou leaned over and pecked him on the cheek just as their antipasti arrived.

AT THE END of the meal, Mary Lou offered to pay but Frank had none of it. She thanked him and they sauntered out the restaurant and walked down the block, hand in hand.

"Fancy going to a pool hall to hang with the fellas, babe?"

"I'd rather hole up in a bar and have another glass. Or we could pop to my place…"

He smiled a full-lip toothy grin.

"I hoped you'd say something like that."

With a quickened pace, they headed to her apartment where Vicky sat in the living room reading a magazine. One minute's conversation and Mary Lou and Frank closed her bedroom door behind them.

They threw off their clothes and, once in bed, investigated each other's bodies. The previous week had been a drunken express train of a fuck. This time, they were more sober and more interested in discovering the other as a person.

After much kissing and licking, Frank found Mary Lou's tattooed rose, an inch below her belly button. She liked the way he didn't ask her about it like everybody else did. He accepted its existence and moved on up her body until she felt his groin near her thighs.

Then it was over before anything had begun. Frank squeezed her breast, rolled over and went to sleep. As he snored, she finished herself off and lapsed into unconsciousness too.

November 1968 to November 1969

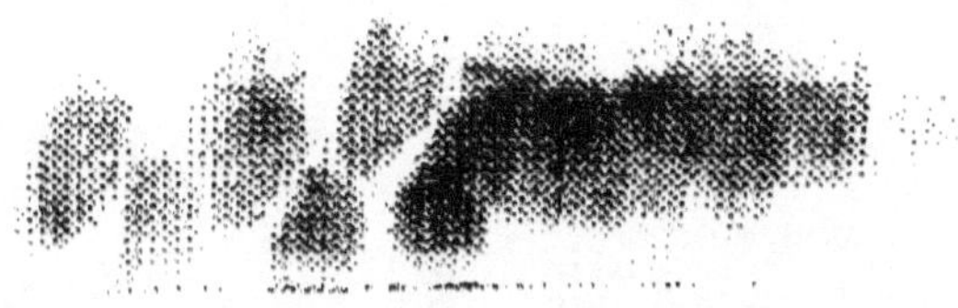

6

CLAUDIA STARR MADE a new life for herself in Canada. When she stepped off the coach, she swapped two hundred dollars for Canadian and vowed not to do it again. Her accent was a big enough giveaway she was a foreigner without turning up at a currency exchange screaming out to the world she was an American.

She considered traveling to the far side of the country in case the Feds or the East Coast mob followed her, but she realized this was paranoia. Mary Lou changed coach en route from LA to Vancouver so there was no way anyone could guess where she ended up.

A year and a half later and not a solitary fat soul turned up in Canada seeking to chase her down. Her escape was complete. She spent the first two weeks in a hotel and found a job working in a dress store. With a paycheck in her back pocket, Claudia rented a one bed apartment on 13th Avenue and Victoria Drive—in between Clark and John Hendry Parks on the east side of the city.

She kept to herself in the evenings, not wanting to make any mark in this foreign community. Within two months she came down with a bad case of morning sickness and she visited a local doctor to find out what her belly and sore nipples already told her: pregnant.

With Medicare not implemented in Vancouver, Claudia worked her ass off to get the money to fund her antenatal care and the delivery itself. In the third trimester, her bump was kicking away in all directions. Three weeks before her due date, she gave birth to Alice and Frank Junior.

WITH THE NEEDS of her two children paramount in her mind, memories of Frank and the loss she felt over his death faded fast. There was no time to pander to her own emotional state.

By the summer, Claudia had organized a schedule at the store which gave her sufficient money to get by and had kept in contact with some women in the maternity suite from the hospital. They were all married and sympathetic to her plight and the old lady who lived on the same floor in her apartment block agreed to look after the twins when she worked.

She was on as even a keel as any single mother with two babies could be, living in a strange city in a foreign land. But she kept her head down and plowed on through these worst of times.

One ray of happiness Claudia gave herself every week was a trip to a park. The area was ripe with gang related violence which ensured inquisitive folks stayed the hell away. This was the perfect cover for Claudia as her discovery was always around the corner.

Given her background—and the fact she walked with a double buggy— she didn't bat an eyelid when a few young guys up to no good appeared to hang out near the swings. They knew better than to hassle a dame with babies. And if they tried anything, she'd have plugged them full of lead.

Over time, the boys acknowledged her presence and she would listen in on their conversations—not that they were interesting, just different from the domestic chaos that engulfed her daily.

They talked about who did what to whom and the hourly travails of teenagers, nitpicked to within an inch of its life. She smiled inside as their chat reminded her of the snatches of conversation she'd heard when she used to go to school. Before she left home and met Frank and everything seemed to be so simple.

Even though it was too early to say, Alice looked like Mary Lou and Frank Jr was the spitting image of his father. At least, that's what Claudia thought as she watched the two asleep in their cots. Her daughter was four minutes older than her son and Claudia knew this would be a bone of contention between them some day.

In the meantime, she worked hard in the store, grabbing any shift going, and when she got home, she'd slave away to make her children happy. Although she hadn't considered herself someone with a strong maternal instinct, truth was she would do anything to protect her two darlings.

The apartment itself was too small for three people but it was the best she could afford. Violence erupted on the streets most nights but none of it affected her. She watched from a window as one young man beat on another or a car was broken into. Cheap robberies by little hoodlums. Nothing to get worked up about.

Anita on the other side of the corridor complained how the neighborhood had gone down hill. She pretended to empathize to keep in Anita's good books, but none of it bothered her. This wasn't her place; this hadn't been her home for thirty years.

As the twins put on weight and grew, Anita felt more comfortable looking after them. So much so that by winter, Claudia went out once a week. She found a bar one block south with leather seated booths and a slightly older crowd who were amiable enough to welcome her into their fold. Her story was known around the neighborhood and Faye was a friendly face in the tavern.

"How you get through the day beats me."

"Oh, you do what you have to, right?"

"Sure but—I'm not being rude—I don't think I could cope with two kids under one by myself without a man to help."

"And David helps with your brood, does he?"

Faye thought for a minute, sipped her beer and laughed.

"Hell no. He's about as useful as a prophylactic with a hole in it, which come to think of it is how we got our third to turn up in the first place!"

They chuckled at the futility of the male of the species and Claudia carried on as the poor girl with the dead husband and twins.

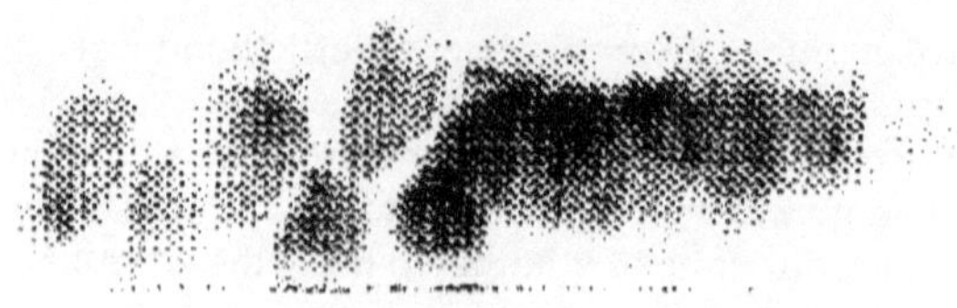

7

CLAUDIA HANDED THE kids over to Anita and traveled to work. It might have been in November but the same set of events recurred daily. The drudge of keeping a low profile bore down on her. The weight of knowing she was a stone's throw from living the high life dragged her feet along the floor.

Alice and Frank Jr were beautiful, wonderful, fabulous sparkling lights in her world. But they couldn't talk and didn't know or care about her troubles. She loved them with all her might but they weren't enough to fill the void in her existence. The gap left by Frank and the absence of spending opportunity offered by the money she kept at the back of her wardrobe, hidden behind a coat and two long dresses.

If she moved somewhere else in this country, she would face the same set of problems. Her accent would make her a stranger and an avalanche of questions would follow. Then she'd find a crappy job so no one would see how much she really had. Here, in the east side of Vancouver, was as good as anywhere.

Claudia kissed Alice and Frank Jr goodbye, thanked Anita for the millionth time in her life and walked down the stairs, off to the Courtney Boutique where Mrs. Courtney held sway over the middle-aged women in the area.

The woman had been kind enough to offer her a job, so there was gratitude at the heart of the relationship but Courtney paid her bottom dollar as there was no better option available. And they both knew it.

One side benefit was the gossip Claudia overheard as she helped dress the ladies or hang back the clothes once they were done. The great thing about women of a certain age—irrespective of demographic, race, creed or color—was their insatiable desire to dig up shit on those near to them. If anything happened in Clark Park, that boutique knew about it almost before it had occurred.

"Did you see that out-of-towner in McAdams last night?"

"Who?"

"A new guy's moved in on 12th and Commercial."

"Do tell."

"I don't know much, which is why I was asking you."

"Oh."

Disappointment in that voice as the customer who'd picked up three jumpers and dumped them back down in a messy pile, carried on perusing the merchandise.

"He's handsome, I'd say. If you like a man in his forties."

"They have seen the world."

A titter.

"Not just the world if you get me."

Another giggle as lewd thoughts permeated across both minds.

"If I wasn't married, I'd be in the market for a dishy guy who knows his way around."

"Wouldn't we all, darling?"

"Where's he from?"

"Dunno but he sounds as though he's from over the border."

"You've spoken with him?"

"Oh no, but I heard him pay for his groceries in the convenience store."

"Well I never. An American in Rain City."

"Don't be like that."

"I'm kidding with you. Tell me more."

"For a guy just arrived, he was well dressed: three-piece suit. And it looked expensive."

"Anyone know what he's here for?"

"Nobody I've spoken to yet."

Claudia's ears pricked up when she heard about a stranger in town and they almost ripped off the side of her head when she heard about the suit. Only Rockefeller and the mob wore a vest…

She told herself to remain calm because the evidence of a gossip was not the best place to start a panic attack. Her stomach muscles tightened and she took herself off to the bathroom for five minutes to recover.

Two nights later, she sat opposite Faye, each with a beer in the hands.

"Have you heard about the new come-over who's moved in down the block?"

"Someone in the boutique mentioned it. You?"

"Bumped into him by the oranges."

"Say what?"

"At the grocers. He's a man who does his own shopping."

"What a modern world we live in."

A chuckle.

"What's he like then?"

"He looks dapper. Wears smart clothes with oil in his hair. Nice hands: clean fingernails."

"Huh?"

"You notice these things when you're both trying to grab the same clementine."

"And he's definitely a come-over?"

"Has an accent, so he was definitely born in the US. Hey, you might know him."

Claudia stared into her beer and counted to five. The next words were uttered with as much calm as she could muster.

"What makes you say that?"

"No reason. It's a small world though, isn't it?"

"Yep."

"If I see him again fondling fruit, you want me to hook you guys up?"

"What? Hell, no."

"What's wrong?"

"Nothing. Sorry. Just not been a good day. Kids were crying and wouldn't settle."

"Must be tough what you're going through."

Claudia nodded.

"You have no idea how difficult it is being me."

Faye smiled not understanding how deep a truth had been uttered.

"What else you picked up about him?"

"I wasn't sure you'd be interested."

"It's not that I don't want to know about fresh blood on the block. I said I didn't need you making an introduction."

"Polite. Lovely fingers. You can tell he's a white collar fella."

"Did he mention what he did for a living?"

"Well enough to afford a sharp suit."

"Seriously."

"Salesman. Sold typewriters."

"You've got to shift a lot of them to make any money."

"Maybe, but he looked like he was doing all right for himself. Did I mention he wore a beautiful hat?"

"No. That makes all the difference."

They chuckled and Claudia moved over to the bar to get another round of drinks in. This also gave her a chance to ponder the information she had on the guy. The more she thought, the greater her anxiety grew.

If he looked like a mobster and he sounded like a mobster then the chances were: he was a mobster. The time had come for Mary Lou to get the fuck out of Dodge.

MARY LOU CARRIED on talking with Faye as long as the beers lasted despite her overwhelming desire to flee. Nothing screams out guilty more than a woman running away for no obvious reason.

Around eleven, Faye called it a night as she received a glance from David that said it was time to go home. They hugged goodbye as they left the bar and Mary Lou walked off without looking behind. As soon as she'd turned the corner, she picked up the pace and scurried in the opposite direction to the apartment. She checked out every vehicle she passed until she found one to her liking.

Opened handbag. Removed a hat pin. Door lock unpicked. Forty seconds later, the engine roared into life and she drove it home. A race up the stairs and she stopped to catch her breath. She snuck past Anita's door so she could get into the apartment and deal without the twins. A suitcase stuffed with clothes. Bags filled with everything else and downstairs to shove it all into the trunk.

Back upstairs. Mary Lou leaned against the wall next to Anita's. Breathe, babe. The woman knows zip and all you are doing is getting your kids like you've done every week for months. She reminded herself there was nothing special about today.

Rat-a-tat-tat.

"Hi there. Hope I'm not too late."

"Of course not dear."

Anita walked away from the door, letting Mary Lou follow her in. The twins were asleep on a mat rolled out for them.

"Have they been any trouble?"

"Not at all. Slept all night."

"Good. Thanks. For everything."

"Huh?"

"Nothing. Same time next week?"

"You betcha."

Mary Lou scooped up the sleeping babes, one in each arm, so their heads flopped onto her shoulders. As she left Anita's, Alice curled an hand around Mary Lou's neck and Frank Jr gurgled contentedly near her ear. She walked toward her apartment and fumbled a little to poke the key in the lock —to give Anita enough time to close her door behind her.

As fast as she could without waking her bundles of joy, Mary Lou slipped downstairs and flopped them into the back seat. She shoved a blanket over them so they didn't get too cold, got into the driver's seat and headed out of town.

Throughout her life with Frank as they fled across country, a simple mantra echoed in her skull: never go over five miles below the speed limit. She hoped the car wouldn't be missed until the morning to give her enough time to leave the vicinity before the local cops were asked to investigate.

Mary Lou's first thought was to hit another town in Canada but if the guy was following her, then he'd know her false name by now and she'd be an easy catch. The mob had tentacles in every city of influence and they'd used Canada ever since the Prohibition.

She figured the trick would be to go to the one place where the trail had grown coldest: the United States. The Feds must have given up on finding her otherwise they'd have done so by now. Hoover and his merry band have bigger felons to fry than a woman who robbed a bank and vanished into the mist.

There was the minor matter of her shooting a Federal office in the leg, but again, if it was that big a deal to them then they'd have tracked her down and they had not.

Over the border in the small hours of the morning without a customs guard even twitching.

"Purpose of your visit?"

"Popping over to hook up with family in Seattle."

"Unusual time to be traveling?"

"Well, they're asleep and it's much nicer to do it then."

She nodded into the back seat as Alice and Frank Jr carried on snoozing despite the rush of cold air from the open window.

"Stay safe on the roads, ma'am."

Men in uniform were the easiest ones to play, she thought. All you had to do was meet their bigoted expectations and you were home and dry.

Four miles down the road, she pulled over and took out the cuticle scissors from her clutch bag. Mary Lou cut up her Claudia Starr ID and ripped up the passport until it was in small enough pieces to chop into shards.

As she carried on down the highway, she grabbed handfuls of the identification confetti and released it out the window. Over the next ten miles, Claudia was sprinkled along the road until there was nothing left of her apart from Mary Lou's memories.

Being back in the US created its own set of questions: the pressing need to escape gave her no time to decide where to head. The east coast was out: living in the backdoor of the people most interested in seeing her dead was a bad plan. And she was damned if she'd return to the south—Mary Lou had spent all her adult life getting away from that hell hole.

That left only two options: the Midwest or the west coast. She needed a city; there was no space in her head for fields of wheat, which took her westwards. Mary Lou considered the craziest idea: who would think she'd go back to the place where she shot the Fed? No one. And LA was such a sprawling metropolis, she could hide in plain sight forever.

The coach ride to the Rainy City had taken over thirty hours and that was without the need to look after the twins. She followed the I-5 down to Ferndale where she ditched the car and stole another, changing the kids diapers in a diner.

Then a stretch to Seattle and a layover in a dive hotel. The journey echoed in her mind, mirroring the days she spent with Frank the last two weeks they were together. Some roads were familiar because she'd seen them the previous year on her way from Burbank Airport and the bloodshed she left behind.

Madness, inspiration: call it what you will, but Mary Lou plotted a return to California with her children in the back seat and dawn's early light streaming into the side of the car.

February 1971

8

NO ONE FOLLOWED Mary Lou into LA. When she looked back on her last few days in the Rainy City, she never could decide if she should have run. It felt right and she and the kids were living through the consequences of her decision.

The City of Angels was warmer and drier than Vancouver and the twins, who were toddlers by now, enjoyed the outdoor life offered by the glorious weather. Another advantage of being back in the States was the cash in her black holdall could be spent—carefully and with consideration. But she didn't need to live on skid row any more.

Mary Lou found a two-bedroom apartment to rent as soon as she could physically place a down payment and six months later, she looked around for somewhere to buy. A year and a half since the heist, she believed it was all over. That she could ease into a life with the children and become part of a community. Have some sense of belonging.

What was the point of having money if she couldn't enjoy a few creature comforts and buy her way into a bunch of acquaintances she'd eventually call friends? As much as she enjoyed LA life, Mary Lou wanted a quieter existence for her family so she moved a hundred miles west into Palm Springs and further away from the San Fernando epicenter.

A new development had popped up on Oakcrest Drive, a square loop of a road. Each house suffered from an enormous backyard, and sculptured lawns beyond, so there was ample play opportunity for the twins even if

Mary Lou got a tennis court built for fun. There were four bedrooms in the south facing home she purchased and an attic fit for a live-in maid.

Downstairs boasted a huge open plan living space, a dining room and kitchen. At the rear was a conservatory leading onto a patio and swimming pool. Beyond was a summerhouse and the rest of the backyard.

As she walked around the area before deciding to buy, Mary Lou noticed how many young families festooned the drive. She and her brood would fit in well here. And she was right.

Within days of getting hold of the keys, she used a local agency to hire a maid. Cindy Magdaleno had barely reached her twenties but possessed impeccable references and seemed to love Alice and Frank Jr.

She sported a tight bun in her head which hid a mane of long black hair. Brown eyes and thin lips. A straight back reflected years of healthy living, which was far from the norm at this point in America's history and not usual in the couch potato paradise of Palm Springs. Cindy was taller than Mary Lou and skinny: like she hadn't been fed enough as a child. She could almost get away with being described as white, but there was a Hispanic tinge to her skin color.

Mary Lou wasn't prejudiced. She didn't care where the woman came from as long as she cared for her children and kept the place tidy. Cleaning would be a bonus.

While Cindy spent her time entertaining Alice and Frank Jr, Mary Lou seized the chance to leave her home and meet the neighbors. She walked from one house to the next holding an empty mug. With a knock on the door, she'd wait until it opened:

"Hi. Sorry to bother you but I've just moved in nearby and I was wondering if I could borrow a cup of sugar?"

The technique worked when she and Frank murdered that girl when they were on the lam. What was her name? And it came up dixie now too.

She first met Janet Frazzini who lived in the house to her left. The woman was a stylish brunette and her son was handled to within an inch of his life by a German nanny. A photo of her spouse, Milton took pride of place above the fireplace. No ego there.

On the other side was Sylvia and Raymond Amante. Again the woman was immaculate and the husband was absent. Mary Lou wasn't surprised. Despite the sexual revolution and the rise of feminism, men worked and their women stayed indoors to tend to the kids. Opposite number twenty— Mary Lou's paradise on Earth—were Vivian and Roy Canepa. Another picture postcard perfect home and missing spouse.

After that day, she thought Sylvia was her favorite, not just because she was the first but because she was the friendliest. Like Sylvia knew how ridiculous her life with Raymond was. While they were sipping cocktails and glancing at manicured lawns, there were sixteen-year-olds losing half their faces and a limb or two in Vietnam.

Powder

The following evening, Sylvia invited her over for a barbecue—the twins too. All the families gathered round, adults and children of various ages. They welcomed Mary Lou as if she was a returning friend they hadn't seen for several years rather than the stranger who landed in their street a few minutes ago.

Wine was poured and the men stood around the grill offering advice to Raymond how best to cook his burgers and hot dogs. Meanwhile, the women huddled on sun loungers discussing home improvement ideas and the state of their nails. This was hardly the conversation Mary Lou was used to, but it was calm and worry-free: an experience she relished due to its absence in her life for so long.

Memories of fleeing Burbank Airport faded for an evening and the bloody pool of Frank's chest melted into the back of her mind. Instead, she smiled watching Alice enthrall a crowd of women and Frank Jr climb up onto the diving board before being scooped up and cuddled to within an inch of his life by Janet.

CINDY AGREED TO move into the attic but explained how she still had rent due until the end of the month. Mary Lou considered paying off the rental for Cindy but stopped herself. The flush of joy from having money to burn needed to be tempered: you only have green by not spending it. All those months of counting out the dollars to eke out the cash to the next weekly pay check seemed to have flown out of her mind.

Instead, she made Cindy commit to arrive in time for breakfast and only leave once the kids were in bed and waited for her to move in. Part of the deal was to have Sundays off—or any other day of the week if Mary Lou fancied.

Only when Cindy left after the first night of work did Mary Lou internalize what her life would be like sharing the home with someone else. It's one thing to share a bed with somebody: there's more than physical space as part of that union. But this was a housekeeper, a maid. There would be no privacy once Cindy appeared on the doorstep.

This meant Mary Lou had work to do. There was a holdall at the back of her closet containing just under one hundred and ten thousand dollars— enough money to last the rest of her natural life.

The financial cost of Frank's death lay in a wardrobe and needed to be secured from prying eyes and sticky fingers. Perhaps she should put it somewhere safe, like a deposit box in a bank. Mary Lou smiled at the irony of that consideration. Not a good idea.

Walking round the first floor of the house, she past the cascading staircase which was far too ornate for a woman of her simple tastes. Into the kitchen: keeping paper money near an oven or a sink? Fire and water were not greenbacks' best friends.

She stood in the living room, staring. In the corner, behind the door that led from the hallway was a loose floorboard. The builders hadn't nailed it completely down. Mary Lou could see the gap from the window. Perhaps this would work. The cash would always be near her but nobody would know it was there. Almost perfect.

On closer inspection, half the plank that made up the floorboard was under the sideboard. To get that baby up would need a saw and then the subtle nook would be a home improvement disaster. She sighed, stood up and walked to the floor-to-ceiling window that led out to the conservatory. Keeping an ear out in case one twin called out, Mary Lou sauntered into the glass enclosure and stared out.

Dusk was falling into the night and she wallowed in the orange, purples and reds of the sky caused by the dwindling sun. The summerhouse looked inviting. It'd be a great place to spend long afternoons with the twins. She could turn it into a playroom. A sanctuary for the kids no matter what went on in the main house—not that she had any plans. She reckoned they'd want their own space as they got older although she couldn't imagine Alice or Frank Jr as teenagers—them going to school was beyond comprehension.

The summerhouse: that was the answer. First, she crept upstairs to check on the children and, satisfied that all was well, she nipped downstairs and scurried outside with a torch. There was a key dangling in the lock and she wandered inside.

The space was enormous—fifty feet by twenty—and empty apart from stacked chairs in a corner. Mary Lou stood at the entrance, shining the light into every cranny hoping for inspiration. Then something caught her eye: two sides were glass to let the sun swarm in. One of the other walls remained solidly brick and the fourth had wooden cladding on it. No biggie. Except there was a door handle.

She strode over and entered. It was an empty store cupboard with no lock. If she removed the handle from the front and added a single hole for a lock, then the walk-in store room would be a perfect hiding place for the money and anything she might acquire that needed discretion. Her firearms were a good example of this. A quiet life was all she wanted right now, but she'd been on the run for so long, she hadn't convinced herself that world was over for her.

The next day she found a local hardware store on South Cerritos Drive: left out of Oakcrest and left again after a five-minute walk. The man behind the counter was more than helpful.

"You want some help putting this into the door, little lady?"

"No thanks. I'll be fine."

"I am happy to come by and finish the job for you, honey."

"Really. You're very kind but I know what I'm doing."

"Oh?"

"My husband died two years ago and I've had to fend for myself ever since."

"Mighty sorry to hear that darling."

Had she revealed too much about herself? There's a world of difference between saying your spouse was shot and killed robbing the Lansdowne branch of the First Bank of Baltimore and admitting he was dead at all. The twins were a testament to the fact she'd had Frank's sperm inside her. He had existed and now he was gone. That was inescapable. So better to glide past the truth as often as possible instead of creating some cockamamie story she would be stuck repeating for the rest of her life.

Armed with a toolkit, Mary Lou set to work removing the handles, adding a lock and making the front appear seamlessly smooth. She reminded herself to buy drawers and cupboards for the room—and some furniture. Later she intended to add steel reinforcement to the hidey-hole so the door couldn't be kicked in but for now she needed to prevent Cindy from opening the bag—and not much else.

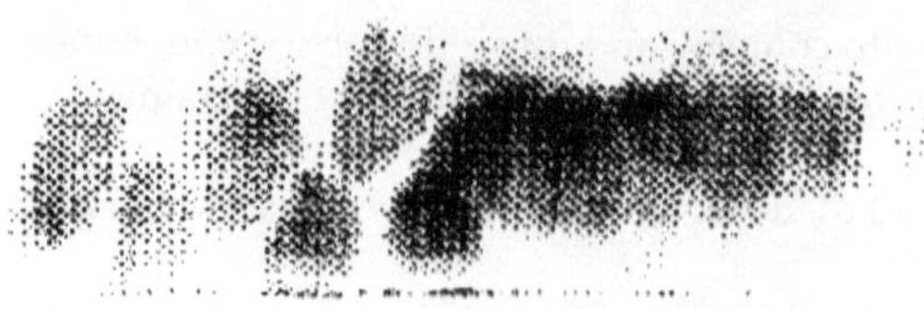

9

THE EMPTINESS IN the pit of her stomach still lingered every day since she held Frank in her arms and watched him bleed out before her. Now there were two things that put a sparkle back in her expression: Frank Jr and Alice.

As each glowing parent in the past has known, they were the light of her life. Despite the pudgy face only a toddler can get away with, Frank Jr's eyes reminded Mary Lou of his father and Alice had his lips without a shadow of doubt.

Time spent with the two of them was magical—in part because she had been forced to work in Canada. Even though Faye reassured her, the kids were all right, she knew they would grow up to be better people if they were with their mom. Her own childhood showed that truth.

Mary Lou converted one bedroom into a playroom—at least until the summerhouse got sorted—and while Cindy dusted and cleaned the place, Mary Lou would sit on the ground playing with Alice or tickling Frank Jr. Small cuddly islands of hope in a sea of loss.

Other times she and Cindy would fight coats and hats onto the twins and Mary Lou'd push them in their two-seater buggy around the area. The sole entrance to Oakcrest Drive had a three-minute walk to flat park land with a view of the white-peaked mountains beyond. For Mary Lou, this was the best of both worlds: she was urban through and through but she enjoyed beauty when she could find it.

She lit a cigarette after she laid out a picnic blanket and released the twins out of their harness. The two sat still for a second and then Frank Jr reared onto his haunches and skedaddled off on an adventure of his own. Alice watched as he raced twenty feet off and kept the same expression on her face as he collapsed and rolled on the ground.

She took longer to get up but made her way over and sat next to him, picking out blades of grass and daisies from the park lawn. Mary Lou remained on the blanket enjoying the view. The giggles of her children causing a mimicking effect on the corners of her mouth. This moment of pleasure sparked a memory of the night she and Frank had met. A judder slithered down her spine as her thoughts turned to darker times.

Mary Lou did not allow herself to wallow. Instead, she leaped up and ran over to the twins and gave them each an enormous hug. Then she pulled at Alice's striped top and blew a massive raspberry on her tummy. The girl created the most amazing chuckle she had ever known. No one could be sad with that noise in their ears.

"Me! Me!"

Frank Jr wanted in on the action and Mary Lou saw no reason to disappoint. His guffaw was fabulous but Alice's was the best.

"Think it. Don't say it."

Mary Lou had no favorites: she loved both the same, but she knew Frank Jr had the advantage of being born a boy. Even though she was older by four minutes, Alice would have to fight to be seen above the herds of young men vying for top dog. She wanted her daughter to be strong enough to beat them.

She returned to the blanket and threw a ball over to the pair. Both children ran toward her and they kicked it around until everyone needed to lie down and rest. Peanut jelly sandwiches appeared out of the voluminous contents of the buggy and, stoked on a sugar high, the twins played chase for ten minutes, returning to her to refuel.

An hour later and Frank Jr got tetchy, so Mary Lou knew it was nap time. Before they arrived home, he was asleep and Alice wasn't far behind him.

"That was fun."

"You've certainly tired them out."

"All three of us will sleep well tonight."

Cindy helped take them upstairs and the two women laid their charges out for the rest of the nap. Mary Lou returned downstairs and Cindy took her post in their room—in case of need. Mary Lou never wanted them to be alone, not for a minute, ever in their lives.

A WEEK AFTER Valentine's Day, Mary Lou attended yet another house party hosted by Sylvia and Raymond, the epicenter of the neighborhood social scene. This time there were more than just the immediate neighbors: people packed the first floor was packed. Some from Oakcrest Drive but most from around town—Sylvia's Country Club buddies, Raymond's business contacts. Mary Lou felt that if you had met Raymond or Sylvia at any point in your life, then you got an invitation to this do.

"Lovely to see you."

"Thanks. Been quite a while since I've been surrounded by so many people."

"Can be daunting, can't it? Don't worry though. They're all nice. And I need to introduce you to loads of them. Grab yourself a drink and we'll catch up later."

The hostess with the mostest swanned off to another part of the house to engage in chitchat with some other social butterfly. Meantime, Mary Lou headed for the bar at the side of the living room and took her beer outside as the air was still warm and hadn't succumbed yet to the evening chill.

The layout of their house and backyard was the same as number twenty; only the decor was different. A scan of the patio showed several huddles of couples and she couldn't face any more conversation about the travails of husbands and wives. It only drew her attention on how much she missed Frank near her.

Instead, there was one guy leaning against a post sipping his drink and watching the world go by.

"Penny for your thoughts?"

"I'll pass, thanks. Nothing personal but you don't want to know what's going on inside my head."

"Oh? Not too malicious I hope. You haven't had time to judge me."

He smiled and clinked his glass against the neck of her bottle.

"Bobby. Pleased to meet you."

"Mary Lou."

"You're the single mother who moved in a week or two ago."

"Yep, guilty as charged. I have other hidden shallows a sentence can't cover too. Don't know about you but I love being reduced to a series of stereotypes."

Bobby laughed and took another sip of what looked like scotch and cola on the rocks.

"You know everything there is about me but you are a Palm Springs man of mystery. Spill your guts, mister."

"Nothing to tell. I have some business interests in LA but I live here. Enjoy seeing the mountains when I wake up in the morning."

"I can understand that."

She glanced at the hand holding the whiskey and saw no wedding band.

"You got family round here?"

"No, I'm not married. Not any more…"

The last words were spoken with a sadness weighing down his heart. Mary Lou echoed how that felt.

"Divorced or dead?"

"Divorced."

"Mine's dead."

"So I heard."

"How long since the ink dried?"

"Couple of years."

"Any kids?"

"Not any more."

Bobby's response caused a chill in the air. Most times when a child dies, the parents split within five years. This was his story, she guessed.

"Fuck. Happy days, huh?"

"Like a fucking Halloween party."

"I'll drink to that."

Another clink and a sip to let the words fade and the images play out in their heads.

"You know many folks here?"

"Fair few. I've lived round here most of my life."

"And you don't need this come-over poking her nose into your affairs."

"I didn't say that."

"But implied."

"Not intentionally. You're right that I dreaded you opening your mouth as you walked toward me. No kidding, but now we're talking I'm warming to you."

"Gee, thanks. Is that what you tell all the girls?"

"What girls?"

"You telling me you go to parties in your home town and always get into bed later alone?"

"You've got me confused with another man."

Bobby smiled. Was it her directness or the fact she was prepared to speak with him and not tread egg shells? Either way he suffered but not in silence. This could go in two directions. Bobby could be a depressing individual who should stay at home until he gets over himself. Or he might be the only person in town who knows the meaning of loss.

"You look just like the one standing in front of me. And I like what I see."

"Straight back at ya."

"And how do people round here to enjoy themselves when they're not hanging around near a swimming pool on someone else's patio?"

"The usual."

For a man who'd revealed his heart to her two minute ago, Bobby was making this conversation heavy going.

"Like…?"

"Golf is good."

"Never tried it. Are there any decent places to eat?"

"You're kidding me, right?"

"Why?"

"The number of people with… business interests… round here. You can find a a decent restaurant or two. You really are fresh to the streets."

"Never pretended otherwise, Bobby."

"I'll show you the sights if you like."

"That'd be good. Real nice."

"Give me your number and I'll call you."

She pulled out a pen from her bag and they went inside to find something to write on. By the time he placed the strip of paper into his pocket, Sylvia had swooped on Mary Lou and taken her to the far side of the room.

"I see you've met Bobby Trevisan."

"Yes, a kindred dark soul."

"Are you that sad?"

"Now and again, Sylvia. I keep a brave expression on my face but there are wounds still sore."

Sylvia hugged her and took her by the hand upstairs into a bedroom.

"Listen, honey. Don't take this the wrong way, but be careful with Bobby."

"Why?"

"He's prickly and you'll only end up in more pain."

"I can look after myself. Don't worry about me."

"But I do. Bobby mistreats women. He pushes them away so he won't get hurt again. And you deserve better than him."

"What if he's the best that there is?"

MARCH 1971

10

MARY LOU SAT in a booth at the Palm Springs Country Club. This was a lovely plush affair where members of the golf club mingled with those who liked to watch and lunch. The seating was red leather and screamed out money although she had never spent a penny since she first visited a week before. The remarkable prejudice in this part of California was that the man always paid. As far as she was concerned, this made the men fools for parting so swiftly with their cash. And she owed them nothing.

Janet and Vivian arrived a moment later, and they settled in for the afternoon with a selection of cosmos and martinis. Mary Lou never finished hers but let the other women get fractious as the hours progressed. They also had the habit of letting their guard down and saying what they meant instead of maintaining the facade built up over the years.

Along with everyone else in America, they were unhappy. They didn't like the houses they lived in, the places they went to and they were dissatisfied with their husbands.

"I know he spends all the week slaving and working to support our family, but when he turns up at the weekends, he's dead beat. No good to me and no good to the kids. And definitely no good in bed."

The two others giggled at Vivian's comments and Janet nodded in appreciation.

"Same here. He goes, returns, sleeps. That's not a life; that's not a way for a man to behave."

"So what do they do to tire themselves out? Running a business doesn't wipe you out. It's not like they are lugging bricks, is it?"

A cold silence descended on the group after Mary Lou spoke: she'd stumbled onto something without realizing.

"Listen, darling. Our men are fine workers. Great providers. You know what they say? What goes on in LA stays in LA."

"And what sort of stuff goes on in LA?"

The words were barely audible from Mary Lou's lips. Vivian eyed Janet, who responded in kind.

"Tell her."

"Okay then, I will. We all come from Italian families with a long tradition running from Sicily, you get me?"

Blank face. Eyes opened wide then relaxed back to normal.

"I see."

She tried to hide the fear within her, knotting her stomach and causing her hands to grip the edge of the table, creasing the white tablecloth. She knew the mob had its tentacles in California but had been unaware that it had an enclave in Palm Springs.

"Don't worry, dear. It is not how you think. Roy and Milton don't go around whacking people who don't pay their bills or nothing."

"It's like a union for business owners. They look after their own and give better rates to their members."

Mary Lou processed these statements, knowing what bullshit she was hearing. Uncle Frankie had ties to the New York mob and look what he had done: raped her, sent men the other side of the country to take the heist money and kill Frank and herself. You couldn't get much further from preferential terms if you tried.

"And that's all?"

"Oh yes. Roy isn't tired from gang shootings. He's tired from banging his mistress. Why do you think the guys stay in the city all week long?"

Good question. These women sipping cocktails at this table produced children, looked pretty and paid someone to keep the house clean. That way, their men could lead a sweet life in the City of Angels and come home to feel great about themselves at the weekend.

"You don't mind?"

"You're kidding me, right? Listen. While he's spending his nights fucking some whore and not making demands on me, I have no problem provided she's clean. And while the cat's away…"

A knowing glance to Janet.

"You mean?"

"Baby. You better believe it."

There were so many double lives being played out, Mary Lou didn't know what to think. She and Frank might have had their difficulties, but

they were sexually honest with each other. At least when he was out the
Penitentiary.

"Jeez, you girls."

"Are you shocked?"

"Surprised to be honest. Everyone looks so normal. I don't mean that in
a bad way. You all appear settled and happy."

"We are, just not the how you thought."

"And your fellas have connections?"

This was Mary Lou's problem. She didn't care who fucked whom in
Palm Springs or Los Angeles. If these guys were hooked up with the New
York mob, she was as good as dead.

"They know members of the club, yes."

"That's not what I mean."

"I understand, but we don't know each other well enough for me to
respond to your question. You a cop?"

"No, I'm not. Are you?"

"Nope."

"So answer my question then."

"Let's just say they have allegiances."

"To the east or west coast?"

"West. Why?"

"No reason. Just interested in the details."

A waiter arrived to deliver another round of drinks. Mary Lou ordered a
coffee: she needed to think straight. While she enjoyed her time with the
twins in the house, she lacked something in the outside world.

Unfortunately she knew what it was: for years she'd spent every day
working toward some goal whether it was to rob the bank, launder the
money or flee for her life and survive. There had been an aim to shoot for
and right now she had nothing. Apart from the kids who she adored with all
her heart and all her soul. But that wasn't enough. she couldn't define what
would be sufficient but she ruminated on the problem.

"Don't worry. The men do their thing and we do ours. Fancy some
olives?"

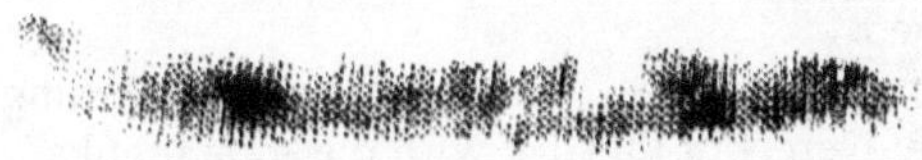

DEEP IN THE center of the West Coast mob territory, Mary Lou sat in the
passenger seat of Bobby's sports car as they drove round town. The twins
were home with Cindy.

The airport lay to the north but Bobby refused to make it one of their
stopovers, despite Mary Lou's fake protestations.

"Don't you love the smell of gasoline spewing out of an aircraft's back side?"

"Mary Lou, you need therapy."

Instead, he concentrated the journey around the more scenic elements of Palm Springs, like the Tahquitz Wash which was a feeder river from the lake to the east toward the west and beyond to LA. The water crossed through parkland and unkempt grass, but the way the town was growing, there would be months not years before the land turned into condominiums or retail space. This was an up-and-coming area where the inhabitants suffered from plenty of money.

Bobby took them around the main drag. It reminded her how she imagined Fifth Avenue was in direct contrast to anything she saw near Clark Park.

"You wanna do some shopping?"

"Not right now. I am getting hungry though. Why not take me to one of the many places you promised me that have good food and an impressive atmosphere."

"Not quite my words, but there is a nice little place around here we could try."

He turned left at the next junction and parked outside a restaurant. A valet in uniform smiled at him as he threw the keys over and the guy swapped them for a ticket. The car vanished round the corner and they stepped inside.

The maitre d' greeted Bobby with a warm handshake and ten seconds later they sat by the window, watching the world chug by as water was served to their table.

"May I recommend the prawns?"

Bobby nodded in acquiescence as the waiter jotted down the order.

"Steak and fries for me, please."

The waiter looked to Bobby.

"You heard the lady."

Then to Mary Lou:

"You want something to drink?"

"A cola would be nice."

Bobby laughed.

"A girl of simple pleasures. I was thinking of something stiffer."

"I'm sure you were, but I'll stick with the soda thanks."

"Make mine a scotch on the rocks."

"As you wish, sir."

Bobby blushed for twenty seconds as Mary Lou's comment entered his head and popped out the other side.

"Teasing. That's all."

She winked and took a sip from her iced water.

"So I don't even know where you live."

"Oakcrest, same as you."

"Where?"

"Number three near the entrance."

"Do you find the noise from East Mesquite Drive too much?"

"Nah. There's a solid line of trees between the house and the road. Besides, the traffic's not that bad most of the time. Not even in what we laughingly call the rush hour."

"And how do you spend your days when you're in town?"

"Sleep, eat, drink. Play the odd round of golf. Nothing special."

"They're playing golf on the Moon now."

He smiled.

"True, but it's hard to figure out your handicap when there aren't any pins to drop the ball into."

Mary Lou imagined him floating around a golf course with baggy trousers and a tightly fitting V-neck jumper.

"And where are the business interests you mentioned at the party?"

"In LA. Like everybody else's."

"Does that mean you're fucking some bimbo during the week and come back here for eighteen holes at the weekend?"

"Woah! Hold on there. I came out for a quiet drive and pleasant company. Not to get a grilling."

"Sorry. The more I discover about this place, the more direct I seem to get. I'm only like this because I am interested in you. Otherwise I wouldn't give you the time of day."

"Thanks for the backhanded compliment."

"You're welcome. Most men round here lead a double life—at least according to their wives and they should know."

"Not me. I have a solitary quiet existence. I have my work and I have some friends here. That is all there is to me."

"Hmm. I don't think that's all you are. Not for a minute, but I'll leave you be for now."

"Why thank you kind lady."

He squeezed her hand across the table but Mary Lou withdrew it onto her lap. The gesture might have been innocent, but she wasn't ready to touch another man—even if he was only a friend. And she didn't know if Bobby was that to her yet.

The food arrived with appropriate ceremony and they hunkered down to dine. The steak was superb, the best she'd ever eaten and Bobby's choice of broccoli as a side dish was well-judged.

After a polite amount of time, the menus reappeared for dessert.

"I couldn't eat another thing, but go ahead if you want to."

"Very kind, but I'm only looking out of politeness."

"A coffee perhaps, then. So in what business are you involved? Everyone is so mysterious about how they earn their money."

"A bit of this and a bit of that."

"Come on, Bobby. I won't be embarrassed whatever you do. Sell blow-up dolls? Nurses uniforms?"

"Jeez, nothing like that. What do you take me for?"

"You are so cagey, you might have been a sex toy sales rep."

"Yeah, right. My work is far more mundane than that."

"And?"

"I used to make accommodations for people, but I'm semi-retired."

"You're in construction."

"Huh? No! Make accommodations: I'd help folk out, y'know?"

Mary Lou thought for a minute and joined the dots between Janet, Sylvia and Vivian's husbands and the West Coast mob—through to Bobby.

"Fuck."

"Stay calm. I'm in semi-retirement. They keep me on the payroll so they know I am safe and because I've been a dutiful soldier."

"Mother. Fucker… You never said how your son died."

"I did not."

"You gonna tell me now."

"Had nothing to do with work."

"And your divorce?"

"That was business, yes."

11

THERE WERE NO need for coats and hats in March. Truth was there wasn't much point the previous month either, but Mary Lou wanted to know she was looking after the twins to the best of her ability.

The trip to the park went without event and she checked out a play area Cindy mentioned the preceding weekend. It would give the afternoon a focus and she might bump into other parents too. A shared experience can be a great foundation for a friendship.

Back onto the sidewalk and east to South Campadre Road as directed by Cindy. And there it was. Swings, slides and a sandpit for the adventurous pre-schooler.

There were a huddle of adults, either sitting on nearby benches or holding the hands of the younger users. Every person apart from Mary Lou conformed to a single racial demographic: Hispanic female, eighteen to twenty-five.

She didn't mind about who they were, just they might be speaking Spanish. She and Frank had always planned on hitting Canada rather than Mexico because neither of them spoke the language.

She let the twins loose on a ladder which reached four steps up into a playhouse. Frank Jr sprinted up without consideration for himself or anyone else in the vicinity. Alice stood at the bottom and weighed up her options. She only tried the lowest rung once her brother was ensconced at the top and had declared the territory owned by the Lagottis. Once she caught up at the top, he allowed her to rule the roost and they pretended their lives away in a game that only existed in Alice's head.

Mary Lou stood apart from the Latino maids and watched her children enjoying the equipment. Three minutes later and she noticed there was somebody next to her. She glanced over and there was a man in a brown jacket, white shirt and jeans. Mary Lou hadn't given herself enough time to make a complete clothes judgment.

"Cute, aren't they?"

"Sure are. Which is yours?"

"Over there."

He half pointed in the vaguest of directions toward the other end of the play area but she was more concerned with checking Alice wasn't getting stuck on the ladder as she journeyed down to the ground.

"And yours?"

"Right in front: there."

Her first finger aimed direct at Alice's back ten feet ahead. The guy felt like he stood closer than when she'd originally noticed him.

"Do you come here often?"

"First time. You?"

"Constantly. Great location and wonderful facilities, wouldn't you say?"

"For sure."

Again, when she glanced at him next, he was within two feet of her. Something wasn't right in the state of California.

"Where are your brood again?"

He leaned into her so their shoulders touched.

"Just there."

Mary Lou followed his arm and his finger, by extension, but there were no children in the line of sight.

"See them now?"

He put his hand on her shoulder so she could follow his direction more closely. No one else appeared to have noticed what was happening. She could smell his breath on her cheek and she was not happy about it.

The inevitable consequence of his actions came to a head as his groin nestled against her side, just above her hip. On instinct, she elbowed him in the stomach and used her weight to spin around and push him to the floor, all the while grabbing a hand as he fell so she could twist the attached arm.

He rolled over causing his elbow to flip round his back and Mary Lou pulled upward until she thought the upper shoulder might pop out of its socket. A kick between the legs finished him off. She leaned in and whispered through clenched teeth.

"I see you again: I'll kill you, you motherfucker."

By now, four of the Hispanics had gathered around her but Mary Lou ignored their inquisitive stares.

"It's all right ladies. He just had a bit of a fall but everything is okay. Isn't it, buddy?"

"Yeah. All fine."

The guy still had one hand on his groin reflecting the aggressiveness of the kick. She marched over to the twins and, without making a scene or scaring them, took them softly by the hands and walked away from the play area. The dude limped off refusing to speak to any of the enquiring housekeepers and maids surrounding him.

Mary Lou considered calling the police but thought better of it. The fella wouldn't go bothering her for sure and the chances were he would not be seen in this part of Palm Springs again. Not unless he had a death wish.

She took the most direct route she could to get home but only picked up the pace when the twins were safe in the buggy. Back in the house, she reviewed what happened and realized how quick her reactions had been and that she could still handle herself.

If she'd had a knife in her hand, she knew would have sliced his throat open from ear to ear. A gun would have created a large red hole in his chest. All the years which brought her to this point in her life conspired to make her ready for anything. She was an unashamed fighting machine and that could never be taken away from her. Never.

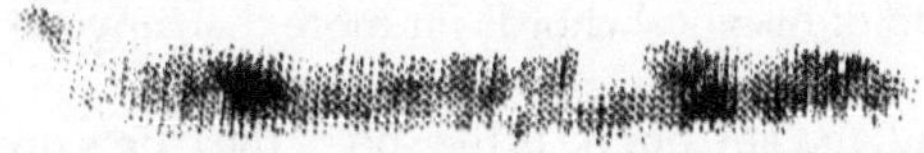

NOT FOR THE first time, Mary Lou sat in an upmarket booth at the Palm Springs Country Club surrounded by her girlfriends. Today's topic of conversation was whether there was any point in having a golf course next to this eaterie.

"It keeps the men away for a few hours."

"Longer if they don't haven't learned how to swing a club."

"Less if they know how to get their thing into the hole."

"Stop it!"

Janet was unaware of the double entendre that came out of her mouth. And the others were feeling frisky. Mary Lou hoped they'd catch up with their boyfriends soon because they were getting hysterical and it was doing her head in.

"Have any of you ever been tempted to have a go?"

Laughter all round.

"Darling. A lady who lunches should not be a lady who swings."

"Not like that, anyway!"

Janet continued to appear bemused while Vivian and Sylvia tittered over the cleverness of their wordplay.

"I'd be up for having a go. Anyone with me?"

"Would cut into my cosmo time."

"Same here."

"Me too."

Mary Lou looked forlorn. None of these women were prepared to do anything. They sat on their well-toned asses and did nothing but prepare for the next cocktail hour. She couldn't stand it even though she liked them as individuals. Each of them at the table had been so welcoming when she arrived in town and had continued to be friendly since then.

"If not a round, how about knocking a ball around a putting green?"

Blank expressions across the board. This group was not for budging off the red leather. Mary Lou didn't think her expectations were too unreasonable. Women had been admitted as members here in their own right for at least three years. No blacks as yet, but girls were acceptable.

A flicker of memory of Martin turned into a red soaked scene of Frank's blood drying on her arms and legs on the way to the Clements.

Back in the moment, Mary Lou shrugged and allowed the chatter to meander around whether the men should spend longer on the course. This being a weekday, there were few males out playing anyway, but there was a guy four tables down who was punching the hour with his voice. Sylvia called a waiter over.

"Is there any way someone could have a word with the fella over there. He likes the sound of his vocal chords far more than anyone else in this place."

"I understand, ma'am, but he is the son of the club's owner so I can't make you any promises. Would you rather move to a table further away?"

"I'm damned if I'll shift because that man's being an oaf."

The waiter shrugged and walked off, knowing his job would be on the line if he told the twenty-year-old boy to shut his trap. Sylvia remained unhappy with the situation.

She bowled over to him and words were said—too soft for Mary Lou to hear. The boy replied, Sylvia slapped him and stormed back, sat down and finished her cosmo in one gulp. A calm descended on their table but the guy kept his volume down, not least because a trickle of blood rippled from his cheek toward his neck. Sylvia ensured her nails hit his skin instead of the palm of her hand. Clever girl.

MARY LOU WAS true to her word and spent the next week getting private golf lessons. She was not a natural—and it involved the purchase of a new outfit comprising some shockingly unflattering trousers and unpleasant-looking shoes. But she kept at it, practicing daily until she believed she could face a hostile golfing world. Then she got Bobby to agree to a round with her.

"Don't be too critical and we'll see how we get on."

"Golf is the only game I know where you play against yourself and nobody else."

She had no idea what he meant by that but she'd heard others say the same.

Two holes in and Mary Lou watched Bobby tee off. His swing was smooth and effortless. He stood over the ball, moved the club back and forth and the little white sphere flew in an arc heading straight for the flag. A joy to behold.

Her effort continued to involve staring at the ball and waiting for the anxiety to subside long enough to ignore the eyes she imagined bearing down on her, a rush of metal and the ball popped forward cutting the fairway and rolling to a stop within a hundred feet walk.

"Slow your game down and you'll have a better chance to control what you are doing."

She nodded and agreed she was rushing.

"Take your time and focus on the moves you will make. Ignore me, the wind, the world. Keep your head over the ball and everything will flow from that."

His voice was calm. Soothing. There was no annoyance at how she was dragging down his game to a crawl. No sense he'd rather be playing with somebody else — anybody in fact. Bobby was a classy guy.

When the eighteen holes were over—several hours later—they changed out their golf clothes and Mary Lou took a shower. Once suitably refreshed, they met up in the Country Club.

"Hope that wasn't too painful for you."

"Not at all. We all started with our first game. It's normal—and you showed promise."

"Yeah?"

"For sure. You have a good, natural swing. Once you stopped overthinking what the coach told you, the ball flew onto the fairway and your hand-to-eye coordination makes you a solid putter."

She smiled. Compliments were scarce and she wasn't intending to fish.

"You're a good golf buddy. You are patient—and to be honest, you are the only person I know who wanted to play with me. None of the ladies in our little group were prepared to leave this room."

Bobby laughed.

"Cocktail versus a long walk chasing a ball? Most would choose a mojito."

Mary Lou's turn to chuckle.

"It has its own attraction."

She briefly touched his lower arm, near his wrist. Something she had not planned. Involuntary. And, as she was aware, definitely flirtatious.

12

ANOTHER DAY, ANOTHER party. Mary Lou found the constant get-togethers quite tiring. She had no problem being sociable, being in the company of other people. As days and weeks rolled on, she realized she felt less of a loss when she had her nose to the concrete in Canada.

With time on her hands every day, there were greater opportunities to recall Frank and the life she had with him. It had been far from plain sailing —his time behind bars; her time sleeping with other men—but they had been good together for so many years.

And the parties got her down. This lifestyle was not hers. She might have bought the swanky house and have money to burn, but that didn't make her like the neighbors. Mary Lou worked hard for everything she had and would defend her children to the death. Literally.

Part of her needed to keep busy and her recent sporting exploits had been a displacement activity. In the absence of anything meaningful to do, she found an excuse to learn a skill and spend time with Bobby.

But golf was not a sustainable option. While the weather was great for a year-round outdoors pastime, Mary Lou understood herself well enough to know that hitting a small ball was not sufficient to keep her mind from atrophying. And as much as she loved Alice and Frank Jr, she could not spend all her time looking after them. Cindy was better placed to do that day in, day out than her.

That didn't mean she'd ignore her kids. Far from it. She vowed never to disregard them, the way her mother had disregarded her. There would never be a Pastor Neil in her children's lives.

All these thoughts bundled into her brain, Mary Lou stood in Janet's living room with a beer in her hand and Roy, Milton and Raymond talking on the sofa four feet away.

"Will he recover long enough to keep running things?"

"Hard to tell. The Feds are breathing down our necks. That's for sure."

Roy looked up and noticed she was within earshot. A hush descended as they hoped she'd walk back out to her girlfriends sat next to the pool but she remained resolute in her stance. The men changed tack to discuss football while she stood her ground.

"The Baninno Family have always held interests this side of the country."

She let these words hang over them so the men were sure she was listening, but also could understand she wasn't some stupid wallflower.

"They have. Doesn't mean any of us must like it."

"No. When I was out east, you always heard stories of the family seeking to extend its reach in California."

"That so? Where d'you say you lived?"

"I never mentioned it before, but I'm telling you now."

"You have connections with the Baninno Family?"

"Me? Oh no. My husband's family did, but I lost contact with them when he died. It was loose at best."

"But you were connected?"

"At arm's length. What do you guys say? Yeah, we had business concerns that aligned with the Baninnos—for a short while."

"And once he passed away?"

"Those interests receded rather fast."

"But you weren't ever in the Family?"

"Nope. Mixed in circles that mixed with them. Only that."

"When did you say you left the east coast?"

"Never did. And at this point in my life, I'm not going to tell you now. It's nothing personal, okay? Just we're in the middle of a house party and this information is precious to me. Capice?"

Perhaps she had revealed too much, but she wanted some action and these guys were the most direct route for her to get to it. As a precaution, Mary Lou took a gun out the summerhouse and kept it with her for the next three days but nothing happened.

No one followed her, nobody asked any more questions. The dust settled on the conversation as though it never occurred. At least, that was the appearance to the outside world.

The irony was she knew next to nothing about the Baninnos. Her most recent info was no less than two years old and had been gained via Frank and his Shylock uncle. The trail was thin as could be. Frank Senior funded local Baltimore operations sometimes, according to Frank, but he always kicked back ten per cent to New York. The Baninnos ran Baltimore, so she assumed they were the beneficiaries of the tithe.

That meant Baninno's men sprawled across country through Las Vegas to LA when she and Frank were on the lam straight after the heist. So Baninno hoods had been in Burbank Airport when Frank was mortally wounded.

A fragment of image: driving with blood drying all over her thighs to avoid capture and get away from everyone and everything.

Back to reality and barbecues, cocktails and more gatherings without the men picking up on her comments from the few days before. Mary Lou couldn't tell if she imagined this, but she got the feeling the women were treating her differently. Slightly standoffish. She was aware she might be distancing herself from Sylvia and the gang but there was a sense conversations died as she walked into the room or sat down at their booth in the Country Club.

Bottom line: she needed to do more than sip cocktails and die a little inside every day.

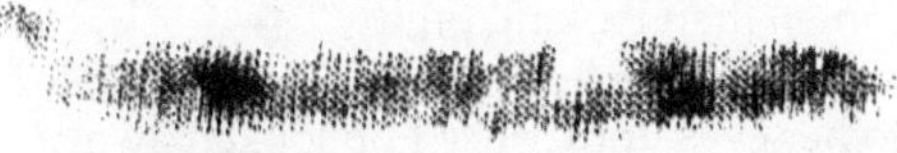

MARY LOU USED her car the next time she hooked up with Bobby because his two-seater had insufficient space for the twins. She reckoned if he was going to be a part of her life then he needed to be in theirs too.

The four headed for a picnic near the base of San Jacinto, the mountain that loomed over Palm Springs like a concerned parent over a toddler. Left onto Mesquite until she turned south on Palm Canyon Drive west of the city. As soon as East Avenida Granada appeared on the left, Mary Lou grabbed the first available right turn.

No more than a dirt track leading nowhere, the turning ending five hundred feet away from the main drag at a flat piece of ground, covered in grass. The base of the mountain rose up almost as soon as the vegetation petered out. Mary Lou had done her homework. Bobby whistled as she stopped the car.

"Beautiful. Lived here all my life and never once came here. This is a wonderful country, isn't it?"

"Has its moments, Bobby."

She patted his knee before hopping out and freeing the twins from the back seat. He opened the trunk and pulled out two rugs and a food basket prepared by Cindy.

The kids ran around in empty circles playing chase while the adults smoothed out the wrinkles in the blankets and checked out the contents of the picnic. Before she sat down, Mary Lou scooted over to the trunk and revealed four cushions.

"I wasn't sure how lumpy this place would be."

She tossed one over to Bobby who placed it near his rump, took another for herself and threw the others down for the twins.

"Want a drink or something?"

"Scotch?"

"Nope. I didn't pack hard liquor. Got coffee, though?"

"Sounds good to me."

"Milk?"

"Nah."

Mary Lou smiled, poured him a cup and one for herself.

"I hear you've been annoying the locals."

"Have I? How'd I manage that?"

"By expressing opinions on men's matters."

"Say again?"

"You spoke to Roy and Milton about the Baninno family."

"Oh, yes. I got bored listening to their hushed tones so I reminded them there's more to women than looking pretty."

"And some sure look cute."

He gazed into her eyes until Mary Lou looked away.

"They said you spoke with some authority."

"I know a thing or two."

"I have every faith you do. Doubt if you care, but you freaked them a little."

"Not much."

"Caring or freaking?"

"Both I guess. Does it bother you I had a life before arriving in Palm Springs?"

"Makes you even more attractive as far as I'm concerned."

"But you had to bring this up as soon as we arrived here?"

"More I wanted to mention it and move on without taking up the whole day. What's past has passed. It's part of who you are, so it is interesting but not to any extent that my finding out about it might stop you from wanting to be with me."

A tentative smile from Mary Lou.

"And if your earlier interests have any interconnection with my current ones: yes, I'd like to find out."

"All my old business affairs have well and truly run their course. Believe me, I have no desire to rekindle my east coast contacts."

Bobby nodded. Just then Frank Jr threw himself on top of him causing the man to exhale a loud wheeze while Alice came up to Mary Lou and gave her a hug around the neck. She scooped her daughter up and swung her to land on her lap, carrying on the cuddle until it had spent its force.

The boys carried on playing rough-and-tumble for a minute more. When Bobby was lying on his back with Frank Jr cudgeling his sides, Mary Lou called a halt. He might have been in control of the situation the entire time, but the boy needed to learn he didn't always have to win every fight. Mercy is an important trait.

To save him from her son, Mary Lou revealed peanut jelly sandwiches and chocolate muffins. Cindy could bake too. Ten minutes of near silence as the contents of the basket were devoured. Their ball was released from captivity and the twins shot off to kick the sphere around, enabling the adults to continue their conversation.

"You said you didn't want to hook up again with your east coast contacts. How do they feel about you?"

"Let's just say there was a parting of the ways."

Bobby chuckled.

"Thought so."

"Huh?"

"I've been thinking—about you, the age of your kids, the death of your husband. And the fact you can afford to live on Oakcrest Drive."

Mary Lou bristled.

"And?"

"And I guess you were in the news two or three years ago."

"Oh, you reckon?"

"Yep. Doesn't bother me. If you are who I think you are then I owe you a huge dollop of respect."

"And who am I?"

"If you haven't mentioned your past, would be rude of me to do so. But I believe there might be a hint of Baltimore about your southern accent."

Mary Lou stared cold at Bobby. Her secret was out. Her fingers felt damp with sweat.

"Who else have you told?"

"Nobody. It's not my story to tell, as I said."

"And why are you letting me in on your thoughts now?"

"So you can trust me and that you'll let me be your confidante. I am growing to like you, Mary Lou and I want you to believe I'm safe—given what went down in Burbank Airport."

"How d'you find out what you think you know?"

"Thought about dates, checked a few public records. Nothing fancy."

"So anyone can work it out."

Her mind raced.

"Well, only if they know you enough to bother. You're hidden away in the heartland of the West Coast mob. East and west haven't played nicely in the sandpit since Bugsy Siegel first cut the turf in Las Vegas. There's no love lost between those two gentlemen's clubs."

"And the others?"

"They can probably guess, but again, nobody out here cares to do anything and no one'll be placing a call to the Baninnos. There's no money in it for them. You are as safe today as you were yesterday."

"Is that enough, though?"

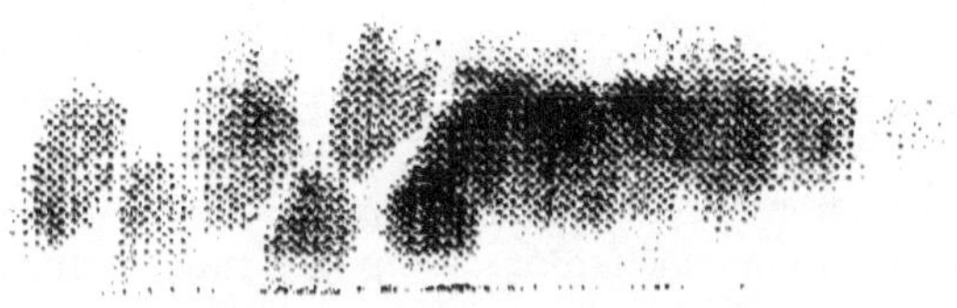

13

MARY LOU WANTED to believe she could trust Bobby, but in reality she knew so little about him other than he had some connections with the West Coast mob. Yes, he appeared considerate—and hadn't tried to hit on her since they first met. Perhaps that was the reason there was any relationship between them: they both respected each other's boundaries enough not to ask too many questions or try to speed matters up through sex.

She wasn't even sure she wanted his dick anywhere near her. The absence of a man since Frank hadn't weighed down on her as much as the pre-twins Mary Lou might have expected. Her loins needed attention now and again but she no longer experienced that pressing yearning inside for a fuck. Either the kids put paid to that or Frank's death. Both had blurred into each other, she couldn't quite remember any more.

If she took the children and ran away again, the good news was she still had enough green to start from scratch and leave the house. Few people had the luxury of being able to walk away from a thirty thousand dollar piece of real estate. Mary Lou knew how fortunate her life had become despite her tenuous circumstances.

She took an overnight trip into LA. The twins would enjoy the razzmatazz of Hollywood even if they didn't know who the stars were just yet. Mary Lou brought Cindy along to ease the burden of the childcare and to have someone to talk to during the adventure.

The two-hour journey passed quickly thanks to the simple plan of feeding the twins before shoving them into the car so they crashed out by the time Mary Lou hit the freeway. They missed the commuter crowd heading into Los Angeles, so they sailed into their hotel and up into their adjacent rooms: one for Cindy and the kids, the other for Mary Lou.

The plan was simple: check out the Chinese Theater, pop past a studio or two hoping to see someone famous, sleep then travel home the next day. The overnight piece was there so the kids wouldn't be trapped in a car for four hours solid. Without the sleepover, there would be guaranteed tears before bedtime.

Feed-and-go meant they stood outside their first studio before one as the crowds abated with pangs of hunger. Fifteen minutes later and there was nothing to see—just like the previous time Mary Lou stopped by the same entrance, only with Frank by her side. Their last days together.

"It'll be more interesting at the Chinese Theater."

"Sure thing."

Into a taxi and off to the excitement of seeing hand prints set in concrete. When they arrived, Mary Lou had a huge flashback: a genuine deja vue as clear as day. The moment she held onto a cab door as Frank was about to rip the head off a mobster who walked past them outside the Theater. Once that had passed and her breathing was back to normal, Mary Lou took the kids and marched them along the road.

Occasionally, they'd stop so Cindy and Mary Lou could discuss some star or another, but generally the twins enjoyed the noise and pizzazz but were oblivious to anything more that that. Impersonators pan-handled their way through the crowd hoping to convince someone to take a photo with them in shot.

Unlike the last time when Frank had sent a Marilyn Monroe off with her tail between her legs, Mary Lou allowed a Laurel and Hardy double act to relieve her of two dollars. The twins giggled and chuckled at the silly antics and she felt the money was well spent.

Ice creams for everyone and then back to the hotel. The kids were ready to drop so Cindy put them to sleep and popped into Mary Lou's, leaving the adjoining door ajar.

"Thanks for letting me come along today."

"Don't mention it. You being here means we're all having a much better time."

"Thank you anyway."

"De nada."

"Your family is a pleasure to spend time with."

"No need to blow smoke."

"I'm not. The last place—you wouldn't believe. The kids ran riot around the parents who did nothing to stop them."

"Nightmare. I wasn't brought up that way and the twins will not be either."

"Of course. Firm boundaries with love in the middle. That's best."

Mary Lou cracked open two beers and handed one over to Cindy.

"I shouldn't when I'm on duty."

"I won't tell your employer if you don't."

Cindy smiled and half-raised the bottle before taking a small swig. The agency would disapprove but she was sitting in a classy hotel having a drink with the client. When in Rome…

"Where's your family?"

"Back in Chihuahua City."

"Do you get to see them?"

"Not the past four years, since I arrived in the Land of Opportunity."

"Tough break."

"I send some of my earnings home—to help out—and I receive a letter at least once a month."

"I'm glad you're still in touch. Families can be difficult beasts."

"Not being rude, but I noticed your family never comes round."

"Because they're all deceased."

"I am so very sorry. I didn't mean…"

"Not a problem. Been dead for years. I was orphaned when I was fifteen."

"Oh man. So young."

"Grew up fast."

"Can imagine."

"Tonight, if you want to go out to a club instead of hanging with me, I'll totally understand. Think of it as an extra night off, if you like."

"Well, if you don't mind."

"Not at all. Just remember not to bring anyone back to the room…"

"I'm a a decent Catholic girl!"

"…and we leave at ten so you must be in the land of the living in good time to help the twins in the morning before we get breakfast."

NOTHING HAPPENED AND no one appeared on Mary Lou's doorstep demanding money or shooting her between the eyes. Bobby had been true to his word: what he knew stayed inside him. She didn't want to trap herself in the house, but she wasn't confident enough to hang out in the local bar.

Palm Springs Country Club was a good compromise with a healthy mix of west coast connections surrounding her. The first time out there since the picnic, Mary Lou sat facing the tables even though her usual position was to have her back to the room.

The weekend's arrival meant Roy and Milton returned from the course as she sipped her second coffee of the day. As they walked to the bar on the far side, she waved at them and they acknowledged her as they bought their drinks.

Despite the unwritten rule that the men and women didn't mingle, the two waltzed over and settled down in the booth with her.

"Hiya."

"Hey, you."

"Drinking alone?"

"A morning Java. The girls are still in the nail bar."

Roy smiled and Milton raised his eyebrows.

"Who won?"

"Draw. We both played appallingly. You deserved the win more than we did."

"Is there a prize?"

"Buy you another?"

Mary Lou laughed and shook her head.

"Keep the coffee all the same, but you could do me a favor."

"How so?"

"At the party last week, we talked about business interests. You remember?"

The men nodded and stiffened their backs.

"Well, would you be able to make an introduction for me?"

"To whom?"

"I'd like to carry out an investment or two and I reckon you know the kinds of people I should speak with."

"What sort are they?"

"Come on, Roy. None of us were born yesterday. There's no need to be coy with me. We've all been hanging round together for long enough for me to work out what's what."

"Nothing personal, love, but my connections won't want me to pass on someone like you for business. Men work with men where I come from."

"Although I have no desire to go into details, I have a track record, which has left me with a chunk of cash which I'd want to turn into a bigger pile of green. If you won't hook me up, is there anything you guys do that needs some extra funding?"

"Really, Mary Lou. The answer is no."

She hid the disappointment behind her eyes as she had no desire to show these mooks what she thought of them. Mary Lou stared at Roy and ground her molars instead. Was it so difficult to get a piece of the action in this town?

Milton turned his head sideways and continued to look at her. Even though Roy had looked at him to join in his smirk, Milton had not.

"Is funding all you're interested in?"

"Not necessarily, to be honest. I'm used to being hands-on in my affairs and it'd be good to jump back in the saddle, if you see what I mean."

"I do. You understand you have no track record here, which is why we're skeptical."

"I get that. The only problem I have is that if I tell you what I've done, I must kill you."

Roy laughed but the other two remained stoney faced.

"Let's say I'm sitting on a significant investment potential and it exists through honest hard work. People have died for me to own this money. Ten. Twelve. I've lost count."

Roy removed the inane smirk from his expression, but Mary Lou continued looking at Milton. She had no desire to work with anyone who couldn't imagine her being a serious business partner.

She carried on sipping her coffee until the impact of her remarks had soaked into their heads and the men swallowed. Milton took a large swig of his drink and placed it back on its coaster.

"So you want to make some more money?"

"Yep. That's what I said."

"I can help. If you'd like me to."

"Sure would. Is that all right with you, Roy? I wouldn't want you to be out of sorts."

Roy mumbled something, stood up with his drink and slunk off. Milton and Mary Lou watched as he sat on a high chair at the bar with his back facing them.

"Don't mind Roy. He's just prejudiced."

"Pig."

"Yes, but I always like the sound of cash registers filling up with greenbacks. I have an opportunity which might interest you. Make tenfold profit minimum."

"Sounds serious. Why d'you want me to get involved? If it's that good, why not handle it yourself?"

"Cash flow. Right now I have no liquid assets otherwise you wouldn't see me for dust."

"And you'll drop me once I make some money for you?"

"I'm loyal. If we work together well, then I'll want us to do so again. Success breeds success."

"And if we both build a stash of cash, then we can invest in ever bigger projects."

"That's how I see it. Yes."

"Here's to a bright future."

They clinked coffee mugs and drank down to the dregs. A smile and she called for the check. Despite Milton's protestations, she made the waiter take her money. Mary Lou Lagotti had arrived in town.

Good Friday April 9, 1971

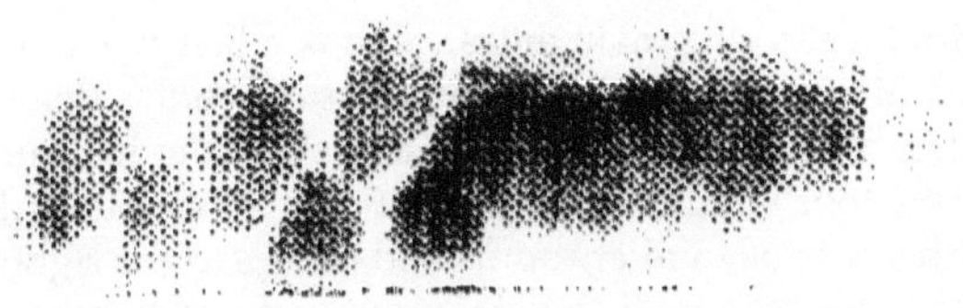

14

MILTON DROVE AND Mary Lou sat beside him. Destination: a warehouse on the far side of town where business could be conducted in relative privacy. All had been quiet since their last conversation until a week ago when Milton knocked on the front door and checked she'd be free today. She wasn't planning on going to Mass: why would she? Mary Lou stabbed god in the balls years ago and slashed his throat for good measure.

"You been to this place before?"

"Couple of times. We usually meet in LA."

"And you trust this guy?"

"He's a capo. Of course I trust him. What's not to trust?"

"Just running through everything in my head. Pay no never mind."

Plush homes flew past them until the buildings got smaller and packed closer together. Then they petered out to reveal some office blocks and light industrial usage. Just before they left Palm Springs altogether, heading north beyond the airport, stood a series of warehouses. Each had four foot high digits on the front, black on a white rectangle.

Too many cars to count were parked outside number five and Milton's vehicle joined them.

"You ready?"

"Yep. You?"

"Sure, but I'm not the one on trial today."

The hundred feet to the main entrance took a lifetime to walk. Mary Lou sensed her breathing getting tighter. Memories of Frank's disused factory and the countless meetings before the heist flashed into her mind's eye.

Through the door and into a large space. An enormous atrium four storeys tall with a row of smaller rooms and offices to the right. A tall and a short guy leaned against a wall chewing toothpicks. A stereotype in all but name.

Milton nodded like he knew them and headed to one of the closed doors. Mary Lou followed. On the other side were another pair of men at a table and three others wearing long coats strung along the walls of the fifteen by ten feet room.

Two chairs stood vacant; Milton sat on one and Mary Lou took the other. No handshakes. No acknowledgment. The two seated guys kept talking among themselves for a minute. Sounded like Italian but might have been Spanish—Mary Lou had no way of knowing.

She remained silent for now, aware there was an unspoken protocol to follow.

"Okay, thanks for agreeing to see us. I appreciate the importance of your time."

"We always have space for our friends. And their colleagues too."

A beady stare at Mary Lou.

"I thought there could be some mutual benefit in us all meeting up. I'll leave you to introduce yourselves."

"My name is Pasquale Bassani and that is introduction enough. Anyone who abuses knowledge of this ends up buried in concrete or stuffed in a sack in the desert."

"Fabio. I help look after Mr. Bassani's business interests."

"Mary Lou Lagotti. I have money to invest in the right project. Thank you for seeing me today."

"That name means nothing to me. What are you to me, Mrs. Lagotti?"

"I'm the answer to your next question. I have significant wealth obtained through illegal channels and I want more of it. Milton told me you were the people to speak to on this. If he was wrong, we can stop this conversation right away and not waste our time."

Both men continued to glare at her and Milton shuffled in his seat.

"That we're in the same room means you've checked me out otherwise you'd be foolish people. And you don't come across to me like mooks. So you should be asking me how we can work together."

Mary Lou fell silent. As much as she wanted to be back in the game, she was no pushover. They needed to understand that from the get-go else no dice.

"Mrs. Lagotti. I mean you no disrespect, but you come here with no track record. All I'm determining is what you have achieved. I am sure there is greatness behind you. As you mention, Milton wouldn't be stupid enough to bring a waster."

"Until now, I have kept my achievements quiet on the west coast. If I tell you, I put my life in danger."

"To be honest, if you don't tell me, your future prospects will be severely curtailed and your two children shall become orphans."

Flat voice. Cold expression. Simple truths. Mary Lou liked his direct approach.

"The First Bank of Boston haul in '68."

Her eyes flit from Pasquale to Fabio and back again.

"Congratulations. That was a million dollar take, was it not?"

"Only if you believed the radio. Nearer to half a mill' dirty. The money's been laundered since then—and is broadly intact."

She watched as Bassani calculated what sum remained in her possession. His eyes widened as he appreciated the potential investment sitting on the other side of the table.

"Thank you, Milton. You can wait outside."

Once the door had closed behind him, Fabio offered Mary Lou a cup of coffee, which she accepted.

"If you want Milton, he'll come out of your end, not ours."

"Understood."

"He will keep the source of your finances with him to his grave. And I'm gonna assume you'd like our business dealings to remain private, which is why I invited him to leave."

"Appreciate it. The fellas lying around the room appear to be okay to stay, apparently."

"If any of these gentlemen make the mistake of opening their mouths, I can assure you, they will lose their tongues."

"Do you have any projects we could work on?"

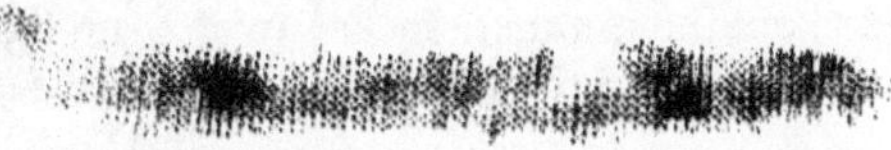

CHARLIE PENTANGELO HAD put on around ten to fifteen pounds since the day he heard Frank Lagotti Senior had been shot in the face. The two events were not connected, but both were true. Charlie was heavier and the Shylock was dead.

The cream sauces and red wine had flowed well for him as the business interests of the Baninno family improved and increased. Their reach had extended from coast to coast. Back in '68, they had made some initial forays beyond the East Sea Board but in the intervening time, the family had consolidated its hold on the other New York families so much that it needed to expand westward to maintain growth. The mob did not differ from any other conglomerate with a saturated market in one part of the country.

Vegas proved to be a wonderful place. Strong connections with high profile New York performers drew the crowds to the shows and the lure of free money dragged people into the casinos. Never had, so many losers deceived themselves into believing they were winners.

This activity fueled projects further west—along with the power wielded by the New York mob inside Hollywood. Those self-same cabaret performers appeared in the movies and Los Angeles became a location of interest.

The natural consequence of these business considerations was the need to have an increased direct influence in what happened in the City of Angels. There had always been an accommodation between the gangs to the east of Chicago and those to the west. Tithes and appreciation flowed in both directions so everyone was content with the relationship.

By the time a man landed on the Moon the amount of cash generated by Vegas—and its money laundering potential—became an object of direct interest to the Baninno clan. It knew Chicago was too hard a nut to crack but Nevada and beyond was a different game, partly because New York families had been the bedrock of both Vegas and LA in previous generations. Their blood had spilled on those streets.

During the same time, the West Coast mob had ripped itself apart with infighting and an unpleasant decision by some members of the warring families to spill their guts to the Feds. This meant that, despite the tremendous opportunities afforded by having one obscenely rich community and another festooned in poverty, money was tight across what was left of the West Coast families.

By 1971, Nick Lica was barely in charge of the west coast operation amid a string of confessions by mafiosi rats. Beneath him was Joe Dip, the underboss in the City of Angels but there was scarcely a structure beyond them as local hoods kept the numbers racket away from the family's touch. As LA was the movie capital of the world, Joe made a pile of cash out of the porn industry.

Pasquale Bassani reported directly to Dip and maintained his allegiance to this failing empire out of habit rather than any belief about Lica and Dip's ability to steer the family to better times.

"I'm sure we can find some project of ours for you to invest in."

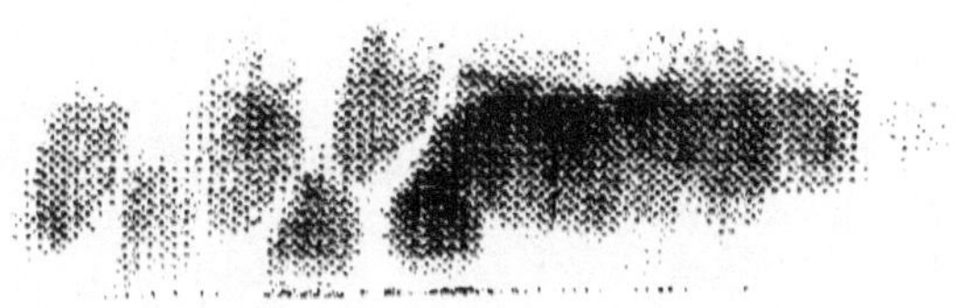

15

"I'M OPEN TO any kind of venture you have in mind."

"If you can't handle yourself in any situation, I'd wonder what you're doing sat here. There are two opportunities to appear recently. One involves brown sugar and the other China white."

"First things first, then."

"There are many the dispossessed and poor living in Los Angeles. For all the obvious reasons, they want to escape from the tedium of their humdrum lives and can't afford to move, get an education or make something of themselves."

"Okay."

"That is where we come in and offer a service to solve their short-term needs. A small bag of heroin enables them to leave their impoverished circumstances for a few hours and it only costs a handful of dollars."

"And how do we make any money if it's all low value?"

"When we ship the material into the US, it is normally ninety per cent pure. That'd kill a bull elephant. So we dilute it to three or five per cent; cut it in with other chemicals like quinine. That multiplies our profit by a factor of twenty, minimum."

Mary Lou smiled. This was quite some business model. Why bother robbing banks when you can rob the poor and ineffectual?

"That means you need somewhere to make the smack cocktail?"

"Yes, that is a cost, but once you are up-and-running with a network of dealers, the money rolls in and the only problem is where to store the green."

"Terrible dilemma to have."

"Right now, there is a factory idle because we need a sizeable amount of cash to buy the first shipment. Within three months, you'd have paid us back and be sitting on a gold mine."

"Pay you for what?"

"The rent of the equipment and manpower. We have a network to sell the material."

"I'd rather you were a business partner than a landlord."

"So be it. Just remember that if we share the profit, then we share the risk."

"I wouldn't have it any other way; it means we must watch each other's backs. If one of us goes down so does the other."

"Understood."

"Tell you what. Why don't we start with a small-scale test? See if we work well together before we get involved in any serious investment. If after a gig either side parts waves then no harm, no foul. We walk away with no malice toward the other party."

"Seems reasonable. Your caution is sensible."

"I'm thinking of a ten grand payment to cover the cost of the rent—just for this first job—of all your resources. And then we split the profit fifty-fifty."

"Mary Lou, a good opening offer but not acceptable. We need eighty per cent. On this job, we take on all the risk. You are merely providing the seed capital."

"My guess is you expect me to run the project and not just cut a check. So there is risk on my shoulders. Besides, without my money, you have no profit and there needs to be an appreciation of these matters. Eighty per cent is not a reasonable figure. I said fifty and I meant it. That is fair and means we can move forward on a similar basis too.

"You know if we are successful, I'll buy the factory and men off you so you'll make your money at the back end. But you will not play me like a sap upfront."

Pasquale and Fabio spoke in hushed tones on the other side of the table. The air was calm and the guys leaning on the walls appeared unconcerned by the discussions taking place before their eyes.

"Your proposal is acceptable."

"Before we seal the deal, tell me about the other opportunity."

"Oh, that is a lot less profitable but much more fun. The high life of the rich and famous in Hollywood is legend. Drugs and alcohol fuel the party atmosphere. The days of Prohibition are well and truly over so we no longer have any interest in that. But as you now know, narcotics attract a very large profit margin."

"Right."

"Cocaine is the substance of choice with the Hollywood set nowadays. In the '60s it was marijuana but a new breed of actor has arrived, wanting something with more of a kick to it. Mellow is out and hyper is in.

"Whatever. There are similar profits to make out of China white in the movie community. Again, funding is the key as we have the connections overseas to get product."

"Why don't we run both opportunities alongside each other?"

"That is entirely possible. Be aware, there is a smaller pool of customers. Even though the product costs more than brown sugar, there is still less actual money to be make out of Hollywood."

"You get to mix with the film stars however."

"Yep. There is that bonus, but it doesn't pay the rent."

"Okay, let us put that thought on hold and focus on heroin."

"I am glad you are prepared to keep your eyes on the prize."

"We are here to make money, not collect autographs. How soon can we start?"

"Depends how long it'll take you to deliver your cash."

"Let's say tomorrow, then."

Pasquale smiled.

"I admire anyone who can lay their hands on ten grand in a day."

"Thank you."

"Half the cash needs to come to us. The other half you use to make an initial purchase with some locals. Once you have the raw product, we manufacture the street bags over the weekend and count the profit before the end of the week."

Fabio went through the details of the job so she was crystal clear what she needed to do. Finally, they shook hands and Mary Lou walked out of the room to start her new life as a heroin dealer.

MILTON LEANED AGAINST the side of his vehicle as Mary Lou returned.

"Everything okay?"

"All is good, thanks."

He slid into the driver's seat and Mary Lou got in on the other side. Out the gates of the parking lot and the car headed back toward civilization.

"You guys work something out?"

"Sure have. You up for working with me on it?"

"Depends what it is. I won't touch child porn but I'm open to almost anything else you got."

"No to child porn? Didn't realize you were a man of principles."

Milton chuckled and Mary Lou smiled, the left corner of her lips curling towards an eye, forming more of a closed-mouth snarl than a positive expression.

"So what is the deal?"

"I'll be looking to use some of your men, if you've any spare. There's a small shipment of heroin needs purchasing, cutting and distributing. Got any expertize in this area?"

"Not directly, no. I've made my money out of the numbers and other gambling pursuits. But I know people who can be very serious minded and handle themselves well if individuals cross the line."

"Good. It's going down this weekend, so I hope you don't have any plans. We'll need heavies for tomorrow when we make the trade and then I'm hiring a lab off Pasquale to cut the smack into five per cent bags. After that, we ship them out and watch the money roll in."

"Tell me the details later and we can figure out how many men we will need."

"I assume this comes with some appreciation from you."

"Of course, Milton. We are not communists. I am sharing the profit with Pasquale so what I give you comes straight from my pocket."

"Spare me the sob story and say me the number."

"Five per cent of the profits and if everything goes well this weekend, I'll add in a one-off brokerage payment too as the introducing agent."

"Is that your best offer?"

"Best and only. If you don't want a piece, then I will hire from Pasquale. All you have to do is supply some fellas and give me some advice along the way because you know the locals. For you, it'll be easy money. I'm the one who'll break into a sweat."

"If it's that great a deal, why offer it to me?"

"Because I am starting out in this town and I want to have friendly faces around when I do business. Someone to watch my back, if you will."

"I can do more than that."

"Don't get any funny ideas, Milton. This is business. If you want anything more from me, it is not for sale. Understood? You've got your girlfriend in LA to look after your dick. Not me."

Silence in the car as Milton mulled over her words. Perhaps she had been too harsh with him, but this was a commercial transaction and Mary Lou didn't want any complications caused by Milton's roving groin. Even if he was interested in her, she flat out did not find him the least bit attractive.

The other thought echoing in her head was that Milton was entirely dispensable after the first haul. He'd given up his connection with no expenditure of money and he was only acting like an employment agency: passing hired hands onto her for a few days paid work. He was not the only source of goons in California.

She figured she was being more than fair: paying him with profit which would far exceed the day rate he might extract from her. That meant she could lean on him and learn how the West Coast mob operated without putting herself as much in the firing line. If the shit hit the fan, Pasquale would look to Milton as the one who introduced her, especially if she was forced to fly the coop.

"No worries, Mary Lou. And no offense intended. Are we okay?"

"Sure are, Milton. All is good. This time next week, we'll be swimming in cash."

"That's the way to drown."

"You could buy Janet a yacht if you wanted to."

"You kidding? Not a word of this to Janet. I keep my business separate from her life. Understood?"

"Fine by me. You organize your world how you want. I meant nothing by it. If you prefer, buy your mistress a sailboat and take the family out for a pizza. For all I care."

Milton laughed and Mary Lou chuckled with him. These men all lived with their double standards and their women did the same. Nobody was honest any more.

"What'll you do with your share of the winnings?"

"Invest it in other opportunities. Stash some away for a rainy day. Might buy a mink coat and something for the twins."

"You sure love your family."

"They're all I got. I've no one to escape from and have an affair with. Nothing personal."

"I love Janet. Really do, but domestic life isn't for everyone and I need other outlets for my… passions. But whatever I do when I go away from her, I always return to Janet. She's my northern star. If it wasn't for her, I'd still be a street punk hustling for quarters."

"My Frank saved me from a life of low-rent alley bootstrappers, but it's just me and the twins left. I gotta do right by them."

"Children are a gift from god."

"They are a gift, certainly."

Mary Lou stared out the window as the smaller houses turned into larger ones. She thought of the night she gave birth to Alice then Frank Jr four minutes later. The agony. And the ecstasy of seeing her charges for the first time.

Milton parked the car outside number twenty.

"Want to come in so we can sort out the details?"

"I'll pop by in two hours. I'm expected home for lunch."

She shrugged and went inside as Milton headed for his fish lunch. Nothing in this world like a good Catholic.

THAT AFTERNOON, SHE phoned Bobby and asked him to come round. He started the conversation after she'd handed over a mug of coffee.

"Is there anything wrong?"

"No, I wanted your advice and some things are best kept off the national phone lines."

"What are you up to?"

"Why do you assume I'm up to something?"

"If you are concerned about a wiretap, you're not baking cookies for the Girl Guides of America."

"You acquainted with a guy goes by the name of Fabio Abate?"

"Do you?"

Another silence.

"That's a yes, then."

"You meet Pasquale too?"

"Sure did."

"Are you about to go into business with them?"

"Planning to."

"You know much about them?"

"Yep. Known them for years."

"Done business with them?"

"Worked with them. Now I'm out of that sort of work, like I told you."

"What did you do?"

"I don't want to talk about it."

"But this is important. Could help me over the next few days—the more I know about them… Can I trust them?"

"They are straight down the line fellas."

"And why did you stop working with them?"

"Number of reasons, nothing specific to them."

"Tired of the life?"

"And some, but we're all weary of something. That's no reason."

"So what was your excuse?"

"Something happened. Totally in my control."

"And completely tragic?"

"You betcha."

"A death?"

"U-huh."

"Won't ask any more."

"Thank you for that."

"All things being equal, would you work with them again?"

"Ye-es. The hesitation in my voice is because of how they behaved at the end."

"Something for me to worry about?"

"Nah. Lightning doesn't strike in the same place twice."

"I am still not getting a great vibe off you."

"No need to worry. Really."

"Okay, but I'm not convinced."

"Would you like me to ride shotgun?"

"What?"

"Be by your side?"

"No thanks. I think I've had more recent experience of shooting someone than you have."

"Maybe so. The offer's there if you change your mind."

Mary Lou liked Bobby, but he came across as quite passive nowadays even if had been a hustler in the past.

"How about Milton?"

"Into anything that'll turn a buck. Like the rest of them."

"Oh?"

"Yeah. I've heard he's quite the reliable type, but expect nothing requiring imagination from him. He knows the numbers racket and moneylending."

"That goes with extortion and violence."

"He's handy with a crowbar and a gun, yes."

"And reliable?"

"You can rely on him to follow the money. If you keep him greased, he'll stay with you until the end of the world."

"And if he sniffs a better offer round the corner?"

"Then you won't see him for dust."

As he walked out, Mary Lou gave him a hug. One day she'd find out who he'd killed to leave the gangster life. But not today. Bobby squeezed her waist and let his hand hang there a while as she stepped away.

"Take good care of yourself, Mary Lou Lagotti. I'd hate for anything to happen to you."

"I'll be fine, Bobby Trevisan."

"Hope you're right."

She closed the door, had dinner with the twins and put them to bed. Cindy had the night off, so she'd stay late the following night. Who knew how long it would take to buy five thousand dollars of brown sugar.

Saturday April 10, 1971

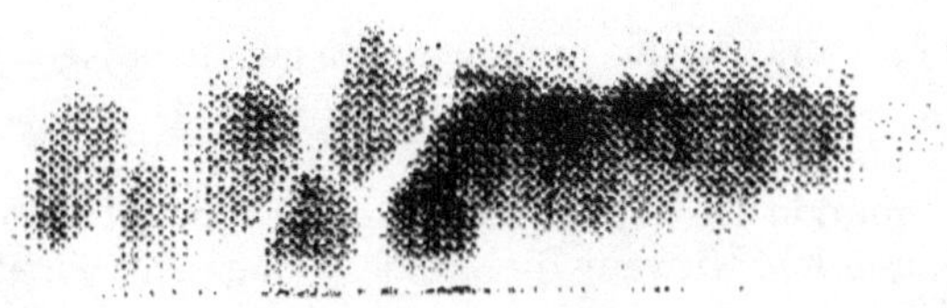

16

MILTON DROVE AGAIN with Mary Lou in the front passenger seat. Stephen Franco and Albert Nardi sat behind them, two of Milton's fellas. He assured her they were good guys as he introduced them in a diner on the outskirts of town.

They ate breakfast together—a team-building suggestion from Milton that made sense. Reality was that Stephen and Albert were not the talkative type. As Milton and Mary Lou discussed their plan for the morning's activity, the other two chomped on eggs, toast and coffee.

Neither had a discernible neck and their bodies had been invented for the word 'thickset'. She noticed a bulge in the left-hand side of each of their jackets so she drew comfort from the fact they were both packing a piece. Never walk into a gunfight with a smile and a knife. Not that this should turn into a gun battle. The contact had the heroin and they had the cash. Straight exchange and the four would be out of there before you could count to ten.

That was the intention. Milton preferred to consider what Plan B would look like if things didn't go exactly as intended. His attention to detail echoed Frank's approach to business; he might be a goofball, but she respected Milton for the way he was handling himself this morning. There was more than a fatuous grin and roving dick to the man.

"Albert: whatever happens, you make sure you cover Mary Lou. She is our number one priority."

"Got it."

"And if they are not forthcoming with the merchandise, what'll you do Stephen?"

"Wait on your instructions."

"Correct-o-mundo. Do not decide for yourself to grab the product. Second, do not interfere with any discussion taking place. Finally, do not use your piece unless someone is aiming a barrel at your head or I give you permission."

"Sure thing, boss."

"When we arrive, let me do the talking, okay?"

"Not really. It's my money, my connection and my deal. If they can't speak to me the first day we meet, how are they going to cope with doing business with me in the future?"

"These are old-fashioned men…"

"Who live in the modern world. They like it or lump it, but they must trade with me either way."

Milton was silent and the other two stared blankly, waiting for their next instruction. He sipped his coffee and let the tension subside.

"If you say so. I counsel against it, but it is your party and I am merely a bit player."

Mary Lou nodded to emphasize a decision made but she could see Milton wasn't happy with the outcome. Sometimes being stubborn was not the best way to deal with people.

"I've brought some test equipment which we must use before we accept the shipment. And they are bound to want to count the money. While all this is going on, you two need to keep your eyes open for trouble."

Milton turned to Mary Lou.

"If something goes awry, it's normally when everyone's attention is on checking the goods."

"Have you tested this kind of product before?"

"Yes. Not for a year or so, but I have experience and know what I'm looking for, if that's what you mean."

"It does. What a wide set of business interests you've had."

He smiled in appreciation of her comments and that he couldn't have been very successful in the heroin trade. The profit was too vast compared to the numbers. If it had worked for him, he'd have left small-scale gambling behind.

"Mary Lou, while I'm mucking about with the scales, you must keep your eyes on our hosts, not on me. No matter how fascinating you think I may be, watch them like a hawk, okay?"

"Understood."

"And if the deal goes south, stick your tits out. Might confuse them long enough for us to get the initial shot."

Mary Lou glared at Milton, self-conscious. This was the first day she'd worn jeans and a tee shirt since she'd fled Burbank Airport. After that, she had lived in tie-dyed below-the-knee skirts and dresses. But today, she needed to be ready for action and a skirt wasn't appropriate. The red glow on her cheeks subsided and she took a glug of coffee.

"Just you make sure we're walking out with the right kind of powder, mister. I have no intention of paying five grand for a pile of talc."

"It'll be cool. But if it's not, let's meet up here at three this afternoon and pick over the bones of what went wrong."

Nods all round as they finished their drinks. Mary Lou picked up the check and they split up in their two vehicles.

"How reliable are Albert and Stephen?"

"They've got me out of enough trouble in the past. Got an issue with either of them?"

"Not at all. Just running through everything in my head. I don't know them so that's a concern until I see how they handle themselves. I get you wouldn't bring along a doofus or two to mind the bags, but there's a difference between what you see and what you know."

"Sure. I'd think the same if I was in your sling backs. But they are reliable fellas. Not the brightest, I'll admit, but they have a good nose for situations and respond well to trouble."

"That's what we need."

"Although Albert is prone to shoot first and ask permission afterwards."

"Kidding me?"

"No, each time he's been right, but he generates that split second of panic when everyone thinks they will die, because no one expects him to fire first."

"Something to look forward to."

"We'll be fine. In the general scheme of things, this is a small amount of China white and chump change for our contacts—with all due respect to your hard-earned money."

"None taken."

The rest of the journey took place in silence as Mary Lou stared out the window and watched the world fly past.

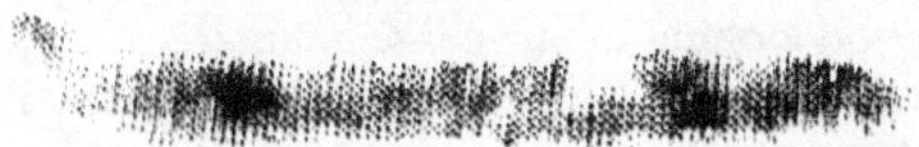

NORTH OF THE airport lay a handful of buildings that bled away into the desert. Close to transportation for drug mules and far enough from anywhere citizens might want to go to, which meant the local cops wouldn't bother with the area, not even an occasional drive by. There wasn't sufficient property to be defended to warrant the police time. Perfect.

Milton drove to a building that a realtor would describe as a light industrial workspace. There were two cars parked in front before they arrived.

"Looks like we got company."

"Take everything nice and easy. Let's only bring the money inside when Stephen and Albert get here."

Almost on cue, the two men lurched to a halt next to Milton's vehicle.

"Keep sharp."

Into the building and a hallway leading to a back room—an open space covering most of the first floor. In the corner were spiral stairs heading up to who knows what. There were cardboard boxes and shelving running all along, creating a miniature labyrinth to work around to reach the guys stood at the far end of the room.

Milton raised a hand in recognition as the four picked their way through the controlled chaos of the box-and-shelf maze.

"Nice place you got here, Candido?"

One man nodded to announce himself while the two others remained still. Statues.

"Glad you could make it. Any problems getting here?"

Mary Lou shook her head as a plane roared overhead. No one flinched even though the noise was close to deafening.

"Nice place you got here."

"It'll do, lady."

Alberto and Stephen stood as bookends with Milton and Mary Lou in between. One stranger wore a cream suit, while the three others had jeans and brightly patterned shirts. Straight out of Hawaii.

"We've been informed you have some product you're hoping to put our way."

"Reckon you might be right. You a cop?"

"Nope. You?"

"No."

With formalities over to confirm neither was working for Hoover, they could concentrate on the business at hand.

"How much you looking to pur-chase, mama?"

"We'll get there, my man. No need to rush to the end. First, introduce me to your friends, so we can all know each other better."

He pointed at the other two.

"Silvestre and Barclay. Now we're buddies. Can we get down to business?"

"Sure, man. We can get this done in a matter of minutes."

Mary Lou glanced at Milton, not understanding why he butted into her conversation.

"How much you got?"

"Lady, you have this all upside down. You tell me how much you carrying and I'll say the quantity of product we're prepared to part with."

"Five thousand."

"What the fuck?"

"You heard."

"You dragged us here to buy half a pound? That's not worth switching on the lights."

Why hadn't Milton said something? And what about Pasquale? They were in a dark and dangerous hole, slowly sinking.

"Listen, Candido. There's been a small misunderstanding but nothing we can't sort out."

"Are you fucking with me?"

"No. I was given false information. We can turn this round if we work together."

"Candido, the lady is out of her depth but you and I have a history. You know we can make this good."

Mary Lou shot a fiery stare at Milton, who had undermined her at just the wrong moment. You didn't need to be a psychiatrist to sense trigger fingers were getting itchy. A quick glance at every expression in the room told you everything.

"Stand firm, Alberto. You too, Stephen."

"On it, boss."

"Look, if we talk about ten grand does that buy us a pound of China white?"

"Still hustling us."

"Not at all. Just attempting to get back on an even keel."

"Sounds more like you're trying to run the show."

"Your show and no mistake. If you want to, I'll reach an agreement with you. If not then no harm, no foul and we'll leave you be, straight away."

"No need to go running off, missy."

"None of us are going anywhere, just yet. Depends on the deal you eventually offer me."

"You in charge are you, little lady?"

"Yes. I assume that will not be a problem for you."

"Doesn't have to be. I'll let you know later."

"Waiting on bated breath. So do we have the makings of some accommodation here?"

"Yes, Milton. A pound of raw for twelve thousand."

"That's too rich for our blood."

Mary Lou fumed again at Milton's indiscretion and poor decision making. She did not understand why he thought he should lead the conversation when he was only getting five per cent. The chances of a finder's fee was fast diminishing.

"Then twelve thousand can procure you a pound and a half."

"You weren't listening to Milton. The twelve was too high. We aren't negotiating over the amount it might buy us. In case you forgot, we're here to purchase a pound of your finest."

"No need to get tetchy, mama."

"So how much for a pound?"

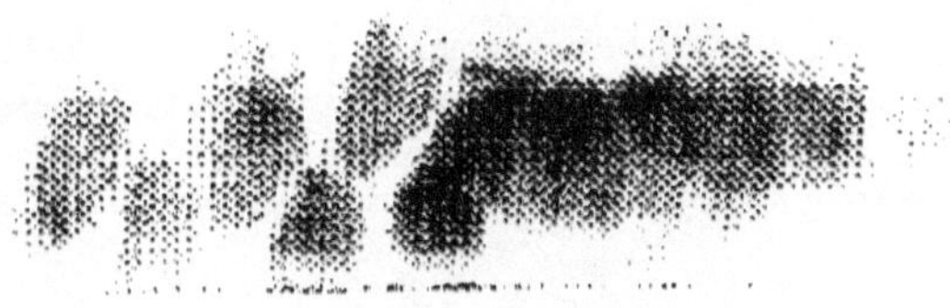

17

"TEN GRAND FOR one pound. If you come back with a bigger order, then we'll have more room to maneuver."

Mary Lou knew this was twice the amount Pasquale expected her to spend which meant she was getting fucked by these two strangers. But Milton didn't appear to flinch at the price. So either he had a side arrangement with Fabio and Pasquale or he had set her up to fail. Neither were good news.

On a positive note, she hadn't been stupid enough to only bring the exact amount of cash. Mary Lou thought there might be a better deal on the table if she doubled the quantities so was in a good position to close the transaction Candido proposed.

She opened her money purse and removed ten thousand. One of Candido's guys flipped the lid on a cardboard box and pulled out a bag of white powder. Milton took it and Mary Lou handed over the cash for counting.

He produced some scales and vials of clear chemicals out of his toolkit and kneeled down to test the product. A small quantity of powder weighed out and he added a pipette of liquid onto the spoon. Twenty seconds wait and then he held the cutlery up to the light. It remained transparent.

He scrunched up his face like he didn't understand what was going on. Then he wiped the spoon clean on a cloth and picked out another peck of powder and added a pipette of chemical. Same result: clear liquid.

Milton raised the vial to show Mary Lou and she nodded by reply. Then she looked at Alberto and blinked once to show the seriousness of the situation and to alert him there may be trouble ahead.

"What gives?"

"Huh?"

"You've seen the test result. Twice. What are you trying to pull?"

"Nothing. There's four bags of the China white you asked for and paid for."

"Don't treat me like a fool. That's not heroin and you know it."

She looked around where they were standing and couldn't see her money. They must have stashed it in one of the boxes while Milton was testing the gear. He'd told her to stay sharp and she'd fallen for the oldest trick in the book.

"You have yourselves a problem, but it's easy to remedy. Two options: deliver me a pound of base or return my money."

"Look see, little lady. You got matters all upside down again. Your money's gone—right, Silvestre?—and there's no heroin round these parts for me to offer you. The only thing you and your compadres can do is to walk out and keep going.

"The options you're offering ain't gonna happen, so you gotta decide how you want to end this."

"Listen to me carefully. I do not intend to repeat myself and I need you to be clear I mean what I say."

"I'm hearing you."

"Good. The money or the smack. That's all you got left to choose."

Alberto shifted his stance slightly but everybody else remained perfectly still. Mary Lou eyed Milton, who checked on Stephen. Alberto and Stephen gazed at Candido, Silvestre and the third guy. They soaked in every inch of how they stood and what they did.

Candido took a pack of cigarettes lying on a shelf and lit one, throwing the rest of the packet on the floor. Silvestre, straight and tall like he was somebody, but she knew he was nothing more than a hired hand. A hush descended on the room and, for the first time since their arrival, Mary Lou heard the ticking of a clock.

"Stash or cash. I'll give you five seconds to decide."

Candido blew smoke rings and smiled a cheesy grin, looking to all the world as though he didn't care what she said or did.

"One."

Milton put his drugs paraphernalia back into his toolkit.

"Two."

Stephen and Alberto stood firm.

"Three."

Milton finished clearing his stuff from the floor but hadn't closed his toolkit—a hand drifted near the opening, resting harmlessly. A finger drooped inside.

"Four."

The corner of Silvestre's mouth twitched and a bead of sweat plummeted from his nose onto the floor. Candido stared straight at Mary Lou and Alberto kept staring in front, not even blinking.

"Five."

A SLUG RIPPED through Candido's shoulder causing him to fly sideways with the force of the impact. Mary Lou hit the dirt as Alberto added a bullet to Candido's back.

Milton whipped out a gun from his toolkit and blasted in the general direction of the three men, but not one shot reached human flesh. Stephen stepped aside, behind the corner of a shelf and took aim at Silvestre. A red pool in between his eyes showed the trajectory of Barclay Valdez's slug and Stephen keeled over.

Alberto maintained his shooting rate at Candido and Mary Lou focused her attention on Silvestre, who refused to go down. Milton opened a barrage of fire at Barclay until bloody circles appeared across his torso and he collapsed dead.

That left Silvestre who was scurrying along the floor, trying not to be in anyone's line of sight. A bullet popped into a box and a ball of powder erupted out. Holes plastered the wall and Silvestre cowered round a corner to escape the shower of firepower directed at his body.

Mary Lou aimed square at his chest as the hail of bullets descended around him and pop. He went down as one of her slugs entered his torso and ripped through his heart.

An eerie silence took over the room as Mary Loushe surveyed her people to see who was left alive. Only Stephen had bought it. The rest stood up and headed toward the bodies to ensure they were goners.

They picked up the spare guns and she walked around systematically checking the boxes to find the real China white they'd come for. Alberto recovered her money from a box near Candido's corpse.

After fifteen minutes searching, they had uncovered twenty four bags which Milton confirmed contained heroin and two sacks of more or less flour.

"Six pounds of smack for zero dollars. Nice work if you can get it."

They removed Stephen's body and dumped it in Alberto's car then returned for the money and drugs. If there'd been any gasoline, Mary Lou would have torched the place but there was none. Instead, they shut the door on the way out and relied on the fact that few would worry about the absence of the inhabitants for quite some time.

Alberto knew to drive to the far side of town—south and still further—and bury Stephen in the desert where no one would find him. Mary Lou and Milton returned to her house, coming in the back way, past the summerhouse. Cindy was playing with the kids in the living room.

While Milton stayed in the indoors out of sight, Mary Lou scurried upstairs and took a shower and changed her clothes. The dirt and dust from their earlier escapade clung to her like a shroud. Then back past the pool.

"You want to freshen up before we shift the gear?"

"Thanks, don't mind if I do."

She stayed with the white while he popped indoors and sorted himself out. Mary Lou took the opportunity to put her money away.

"You ready?"

They walked out the front of the house and transferred the bags into Mary Lou's car—at her insistence. She wasn't sure why the situation had gone so awry, but she was damned certain she hadn't caused it. Until she figured that out, she needed to keep an eye on Milton. And have a conversation with Pasquale too.

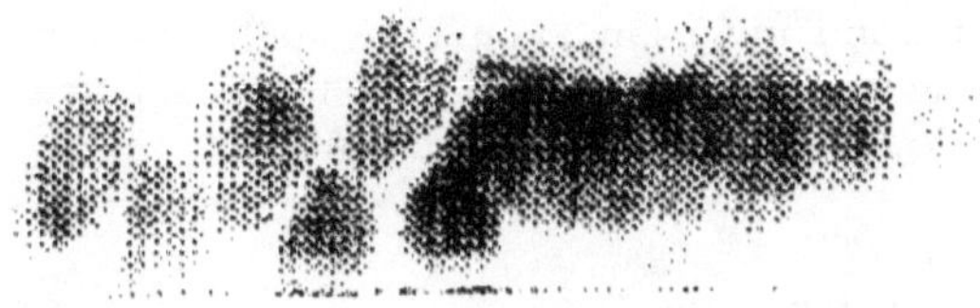

18

BACK IN THE room with Pasquale and Fabio, but this time Mary Lou was
not in a good mood. Milton sat next to her and knew she was angry based on
the silence in the car on the way over. She hadn't said a word since he came
down from the shower in her house.

"What kind of stunt was that to pull?"

"Did you strike a deal?"

"We'll come to that in a minute. Answer my question first."

"You appear quite emotional right now. Do you need a Java to calm
down?"

"I'll take the coffee, but you have to explain why you let us walk into a
situation where the vendor wanted twice as much as we were prepared to
pay. You brokered this deal and it went south almost before I opened my
mouth."

Milton nodded agreement, but he couldn't bring himself to look
Pasquale in the eye. He shuffled again in his chair as though he hoped
somehow to vanish from sight and leave Mary Lou on her own with her
anger and Pasquale.

"Mary Lou, I respect what you achieved in the past—back east—but
please remember that we judge you on what you do now. And you are not
speaking to me in an appropriate manner. I have forgiven you so far, but my
patience is wearing thin."

"Listen to me and understand: you set us up this morning and I want you to give me an explanation. If you can't do that, just let me know and I'll be outta here. Along with my six pounds of smack."

"Six?"

"You heard me."

"We can come to that later."

"You betcha."

"Candido and his crew have been a thorn in my side these past few weeks and I was hoping you could sort them out.."

"We sure did. But you could have told me beforehand. I don't mind doing someone else's dirty work. I prefer to be informed in advance."

"Think of it as a small test of your mettle, if you like. For your bank job, you were surrounded by many gang members. We needed to be sure you could handle yourself."

A smirk spread across Fabio's mouth as he glanced at Pasquale every few seconds.

"What's your problem, motherfucker?"

She jabbed a pointing finger in Fabio's direction. He sneered back, not caring what she thought or what she said. The coffees arrived and one of Pasquale's men placed them on the table. This interruption defused the tension but she continued to glare at Fabio as he ignored her and sipped his piping hot drink.

"We appreciate your efforts, Mary Lou. Truly. If you suffered any inconvenience, then we can discuss any necessary compensation."

"A bunch of flowers sent to Stephen's widow would be a good start."

"Just the one fatality?"

"Yes."

"Consider it done. We will look after the family directly. Milton: my condolences to you and those who mourn. He was a solid fella. Rest in peace."

Milton, Pasquale and Fabio made the sign of the cross in front of their upper bodies. Classic Catholic auto-response.

"On the positive side, Stephen was not the only death. Candido and Silvestre will no longer be a problem for you. They breathed their last."

"Good news. That explains the volume of product in your possession. And I assume your stake is intact?"

"Sure is."

"Excellent. Pleased to hear it."

"Not as much as me."

Pasquale allowed himself a brief smile. The tension was diffusing as the two protagonists eased into their conversation.

"Probably not, but they had been costing me plenty—ever since they moved into the area Christmas time."

"And now we have freed you from these concerns."

"More or less."

"How so?"

"Well, as much as Candido was a pain in the ass, he was the front. A guy name of Sancho Mendoza was backing him and will no doubt look to replace the fella with another. Until he does, we take over his territory."

"We?"

"Your hard work from this morning deserves to be rewarded. Assuming you can lay off the six pounds, we can go into partnership on a more extensive basis."

"Partnership?"

"The fifty-fifty deal we agreed when last we met."

"That still alive?"

"Always has been. I enjoy working with professional operators like yourself."

Mary Lou nodded to receive the compliment.

"Once we have the operation up-and-running, we can discuss the financial terms of the partnership. I am expecting to show you appreciation moving forwards, but if this business is as profitable as I believe it is then I should be able to own my own facilities sooner rather than later."

"The future is all to play for. Let us focus on the Mendoza matter and we can deal with the rest afterwards."

"Okay."

"You will need to convince Mendoza to relinquish his control. Either by giving up on the territory or by drawing his last breath."

"How far back does the bad blood between you and Mendoza go?"

"A matter of months. This is business and is nothing personal. I have no desire to see the man dead, but I don't care whether he is alive. What matters to me is that he ceases to impede my business interests."

"Got it. And must I use Milton's firepower or will you be able to offer more tangible support on this occasion?"

"My resources are at your disposal. All you need to do is let Fabio know your needs and he will get it for you. We want you to succeed because your success is our profit too."

"How many men does Mendoza have?"

"Around ten or twenty. They run the north of Palm Springs but there's a sizeable force in LA. That is where I'm keeping my eye on. The local operation is useful to get only in so far as we can leverage it against his main area of control."

Mary Lou contemplated what Pasquale had told her. Chances were he was honest with her and they set her up as a test to see if she could handle herself. And she had passed their exam. But she wondered if she would have been lured into such a stupid situation if Frank had been by her side. In her eagerness to get back into the game, she'd forgotten how easy it was to be suckered into a dumb plan.

"Let's take the fight to Mendoza, Pasquale."

MILTON AND MARY Lou had a bite of lunch in a local restaurant. Nothing fancy: a bowl of pasta and a glass of wine. Simple Sicilian fare.

"Did you know what would go down?"

"Not in the slightest. I was as surprised as you."

"I see. Next time we cut a deal with my money…"

"Yes?"

"When I said to leave me to do the talking: I mean it. You spoke for me back there before we shot them full of holes."

"Did I?"

"Yeah, sure did. If you want to carry on working with me, you need to listen to what I say. And act on it."

"Okay. Understood, I guess."

"Milton, do we have a problem here?"

"What? No. This is the first time I've worked with a woman."

"Get over it. You play straight with me. Don't assume I'm a pushover just because I have no dick between my legs. Then we'll be fine."

Milton ruminated on Mary Lou's words while she enjoyed her fettuccine. She understood her money might give her power but the men around her needed to see beyond her womanhood to bow down to her green.

"Are there any other guys to call on who are reliable like Alberto or Stephen were?"

"One or two I can lay my hands on at short notice."

"That'll be helpful. The size of the pie for this first deal has become a whole load bigger and we need to make sure we secure our investment."

"That's a polite way of putting it."

"Mendoza will come after us—for killing his people and stealing his drugs. Shame we didn't find their cash or we could have lifted that too."

"If they were there, the notes were well hidden."

"Didn't have the luxury of time. Where do you think we should offload the China white?"

"There's a small group of users in Palm Springs which is one reason Candido based himself here. The biggest source of eager customer will be in the LA projects. Watts in the south should contain enough demand for the amount we are seeking to shift."

"And do you have any network to leverage or are we going to go in dry?"

"I shall find out if anyone has any useful connections for us."

"And if not then we can take Pasquale at his word and ask for his help."

"Yep. Let's remember that his help comes with a price tag attached."

"I know but even forty per cent of something big is better than a hundred per cent of nothing."

Milton nodded, realizing Mary Lou's logic was flawless and acknowledging her pragmatism.

"AND WITH SIX pounds, will that impact the price?"

"Only if we dispose of it all on the streets at the same time."

"You saying we should spread the sales over six weeks?"

"It'll keep the price steady, but the longer we are on the streets, the better chance Mendoza has of attacking us."

"Do you think we should dump all the white this week?"

"I'm not suggesting that either. Just we'll make more money if we restrict supply a little. The risk is that this'll give Mendoza more opportunity to get to our men and kill them."

"It's almost all profit though, isn't it?"

"Apart from whatever fee we pay Pasquale: yes, the white cost us nothing but blood."

"And we don't want Mendoza in our face until we are ready to deal with him."

"Not particularly. He has a fierce rep. His name precedes him."

"That doesn't bother me. So some locals have heard of him: big whoop. I've never known of him so he's not that important. And every man can be felled with a single bullet between the eyes."

"Or a kick to the groin."

"You said it."

They both laughed a little, having regained some trust in the aftermath of the morning's events.

"We should flood the market then. We make some money to fund our next deal and Mendoza will find his prices drop too. Double whammy."

"And this time next week, we divide up the spoils."

"He must die or leave the state. Nothing else will be good enough."

"Fighting talk."

"I'm not in this for the good of my health. I want to make money and build something lasting for my children."

"Flood the market this week and fuck Mendoza the next?"

"Pretty much, yes."

"If we're selling small bags by Monday, we'll need quite an operation to refine the heroin over the weekend."

"I'm sure Fabio will oblige us with the facilities. Remember, they get rich when we make money."

"We should still get going."

Milton looked round until he found the eye of a waiter and gave the universal hand gesture of writing on his palm to get the check.

"Taking out Mendoza is no mean feat. He's surrounded himself with major security and even if you get past his goons, the man is built like an ox."

"That may be so, but there is always some way to bring a man down. We need to find his weakness."

"Do you believe you can take over Mendoza's territory, the time it takes most people to get out of bed?"

"I am a determined woman out to protect her children from the evils of the world. Underestimate me at your doom."

"Right, but you didn't answer my question."

They both chuckled and the waiter arrived with the check. Mary Lou dipped into her handbag and pulled out few notes. Milton's eyes widened as he took out his wallet from his pants pocket.

"I'll get this. Think of it as the first costs of my new operation."

"Apart from Stephen's blood."

"Pasquale already said he'd compensate you, so Stephen is taken care of."

Cold. Stark. Mary Lou'd never been so direct before losing Frank. She thought she'd be more sympathetic, but truth was she didn't give a damn. Stephen was expendable and, come to that, so was Milton. The important thing was to know who you care about and who you do not.

"Is that how you treat everyone who dies for you?"

"Stephen died for you, not me. I can't grieve for a person I knew only a few hours and I won't pretend just to help you feel better."

Milton looked at her, wanting to respond but knowing there was no point having a row about the guy. He was dead, they were alive and that was all that mattered. Mary Lou was right, but she didn't need to rub his face in it.

He drove them back to her house and pulled up outside the front door.

"You contact Fabio and get the processing underway. I'll secure my stake money and we can meet in an hour at the Country Club."

"Sounds like a plan."

Mary Lou hopped out the car and gave Milton a quick salute as he drove away. She turned to face the house and noticed the front door was ajar. Strange. She grabbed her gun and pushed the door with her other hand. Something was not right in the state of California.

19

SHE BRACED HERSELF and stood in the hallway. Scanned the stairs: nothing and no one. Deathly silence. Mary Lou's heart rate increased and a dull sickness in her stomach felt like it would erupt out of her mouth. The kitchen door was closed but, as usual, the living room was visible. She edged toward it, gun in hand.

"Cindy? Alice? Frank Jr?"

Nothing but the ticking of the clock on the mantelpiece. An armchair turned on its side and the contents of the coffee table strewn on the floor. Everything else in the room remained resolutely unchanged—as though nothing was wrong at all. The oppressive lack of noise in the building. Mary Lou's breathing stormed into her ears and her heart provided an undertow of rhythm.

The entrance to the conservatory: closed. The kitchen door open. Dining-room door shut. She sidled up, took a deep breath and whipped the wood open and swung her body sideways in case anyone was hiding inside. Just the table, armchairs, sideboard. Nothing out the ordinary—everything in precisely the location as when she'd been in it last night for dinner.

Back to the living room and over to the kitchen. She peered in at the open cupboard doors and chairs lying in a mess on the floor. A chill ran down her spine as Mary Lou noticed the knife block was missing one blade. The hole screamed to her from the other side of the room. Slowly, slowly into the room, she pointed the gun left and right but there was nobody to fire at and her children were nowhere to be seen.

"Alice!"

Silence.

"Frank?"

Nothing.

Through the kitchen and back out to the hallway. Upstairs. First to her bedroom at the front. Immaculate. Everything in its proper place. No one had been here since she left with Milton for lunch. There was nothing to see in the en suite either.

Next, over to the kids' bathroom, which Milton had used. Nothing untoward but he hadn't done a great job of tidying after himself when he left. No biggie.

A creak. Mary Lou stopped in an instant and tensed, ready to pounce on whoever was creeping around the house. She eased onto her front foot to give herself greater stability and the noise recurred. For a moment, she relaxed as she realized the floorboard under her toes caused the noise.

Still holding the gun in one hand and keeping the other on her bag to stop it swinging in her way, Mary Lou popped her head round the three other bedrooms. All the doors were open and half a glance inside showed there was nothing to see—apart from a spare bedroom, Alice's princess-themed palace and Frank's whirlwind debris-littered crash pad.

The only place left was Cindy's attic space. Again, the room might have needed a tidy but there was no one there: not under the bed, not in her wardrobes. Nada.

Mary Lou stopped for a second and tried to concentrate. Perhaps she had overreacted. What if they'd all gone out for a walk and Cindy had just forgotten to shut the front door properly? That didn't explain the upturned furniture. Her paranoia was well-placed.

With nothing else to see, Mary Lou descended to the living room. Her eyes cast round until she remembered she hadn't checked out the conservatory. And it's sliding door was closed, covered by the drapes. She them up so the kids could be in one part of the downstairs and adults could be elsewhere without interfering with each other. Close but separate. Now the blue velvet material of those drapes bore down on her. She was afraid what she would find on the other side.

She pulled the drapes back and leaped into the conservatory where she found: couches, rugs, a box full of toys with its lid shut. But no people.

"Cindy! Frank! Alice!"

Still no reply.

She plopped down onto a couch, looking out at the patio area. The room stuck out so three sides were glass although the far end was covered by drapes. On each side, Mary Lou saw patio furniture and empty space—just as it had been two hours ago when she sat in the summerhouse waiting for Milton. She leaned forward, placed the gun by her feet and rested her elbows on her knees. What to do? Where were they?

This change in body position gave a different angle to her view of the patio and now included a corner of the swimming pool. Mary Lou stared blankly into the abyss of her soul, losing focus on her surroundings. Then she blinked and noticed the pool and the wooden steps leading down into the water with their metal handrail.

She froze at the image before her. While her eyes remained trained outside, she lowered a hand and felt around until her fingers clasped the gun again. Pushed herself up off the couch, grabbed a handful of drapes and yanked them out the way.

The glass doors revealed what she knew was behind them and what she was certain she'd noticed by steps: red. The entire pool was filled with red liquid. Although the shade was quite pale, Mary Lou knew this was the color of diluted blood.

Out onto the patio, gun dangling by her side, she scanned the sides of the pool but no one. In the pool was another story: at the far side, near to the summerhouse, a body floated face down, fully clothed. Mary Lou didn't need to move from her spot to know who it was.

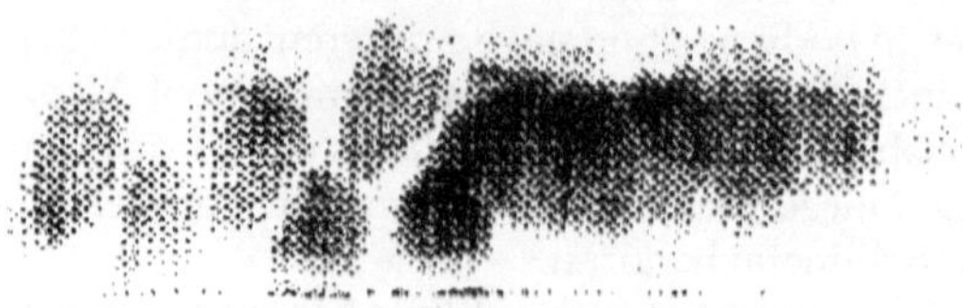

20

CINDY'S ADULT-SIZED corpse floated, bumping the far edge of the pool. As Mary Lou walked round, she raised her gun again in case there was anyone to shoot, but by now she knew the chances were slim to none.

She rolled up her sleeve and grabbed at the body, trying to flip it over. Failed at that, but there had been enough sideways movement for Mary Lou to know Cindy's throat had been slashed. At the bottom middle of the pool, she made out a shiny object glinting in the sunlight, despite the red mist surrounding it. Must be the knife from the kitchen.

Still no sign of the kids. Her only hope lay inside the summerhouse. Mary Lou dried her hands by wiping them on the tiles next to the pool and finished the process by rubbing them on the back of her jeans.

Her bag lay by the conservatory door and she cupped one hand against the glass window of the summerhouse to peep inside, but the sun's reflection prevented her from seeing anything meaningful.

Pulled the door open and shot indoors. A quick look around revealed nothing and the door to the safe room remained stoically locked shut.

She'd lost Alice and little Frank Jr.

First Frank and now the twins. She had nothing. Nothing at all. The absence of her boy and girl twisted her stomach inside out until she felt it spasm violently. The taste of acid hit the back of her throat and she vomited onto the floor.

Still standing, Mary Lou staggered backward and leaned on a chair, not knowing how she would cope. What should she do? Who had taken them and how was she going to get them back?

Her first instinct was to call the police. Not the cops who'd chased her across the width of the country. The local police who would understand a mother's despair and might have already gathered intelligence about their likely whereabouts. They might have been spotted somewhere about town.

Then she slapped her thigh as she perched on the arm of the chair.

"Get a grip, girl!"

Cops were cops wherever they were from. And how exactly did she intend to explain her housekeeper's throat slashed from ear to ear and floating in the pool? Is that what a normal kidnapping involves? Besides, abducting children meant the Feds would be called within the first five seconds. As sure as hell, they'd have a description of her on file. What if McNamara came to investigate? Mary Lou would not be calling the cops. To quash a parking ticket perhaps, but not to get the twins back.

The stench of her own sick lying on the floorboards by her feet made her stomach wretch again. She lurched out the summerhouse. Back onto the patio where she sat down on the ground, back against the summerhouse wall, feet apart, knees up. Mary Lou stared into the empty space between her legs and at the pale crimson expanse of water before her.

Tears squeezed out of both eyes and she let the gun slip onto the floor. Crash. The drops of salty water became a cascade and her shoulders rocked up and down as the sadness engulfed her. Memories of Frank's bloody body flickered across her mind and melded with images of Alice smiling and screaming or Frank Jr scampering and hollering.

Mary Lou allowed herself this silent howl because she felt so powerless. One minute she was having a shower and going off with Milton for lunch, the next her world was turned upside down. Nothing would be the same again. She was angry for allowing herself to believe everything was safe when she'd spent so much of her life waiting for the next time to run, to move on.

Why was she so stupid to think anything was any different, just because she'd wound up in a community on the west coast? Life was filled with broken glass wherever you were and whatever she did.

While she wouldn't get the cops involved, Mary Lou still needed help. She thought about calling Bobby but what was he going to do? One lone over-the-hill gunman? Nah, he wasn't any good. Fabio was probably the only answer available to her although how could she tell whether the west coast mob hadn't had a hand in this? As some way of keeping her in check while she built up their heroin trade?

Strange: there was no ransom note. If you extort somebody, it's best to let them know what they need to do to get their loved ones' safe return. This pointed to the kidnapping not being about money—although she had hardly spent long enough in the house this afternoon to take a call for ransom demands. More time.

If it wasn't a money play, then this was about revenge or power. Mary Lou heard the ringing of the phone. She scrambled to her feet and rushed indoors to the living room and the nearest handset.

"Hello?"

Just as she picked up the receiver, she heard the line go dead. Damn. Goddamn. Was that the kidnappers or Milton or…

She sat on the couch and rocked backwards and forwards trying to get sufficient focus on events to see matters clearly. But every time she tried to think things through, some horrific image flashed across her mind and she had to stop before the pain became excruciating.

Who had taken her children?

THE THREE MOST obvious culprits were the New York mob who finally had caught up with her, Mendoza and the Latino connection or Pasquale and Fabio. The idea it was the west coast mob sounded plain stupid as they had already played their games with her. She'd come good and looked like she would earn them decent bucks, so Mary Lou discounted that option almost immediately.

That left the east coast contingent. If they had come for her, they usually were more direct in their behavior. In their eyes, she'd stolen from step uncle Frank Senior and his loss was shared with them. But their notion of revenge would involve a simple hit on her. There would be no interest in getting involved with her children. A knife in the back or a bullet from a long-range rifle was more likely than a kidnapping and the hassle of dealing with all that before they whacked her.

Mary Lou had heard stories of more complicated tales of revenge. They could have become annoyed the time it had taken for them to find her—they might be vexed at the cost of the resource needed to track her down. If that was the case then maybe they might have operated against type.

The trouble was they would have left a clear message that the twins' disappearance was their handiwork. A note perhaps and, if not, then a phone call with a menacing tone. But nothing? Made the New York contingent unlikely as the perpetrators.

This left Mendoza, who'd have had to act super fast after they did for Candido and Silvestre. Difficult, but not impossible. If it had taken them an hour to find out the white powder was gone and the two men were dead, they could have been round here as soon as spit and carried the twins off before Mary Lou'd had her first mouthful of fettuccine. A cold shiver along her back at the meaning of the words she'd just uttered to herself.

The probability was Mendoza, although why hit someone's family if they'd only made a small gouge into your business? This was not a proportionate response by the man. It also meant she needed to be very careful when dealing with him. He didn't follow the usual rules of the game, which meant he was dangerous and hard to handle.

The other thing was it gave her no better idea where to find Alice and Frank Jr. Even if Mary Lou could get hold of Mendoza, chances were the kids wouldn't be with him. Some hideout, surrounded by a bunch of goons who didn't care if her babies lived or died. At this point, she had to stop thinking for a minute as the ideas rattling around her head were too dark for her to cope with. Terrible images of their tortured limbs permeated the back of her eyelids.

Then the final possibility was plain random: some guys saw the expensive house, the housekeeper and decided Mary Lou was good for a buck or two and tried a kidnap. But again, surely they'd have left a ransom note. Some clue what they wanted and by when it needed to be delivered.

No. Mendoza was the man.

IF MARY LOU was going to do anything, then she needed to deal with Mendoza. She wondered around outside on the patio, trying to remember quite where she left her bag. Truth was she'd kept it near her all this time—a subconscious act. Mary Lou walked a full circuit around the pool. When she arrived back at the corner steps, she noticed the bag in her hand all along. Like an old maid searching for her glasses on her forehead.

Back into the summerhouse and Mary Lou fumbled for the keys to open the hidden door. She put the pile of greens in a locked box and returned it under the floorboard she'd previously jimmied open.

She perched on the arm of one of the summerhouse chairs, getting her head together so she could think straight and figure out the best next step to save her children. With or without Milton, she needed to contact Fabio and get some local help. If Pasquale wanted a real partnership between them, then he should be there for her in her time of need.

Mary Lou returned to the house and stood in the kitchen to dial his number.

"Can I leave a message for Fabio?"

She couldn't decide whether to read too much into his absence. Was he avoiding her or just not in for a million possible legitimate reasons? There was no way to know—not with the information she had right now. The doorbell rang and she automatically headed to the hallway, stopped herself and checked her gun was loaded.

With the pistol hidden from view, Mary Lou opened the door with her left hand to reveal a man dressed in a three-piece striped suit topped with a Fedora.

"Mary Lou Lagotti?"

"Who's asking?"

"Arnold Roach. You owe me money and I'm here to collect. Please take your hand from behind your back. Would be a tremendous shame to kill you after the time I've spent tracking you down."

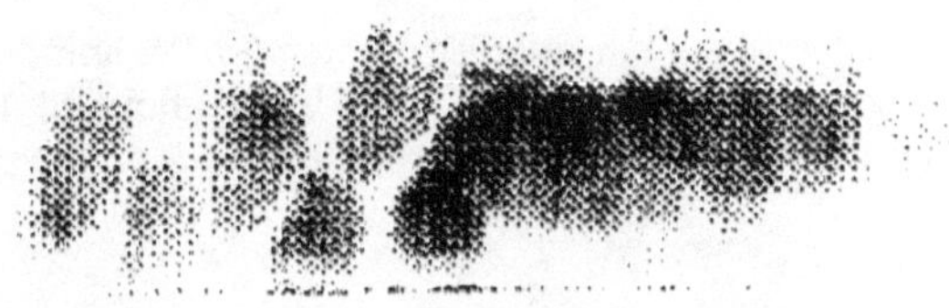

21

MARY LOU LET her right hand slip to her side so Roach could see her piece.

"You'd better come in."

As she closed the door behind him, Mary Lou noticed a three inch smear of red on the doorjamb. She missed that sign when she first came back from lunch. Was it Cindy's or the children's? Didn't bear thinking about. Besides, there was a mob hitman in her hallway she'd hired two years ago to whack Uncle Frankie.

"As you haven't taken out your gun and shot me between the eyes, I'm guessing killing me is not on your agenda."

"Mary Lou, that all depends on you. Like I said, we had a contract and you only paid me half my fee even though I carried out one hundred per cent of the service."

She craned her head back in the hope the position of her skull would somehow alter her ability to remember whether she'd paid the second installment. Nada. Ran away from California? Check. New life in Canada? Check. Heard the Shylock was six feet under? Nope.

"I appreciate you will not believe this..."

"Try me. You'd be surprised the stories people have spun over the years."

"The hit was aimed at a guy who was financing a robbery I was involved in."

"Mary Lou, I know all about the First Bank of Baltimore heist. You made the news in New York."

"Okay. Well, when the job headed south, ten tons of shit descended and I ended up having to skip the country. I never heard about anything that was happening in Baltimore from the day I turned my back on the place to today."

"U-huh."

"So I never heard you'd carried out the hit."

"I see."

They were standing in the living room by now although neither seemed interested in squishing down into the comfortable couches only feet away.

"Let me ask you a simple question. All I want is some honesty. Can you deliver that for me?"

"Of course, Arnold."

Mary Lou didn't feel right using his first name—a man she hardly knew—but he was pointing a gun at her chest and she had placed hers down on a coffee table as soon as they walked into the room.

He smiled. If she was going to disarm him with familiarity, he could do the same with a look.

"Is the payment available for my second installment?"

"Yes it is."

"Then if you would be so kind as to give me the money, I'll be on my way."

Mary Lou swallowed hard. She had the cash in the summerhouse and it was not a huge amount—certainly not for what it bought her. But she had a nagging doubt at the back of her mind.

"Thing is, Arnold, there's a problem, which I need to tell you about and you'll understand why I am nervous about paying what I owe."

"Oh?"

"Will you be honest with me?"

"I only ever kept my word to you. I intend to continue to do so."

"If I hand over the greens, what's stopping you killing me, anyway?"

Roach laughed and sat down. Mary Lou echoed the action.

"Good question. Usually I don't meet my clients, just their victims, so this isn't a situation I've had to deal with before."

Mary Lou allowed him the time to think as her life was on the line.

"I want to say there's nothing to stop me, but that won't encourage you to hand over the paper. The truth is that I won't kill you because no one has paid me to. I am a businessman and offer a very particular service."

"And if there isn't a fee in it then you don't whack people?"

"Pretty much, yes. I mean, if we were playing poker and you cheated, I'd say there was a justification. On the flip side, if you don't pay up then I will most definitely kill you this afternoon. In my business, I can't afford someone to welch on a deal with me and survive. That is very bad for future earnings."

"I can understand that."

"So you must trust me or you will die. You asked me to kill Lagotti and I did. No question why. Your wish was my command. I played fair and I have been exceedingly patient to wait this long for the second amount."

"I was in Canada..."

"...but you've been back for quite a while, I'd say. Yes?"

"True. A lot has happened since we last spoke."

"I am sure. Time passes quickly when you live our kind of existence: inside a criminal world."

Mary Lou nodded. Even though the man had tracked her down from across the other side of the country—more than the East Coast mob, the cops or the Feds had done—he didn't appear angry.

"I'll get your money."

"I am sure you will, but given you haven't kept your word to me so far, I shall accompany you in case you seek some alternative ending to this conversation.

Roach followed her through the conservatory and out onto the patio. He glanced down at the red water, but said nothing as they entered the summerhouse. Mary Lou unlocked her hidden room.

"I'll need some privacy in there. Look around first if you like, but you can't stand over me while I get your cash."

"So be it. Your personal affairs do not interest me. Only my money. If you come back out of that room without your hands in plain sight, you know what'll happen."

One minute later, Mary Lou walked out with both hands in front so they were visible to Roach before any other part of her body. Open palmed, she gave him the second half of the fee and sat down. This offered Roach an opportunity to count his cash and satisfy himself that all was well.

"Some trouble earlier on?"

Roach pitched his head toward the pool where Cindy's body remained face down. Floating.

"You know anything about it?"

Roach shrugged, lit a cigarette and sat down in a cushioned chair.

"Wanna tell me a story?"

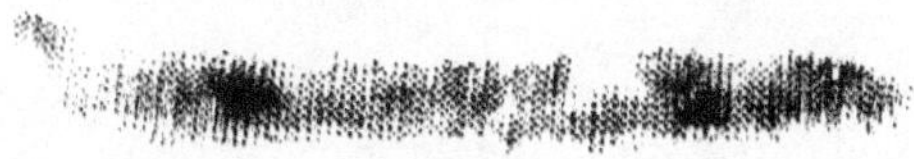

"YEAH, I GOT issues but before I tell you all about it, I need you to tell me how you found me, because..."

"...I'm not the only one looking for you?"

"Something like that."

"I took out Lagotti two weeks after you hit the bank, as agreed."

"We were hoping to launder the money by then but everything went crazy before we even left the vault."

"Uh-huh."

"Then I waited a week for the cash to appear and when it failed to do so, I made enquiries. Took me about twenty minutes before I discovered the extent of my problem."

"Oh?"

"You see, I have a primary client."

"Your fame goes before you."

"Very kind. I don't seek fame, only money. They'll never erect a statue."

"Sure, but in our circles, your name is legend."

"Shame Arnold Roach isn't my real name then."

He smirked, almost appearing to regret the line of work he excelled so well at.

"Let's say that shortly after you fled Baltimore, word was out there was a price on your head."

"Who had issued the order?"

"Does it matter now? Will it make any difference to you?"

"Not really. I'm interested, is all."

"Suffice to say, word came from New York and that meant only one man: Charlie Pentangelo."

"Is his the voice of God?"

"Not quite, but he's only one removed from St Peter for sure."

Mary Lou whistled to show her respect. She never imagined their escapade had been noticed by anyone of importance in the mob. She'd assumed Uncle Frankie had pleaded for help and he'd just leveraged his connections.

"Why were we even on his radar?"

"The size of the haul?"

"Don't believe everything on the radio. They made up that number."

"Quite possibly, but Charlie explained they used that bank as a laundering facility and were not pleased that the person who was supposed to be overseeing the business had skimmed half a million off the top right under their noses."

"Jeez Louise."

"At first, they thought you guys were behind it but a small amount of investigation proved that assumption wrong."

"How so?"

"I terminated the guy that July on a trip to Florida. Anyway, they knew you had lifted the money once the moneylender told them the size of the actual take. To be honest, if you hadn't paid me to plug him, Pentangelo would have done so."

"And you'd got paid either way."

"It is how I make a living. No mess, no fuss, no trace."

Roach's eyes veered toward the pool as if to assure Mary Lou he had nothing to do with the slaughter which took place here earlier. She ignored his gaze—for the moment.

As much as she had to deal, she also needed to be sure she could trust him. Also, she had no idea if anyone had followed him from the east coast and had taken advantage of the man's tenacity to get a bill paid. It might all tie together with whoever stole her children from her.

"We had a lot of heat coming down on us—from all sides."

She felt almost confessional with Roach—partly because of what he knew about her time in Baltimore and partly because of the simple, calm way about him. He might be about to kill her—who knew—but he was respectful to her and for what she had gone through at that fucking bank.

"But that was a long time ago. When did you pick up my trail?"

"In-between jobs, I came over to LA and asked some people a bunch of questions. Didn't take long to figure out you went north. Then three more trips and I tracked you to Clark Park."

"It was you that night?"

"Huh?"

"One night a little over a year after I got to Vancouver. There was a new guy in the neighborhood who sounded like he might be from the mob. So I packed up and left there and then."

"Yes, it was me. I thought I'd found you, but you slipped away. Vancouver is a beautiful city, but Clark Park was a hole. Why d'you stay there? Didn't come across as a good place to bring up young children."

"I thought I'd stick out too much as a foreigner if I splashed out on a fancy pad somewhere real nice."

"Where are the kids, by the way?"

"Not here at the moment."

Mary Lou didn't want to reveal her hand yet, although her voice faltered half-way through the sentence. If she wasn't mistaken, a small bead of liquid rolled out her right eye. Roach didn't appear to notice as he was engrossed by the spectacle of Cindy's corpse bobbing on the pink water.

"We can come back to that later, perhaps."

"That was two years ago—or more. You been tracking me down ever since?"

"Oh no. Nothing personal but I had better things to do with my time. I've been busy, shall we say?"

He took out another cigarette from his pack and lit it with the butt he hadn't quite finished.

"Two months ago, I was in the state and thought I'd see what I could find out. The West Coast fellas had hired my services and I picked up some ideas from them. I thought you'd changed your name again. To be honest, I wasn't expecting you to call yourself a Lagotti."

"Yeah, if I had been on my own, I'd have bought more fake ID and carried on. But I wanted my children to know who they were. And for them to live in America."

"Where did you say the kids were again?"

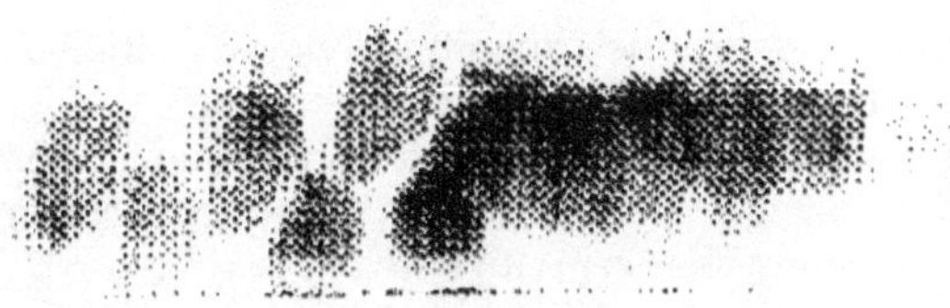

22

CHARLIE PENTANGELO KEPT his black armchair despite all the other changes in the family apartment over the years. He found comfort in the creases which contoured to his body shape. Decades before, the smell of the leather merged with his own natural oils to produce an aroma he could only describe as comforting. The familiarity of the scent enabled him to relax as soon as he sat down—irrespective of the decisions he made or tales of woe that confronted him on an almost daily basis.

In the two years since he'd ordered the hit on Frank Lagotti Senior's killer, Pentangelo had gained more gray—or at least the remaining hair was grayer than before, although the overall quantity had reduced. His patience had diminished in almost direct proportion to his scalp follicles. This was a function of age rather than of his baldness.

Problems he had plenty. Failing to find Lagotti's killer was of little concern anymore. He'd wanted to make a clear statement that people shouldn't go around murdering his men but Lagotti was an unpleasant man. Also, what few assets the guy possessed were picked up within a matter of days and the cash flow continued to roll.

There were bigger Baninno Family problems to resolve that went beyond Lagotti and his now-demised KitKatt Club. Heroin littered the Eastern Seaboard. The tentative approaches by his Sicilian brothers to import opiates proved so profitable that the business line dwarfed the numbers, prostitution and gambling combined. He never thought that day would ever come. The large quantity of low-to-no income individuals addicted to the stuff, and wanting to escape their appalling living conditions, was the cause —public housing had a lot to answer for.

The shift into drug transportation and distribution left some members of the Five Families slow to respond and that created an opportunity which the Baninno clan was happy to seize. With both hands.

As any businessman knows, if your market gets saturated in one place then you need to create a fresh space somewhere else. Baninno saw the way the wind blew—and followed the breeze westwards. At the same time, the upset felt in New York was nothing compared to the fractious relationship between the competing Families in California, who fell apart in the late '60s and no one had recovered their ground since.

With money—and its associated power—from the east coast heroin trade, Baninno made inroads into the West Coast mob. The family funded several ventures and, through indirect means to hide their true intention, supplied narcotics in Los Angeles and the surrounding area—as well as San Francisco.

These thoughts played on Pentangelo's mind because he reported directly to one of Baninno's capos and that meant he stood two rungs below the guy himself. In the last eighteen months, Pentangelo manipulated, murdered and massaged the truth enough to become a right-hand man in the Baninno Family. And they entrusted him with breaking ground out west —a task at which he proved to be highly successful.

Pentangelo recently finished his lunch—a small piece of veal, potatoes and peas with a decent glass of Chianti—when a call came through informing him that a key Latino business partner lay in the morgue. These things happen; not everyone makes it to the end of the day.

One thing jarred: early reports showed a woman might be at the helm of the attack. Charlie was an old-fashioned Italian American and believed a woman's place was standing by the kitchen sink or languishing in his bed.

As far as he was concerned, it didn't have to be the same woman. But there was only one woman who had crossed his path in business and he assumed she was dead: if she was not, surely someone would have found her and blown her brains out by now. The skirt who robbed the bank with Lagotti's step nephew.

He couldn't be sure it was Mary Lou but his ears pricked up at the news, nonetheless. If she was still alive, she needed to die. A call to Roach was on the cards although he'd issued that decree once before and Roach had not delivered the goods. This in itself was unusual which was why Charlie assumed Mary Lou was already deceased. If Roach had found her, she'd have been dead and he would have collected his fee. You could always rely on Roach.

Charlie's thoughts returned to the news at hand and he flicked through images in his head of potential culprits. The candidates were many and varied, so he couldn't narrow down the suspect list enough to send Roach out to get recompense.

Someone would need to go out there and find out what was going on. Although he didn't want to do so, he knew he'd have to wait until after tomorrow as no good Catholic would want to miss Easter Mass. The problem would take a few days to resolve. In the meantime, he'd place a few calls to see if there was any more information out there. Of one thing he was certain: someone would die for this and there was no way Charlie would accept any loss of territory despite this intrusion into his world.

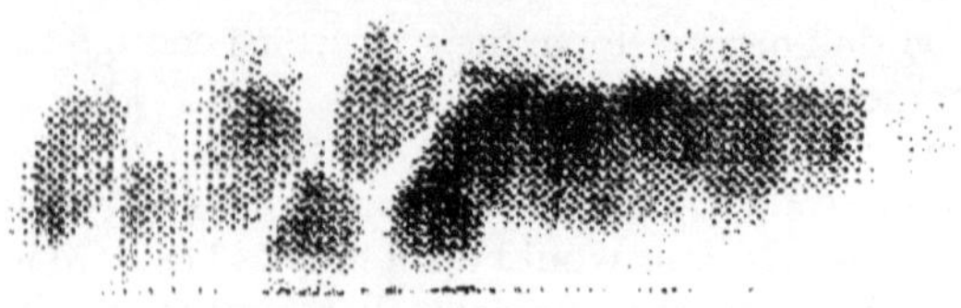

23

"DID YOU INFORM anyone you'd make another attempt to find me?"

"Oh no. You were one of my freelance contracts. I keep them very separate. My New York boss is aware how I fill my spare time, but never asks me about my outside business. And I'd never tell him."

"Good."

"I didn't do it for you, but for me. If you compartmentalize, you get to lead parallel lives with no wires getting crossed."

"I understand that. I've spent most of the last two years trying to keep my past life clear of my current world. It's worked most of the time."

Roach checked outside again: the corpse had moved about one foot since he cast his eyes in the same direction. His thoughts drifted from his day job to his successful search for Mary Lou.

"You should still take care of yourself."

"What does that mean?"

"Two years ago. They offered me a contract on you, which I passed."

Roach revealed no tell as he lied so gracefully.
"Why? You'd have got paid twice."

"Sure, but if anyone found out, then my reputation'd been in ruins. A week after I terminated Frank Lagotti Senior, you should have paid me or I should have killed you. Neither happened."

Mary Lou stopped to think from Roach's perspective. He was right: her departure and disappearance did nothing for his commercial status.

"Did you hear who picked up my contract?"

"Not at all. No one ever does. These things are always kept secret. Means if they want to whack you, you'll never know when it's coming or who will deliver it."

"Life's tough."

Arnold looked at her, deciding whether Mary Lou was being sarcastic, but concluded she was playing things straight.

"Do you think there's a chance the contract holder has found me?"

"What? Because of the mess in your pool?"

"Yes."

"I doubt it. A hit is clean. If they'd caught up with you, you'd be dead. Unless the contract turned into some revenge shtick, but you're old news. No offense."

"None taken. I want to be old news. Gone and forgotten: that's me. Or at least I was until you appeared at the door."

"I am known for my tenacity."

"And will you be telling your New York pals about me on your return?"

"No. Like I said, I compartmentalize."

"And would you have taken the contract if I hadn't hired you beforehand?"

"And you'd have died a week before you ran away from me."

"Was that when you first found me?"

"Yep. I decided to wait and settle into the Vancouver lifestyle as I wanted a vacation and you were my excuse. When I'm on mob business, I don't hang around."

Roach kept his gray hair short because he was of an age when men's hair didn't pass their ears, even though the new decade had ushered in a world of change since he was a boy.

Between the end of the '60s and today, moon landings had gone from being the most exciting event in the history of mankind to a boring TV experience, needing to be bolstered by scenes of astronauts playing golf. Women were robbing banks and running gangs. His own father would never have believed such things were possible.

"And are all Baninno hitmen as tenacious as you?"

"I must say no, but you'd expect me to say that."

"True. I just want to know if anyone is still after me."

"To be honest, someone holds the paper on you, but the chances are that you could spend decades before they'll be stood next to you in line for the cinema or as you walk across the street. Then you'll look into their eyes for a half second and think nothing more of them. Meanwhile, a minute later, they'll put a slug in the back of your head. Bam!"

"Something to look forward to in my old age."

"Yep."

All during the conversation with Roach, Mary Lou tried to get some sense of the man and the extent to which what he said married up to what was true. She believed him over the contract. The reason she'd hired him in the first place was because of his fantastic reputation: as a hitman but also for his discretion.

No one ever knew if he'd been the guy to off a gang member and that made him special. The younger members of his profession would go to a bar and take bragging rights to get inside a girl's panties or to impress his peers. Not Arnold Roach. He didn't hit and tell.

His comments reinforced her belief that whoever had stolen her children from here was not east coast related. The New York mob might have had a hand in it, but he was right: if they wanted to kill her, they would have done just that and no more. There was no extra money in it for them and no pleasure either.

If he was playing a double-cross on her, he was doing a very good job. She'd shown him where her stash of greens was hidden and he sat down and lit a cigarette. A guy who's being paid to whack you points a gun barrel at your forehead within seconds of that and blows your brains out. He doesn't kidnap your children and pop round for a chat. And Roach hadn't come across as the psychotic type.

"I need your assistance."

"Who d'you want to kill?"

"It's not a murder."

"The body in the pool?"

"Kinda. She was my housekeeper."

"Hard to keep good help nowadays."

"Funny man. It's my babies."

"And?"

"Will you get them back for me?"

"HAVE YOU ANY idea who's taken them?"

"Nope."

"Is there anyone who might wish you harm?"

"Several—and most of my enemies became so today. Those that survived."

Mary Lou's words hung in the air for a second as Roach processed the implications.

"Yes, I can help you although I spend more time killing than saving lives. You understand that, right?"

"I do but you are one of the few people I trust at this point."

He nodded but remained silent. This was her show and she needed to run it.

"So what next?"

"We need to figure out who took them and then we go get them back."

"Who is top of your list?"

"That's my problem. I can't see how the guys I messed with this morning had time to do this by the end of lunch."

"You'd be amazed how quickly well-motivated individuals will act."

"What should we do first?"

"People who kidnap want something and the best way for them to get it is to ask. So you need to stay near the phone."

"Sit here and do nothing, you mean?"

"Waiting is doing something. There are moments to run and minutes to sit. You must bide your time."

"And what will you do? Sit next to me and watch me listen for the ringing of the phone?"

"No. I thought I might hit the streets and see what I can find out."

"You don't even know where to begin."

"On the contrary. Most of the connected guys in this town have been my customers at some point or other. I'll be fine. You must promise me to stay put. The lives of your children may depend on it."

"I get it. Don't worry."

"I'll call you every hour to find out if you've heard anything. So just because the phone rings…"

"…doesn't mean it's bad news. I understand—and thank you."

Mary Lou wrote her number on a small piece of paper and passed it into Arnold's palm. He stood up and left the house. She remained seated in the summerhouse trying to figure out how she would do nothing and not lose her mind.

Cindy couldn't remain face down in the pool forever and Mary Lou knew she couldn't call the cops. As the boys in blue weren't swarming towards the house at the minute, she needed to find some trustworthy people to sort out the mess. Pasquale was her best hope and Fabio had the right contacts.

His voice was clear on the line although she thought she might've heard a small click before Fabio spoke.

"I need a cleaner."

"Is extensive work required?"

"Yes. At my home."

"I'll send someone over shortly. I don't want any information right now but you need to tell me what has occurred. Why not pop over now and by the time you return, everything will be sorted out."

"No can do, I'm afraid. Related to the matter in hand, I need to stay by my phone."

"Expecting an important call?"

"Yes."

"I see."

The phone went dead and Mary Lou wondered if she had given away too much or too little information. She'd find out soon enough. Into her walk-in wardrobe and she chose two revolvers and a shotgun. She pushed the pistols into her waistband—round the back—and left the rifle near her feet. Any unexpected visitors would catch a hail of bullets. No questions asked.

Mary Lou picked herself up and headed into the house to position herself by the phone, but also to have a line of sight both front and rear. She propped the conservatory doors open. By sitting on a corner of the couch, she could turn her head one way to view the swimming pool and turn it the other to see her driveway. A hand rested by the phone and the other nestled between her thighs. It had nowhere else to go.

The abject feeling of powerlessness permeated every pore of her skin and crept into each organ. Mary Lou felt the emptiness of her breath as she exhaled and let tears fall from her cheeks as the possibility of what might happen to Alice and Frank Jr seeped through her consciousness.

Who hated her so much, they'd be prepared to harm two innocent children?

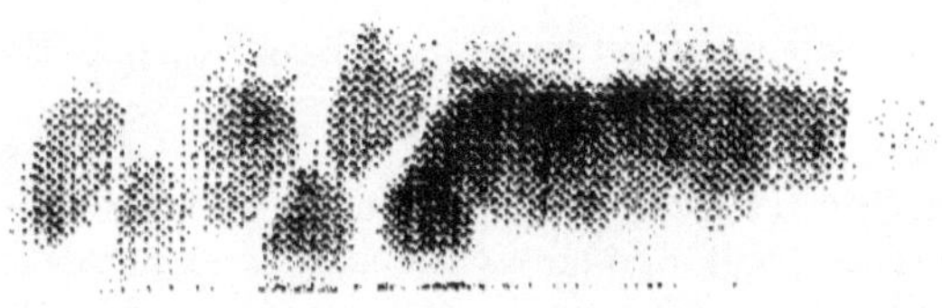

24

TEN MINUTES LATER and a knock on the door. Mary Lou had watched the guy walk up the drive holding a tool bag in his left hand. Fabio must have sent him. In case she was wrong, She grabbed a pistol and hid it behind her back before she greeted her caller.

"Cleaner."

"Come in."

As soon as she could, Mary Lou shut the door behind the guy and replaced the gun in her waistband.

"You were quick."

"Told it was an emergency."

"Like there's no tomorrow."

"I'd better get to work then. Where to?"

She led him through the house until they stood by the far side of the pool. He looked around and dipped his fingers into the water. Removed them and sniffed his fingertips.

"How you want me to deal with the body?"

"Huh?"

"Was it a loved one?"

"No, but show her some respect. At least until you've driven her away."

"Understood. I'll bring in some materials from my truck."

Hands in pockets, the fella padded out and came back five minutes later with a roll of black plastic.

"Need a hand?"

"Best if you leave me to get on with it. I'll call you once the body's out the way."

"Okay."

Mary Lou slipped back into the house unsure what to do next. She returned to the couch and tried not to listen out to the noises confronting her ears from outside. She didn't even know the guy's name. And the thought of what he would end up doing to Cindy churned her stomach, which was already tied in knots with the kids.

She sat by the phone and tried to empty her mind but no can do. Images of Alice and Frank Jr permeated her eyes until she got a headache. Mary Lou popped upstairs to her bathroom cabinet to grab herself some meds to take the pain away. The irony wasn't lost on her that Milton had driven off with enough powder to keep her nullified from life until the day she died.

Her fingers tapped on her knee until the rhythm annoyed her too much. She couldn't think straight with the scraping sounds coming from the pool. Cindy deserved better than this. Her kids needed much better than whatever was happening to them. And here she sat on her ass waiting for a call from the kidnappers or from Roach. Then the phone rang.

"Yes?"

"Any news?"

"Nothing. Fabio sent round his cleaner though."

"That's something, I suppose."

"Anything your end?"

"Nope. I've spoken to a few guys, but no leads yet, although it's early days."

"Keep telling yourself that."

"I know. I'm doing the best I can."

"Sure, but sometimes your best isn't enough, is it?"

"No. It's not."

"Call me in another hour and hopefully one of us will have some news."

"Sure thing."

The line went dead and Mary Lou wondered if Frank Jr was still alive. A shiver ran down her spine and she realized she shouldn't let those kinds of thoughts enter her head. No good would come of it.

"I'm gonna need some help to refill the pool."

She didn't know how long the cleaner had been standing there.

"You catch my conversation?"

"I'm not paid to listen. Just to clean."

She nodded and walked back to the patio. The water was still pink but there was no sign of Cindy. Like she had never been there at all. Mary Lou showed him where the taps were and they watched as the liquid drained away. Then the guy used the steps to reach the floor and applied bleach to every surface he could see. Once done, he hosed down the tiles and she helped him fill the pool again.

"I'd better take all her possessions—unless you're planning on filing a missing persons?"

"Hadn't decided. What you think?"

"You want the cops hanging round here for days asking questions you prefer not to answer?"

She shook her head.

"Then show me her room."

Another twenty minutes and the cleaner was done. Mary Lou remained near the phone as though her proximity would increase the chances of her receiving a call.

"I'm outta here."

"Thanks. What do I owe you?"

"Nothing. It's all taken care of. Including sales tax and tip."

He chuckled.

"I don't even catch your name."

"Good. What you don't know won't kill you."

He tipped his hat and walked out the house, never to be seen again.

MARY LOU SAT on her own until the silence became unbearable and the beating of her heart invaded her brain. The ticking of a clock engulfed the living room and the movie in her head took another turn into an even darker place. Children's limbs and splatters of blood ran through her visual cortex and she screamed, but no one was there to listen. Nobody came to wrap their arms around her to make the pain go away. She was alone.

Mary Lou remained where she sat for a lifetime and then the phone erupted. She grabbed the receiver and listened the voice at the other end.

"Has the cleaner been?"

"And gone."

"Any word?"

"Nada."

"Just a waiting game."

"Sure, I know. But when we find the kids: whoever did this—I want them dead. No questions asked. I don't care who it is or if you're in business with them. Even if it's your mother. She's getting her throat cut all the same."

"Yep."

"There'll be money in it for anyone who can give me the name of who it is and more for the person who kills those fuckers."

"Sure."

"I mean it, Fabio. These are my kids."

"We understand your anger. Honestly. But we also know we have people on the street hunting for your two children and they will find them as soon as they are able—and not a moment before. Until that second, the most you can do is nothing. Sit and wait. It might not be what you want, but it is what you need to do, anyway."

"Feel so helpless."

"You are being strong for your bambinos. When the time is right, you will act—I am certain of that."

"Sure will."

"We understand you have gained a little unofficial help along the way. Are you positive you can trust him?"

"I trust Roach with my life because he hasn't killed me. He is the one man I know feels no ill will toward me. If he did, I'd be floating in the pool by now."

"Not the best testimonial but it must do. I've heard friends say much worse things about each other."

"And we're not friends."

"Not at all. But he's working very hard on your behalf. That's a good worker you've found."

"He found me."

"You're past was bound to catch up with you eventually. The fact he took so long is the miracle, not that he arrived at your doorstep today."

The doorbell rang and Mary Lou jumped out of her seat. She had been so involved in her conversation, she'd stopped looking outside.

"Gotta go. There's someone at the door."

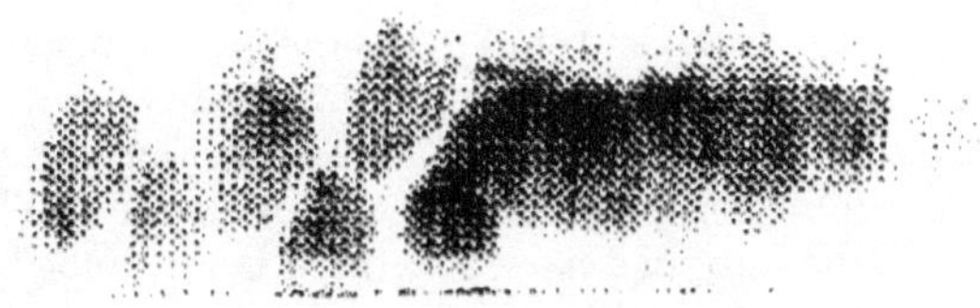

25

MARY LOU PEERED through the fish eye in the door at the unknown arrival. The man standing before her was shaped exactly like Bobby. She smiled and let him in. He pecked her on the cheek on his way into the living room and sat down on a couch.

She followed him inside and slumped next to him. He said nothing and looked at her, waiting.

"Have you heard?"

"About what?"

Mary Lou ran through all that had happened since lunchtime and he remained still, his jaw slowly lowering. By the time she had completed her tale of woe, he was dumbfounded.

"How the hell are you?"

"I don't know, to be honest. All I think about is getting the children back."

He nodded as he tried to imagine what he would do if the positions were reversed. He drew a blank.

"What can I do to help?"

"Unless you plan to magic the kids home, there's zip."

"Is there anywhere I could go which hasn't already been covered?"

"You tell me. I've been stuck on this couch while everyone else is running around town trying to do some good."

"Any word at all?"

"Nothing at all. Nada. Bupkis."

Bobby fell back to silence and stared into the middle distance. Mary Lou couldn't decide if he was recalling some past life moment or if he was having a minor stroke. Neither was helping, and she became impatient.

A tear rolled out the corner of his right eye and landed on his leg. She squeezed his hand, then stopped herself. What was she doing? Shouldn't he be the one consoling her?

"Sorry. Too many bad memories. Stuff from the past, you know?"

"Sure. I just don't need this from you at the minute. In case you've forgotten, some fucker has taken my children and I have no way of getting them back. There's been no call, no note: nothing."

"We'll find them. You can be certain of that."

"No I can't. I mean, thanks for the words of encouragement, but they are useless. If you've not got anything worthwhile to say then keep your mouth shut. You're a lovely man—truly, but I need strong people near me at the minute because I don't know if I have sufficient strength within me to get through this in one piece. Without falling apart."

He nodded as a response and Mary Lou knew that was the best the fella could offer her. Not because he had nothing inside, but because he had spent too many years bottling up all his emotions so he could function in his violent world. The same environment she was now living in. The place where Alice and Frank Jr were in imminent danger and she had no idea where they were or what she could do to save them. Despite knowing these connected guys, they were no good at all to her.

Then a lightbulb went on over her head. If the local hoods didn't know jack then the perpetrators must come from out of town. That didn't give a clue where they may be, but it narrowed down the search for who's behind the outrage. Chances were that Pasquale had figured this out hours ago, but at least Mary Lou had caught up. The single moment of clarity gave her hope. This was the first time since seeing Cindy's body that she felt she might control the world around her. And where there was one drop of vision, others were sure to follow.

She turned her attention back onto Bobby, who remained resolutely silent after his apology and tear. What a waste of humanity that man was proving to be. She wasn't expecting him to save the day, but she believed him had more inside him than this. She appeared to be wrong.

As if to emphasize the quality of his support, he leaned in and give Mary Lou a hug. She let herself remain in his arms and tried to hide within the strength of his touch. He might not have had much to offer, but sometimes little things can count for more than you'd expect. Perhaps Bobby had his uses. She listened to his breathing and noticed the warmth of his chest against her ear. This moment of calm was more than she could have expected when she saw Cindy and discovered the kids were gone.

"Any idea who or why?"

"Only to hurt me. No names yet but they must have come from out of town."

"Why?"

"They aren't known to locals and no one would be dumb enough to kidnap children of a business associate of Pasquale Bassani, would they?"

"Only if their beef was with Bassani and you were a casual bystander."

"Is that likely?"

"Nope. Only happened once I can remember, and the dudes were found four years later in an unmarked grave near the airport."

"Why is it always an airfield?"

"Because the desert was full?"

Mary Lou managed a smile and he allowed himself a minor chuckle.

"Too soon, I know."

"You're okay, Bobby Trevisan."

"Sorry I can't be of any more use. My days of carrying a piece and breaking heads are a long time gone."

"I forgive you—just this once, although by rights I should be angry with you. And I am."

"Times like these, you need people you can trust, like me. Now and forever more. I'm a safer bet than the sun rising in the sky tomorrow."

Mary Lou kept her face touching Bobby's shirt and allowed herself the luxury of doing nothing other than worry about her babies. She had suppressed all the thought that caused the bloody images to pop into her mind, so all she was left with was a terrible sense of anxiety and to exist in a state of fretting. Then the bell jolted her awake.

ARNOLD ROACH STOOD hands in pockets and came into the house with a shrug and a grunt. Mary Lou had hoped deep inside he would deliver for her. The fact he'd tracked her down over all those thousands of miles and the sheer number of years spent on the road doing so. He was the sort of guy who'd be able to find her babies. But she was wrong. He'd given her bupkis.

Roach slumped into the easy chair and let his hands land on the armrests. Mary Lou sat back down next to Bobby. The two men nodded at each other but said nothing, looking into each other's eyes seeking meaning where there was none. She watched them both not speak to each other.

"How's it been out there?"

"Tough. I feel like I've spoken to every hoodlum in town and no one's heard anything about anyone."

"So you've come back with nothing for me. What are you doing here? Why aren't you out there trying to make a difference? Even Bobby wants to do something."

"Doesn't look like he's achieved much so far, apart from warming up the couch."

"That's not the point. You said you'd go out and act for me but you've got nothing. You have failed me, Roach."

The man glared at Bobby whose eyes remained fixed on the ground, embarrassment coursing through his veins. Mary Lou switched her attention between the two, not knowing which way to aim her anger.

"Whoever took your kids is well hidden else I'd have found them."

"Good excuse."

"Don't take your frustration out on me. All I've done today is spare your life and hunt for your children. Once you gave me my money, I could have waltzed outta here without a care in the world. I didn't and now you're giving me shit. Fuck you."

This was stated calmly and free of malice. Stone cold truths expressed with no emotion. Bobby felt Mary Lou bristle in his arms. She sat forward, removing her body from Bobby's touch. Glared at Roach.

"Fuck you too and the horse you rode in on."

Roach was silent, acting as if there was nothing to say. Even though he was right, her frustration with her incapacity to do anything was oozing out of her. She wanted blood and these two men had offered only sympathy and empty words.

"You said you had all these mob connections."

"SureI do, but no one on the West Coast has had anything to do with the kidnapping. I know these guys professionally. They wouldn't bother lying to me because they understand I am only asking for business reasons. If they lie, there are unpleasant consequences."

"You're just full of shit."

"Leave him alone, Mary Lou. It's not his fault. If the attack came from out-of-town then the people he knows will be no good to us. You see that, right?"

"Don't you take his side."

"It's not about sides. It's about the best way to get the kids back."

"Well, you've not exactly been much use to me today either."

"Lash out if you want. Won't change anything though. We are fighting your corner. Despite how you feel, we are on your side. You can rely on us for sure."

"You used to be somebody but now you're a washed-up nothing. Don't go preaching to me, mister."

"Focus your attention on your kids. Not on the men giving you bad news. The important item is that this hasn't come from California. Either it's some local difficulty or, more likely, from Chicago, New York or Baltimore."

"In which case, shouldn't you already have a name and address for me? Those are your towns."

Roach fell silent again, ruminating on her words.

"I've been out west for three weeks. Plenty of time for shit to go down and me not know about it or even hear a whisper."

Mary Lou allowed the heat in her cheeks to dissipate and for a clearer head to resurface on her shoulders. In the pit of her tensed stomach, knowing there was at least an element of truth to what he said. But this was a strange revenge if it came straight from the mob. Perhaps Lagotti Senior was acting from beyond the grave. That cocksucker was a mean hard bastard. Maybe one of his kith and kin was moving in on her.

"Could it be Lagotti's family?"

"Possible, but unlikely. Why move on you now? There have been plenty of opportunities before today."

"What you reckon, Bobby?"

"This doesn't taste of mob, but it is brutal enough. Maybe with some local help who bear a grudge."

"But why my children?"

"It's got your attention, right?"

"Yep."

"There's your answer."

She mulled over the men's statements and considered all the possibilities of their implications.

"I'll give a thousand dollars to anyone who can get my babies back."

"Save your money. We'll do it for free. You need guys you can trust. Your green won't buy you that."

"I know."

She slumped on the couch and let Bobby return his arm around her shoulders. All three sat still for five long minutes while nothing happened. Each of them hoping for the phone to ring or for one of the others to gain some insight. Something. Any idea who had done this and how to organize the safe return of Frank Jr and Alice.

Two figures walked up the driveway and raised Mary Lou's heart. She rushed to the door and let them in.

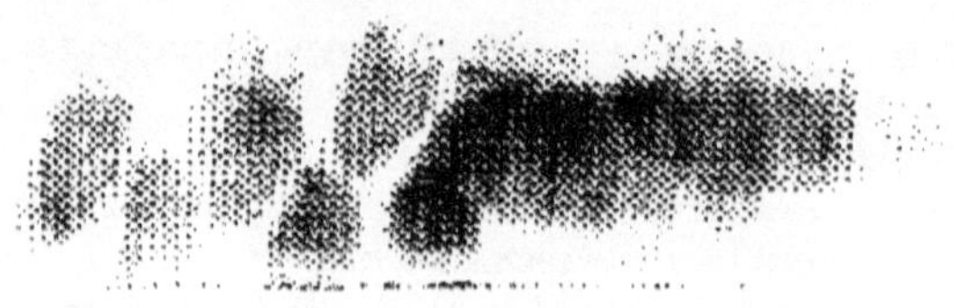

26

HER TWO BUSINESS partners, Pasquale and Fabio, tipped their hats and came inside. Before they sat down and acknowledge the others in the living room, Mary Lou wanted to know everything.

"What's going on?"

Fabio eyed Pasquale, and they both looked round for somewhere to sit. She noticed their discomfort and dragged two dining chairs over for them. Clearly they didn't like conducting business in a domestic setting.

"None of our associates are involved. We didn't think they were, but we checked to be certain."

"Then we ensured our people put the word on the street that an outrage was going down in our territory which incurred our displeasure."

"A measured tone so our men understand when we are angry and when we are curious."

"You are only curious about who's kidnapped my children, right under your nose?"

Pasquale sighed, so even Bobby and Arnold picked up on the exhalation. The two men shuffled in their seats and pretended to keep an eye on the floor. Catching Pasquale's gaze was unwise. The great man stretched his back upright and stared at Mary Lou with abject disdain. He half closed his eyelids and breathed some more.

"Listen. You have asked us for help and that is what we are offering you. We do this because you are our partner and someone has hurt you. Out of respect, we come to you to discuss the matter further. But remember, if your children live or die doesn't change a thing for me. You will still be expected to deliver on our agreement.

"If you can bring yourself to show a modicum of restraint, I am happy for us to continue to support you in your time of need. Although the hour has stretched into most of the day."

Pasquale allowed himself that moment of light relief and then his earlier demeanor returned to his expression. His body remained tense, back straight in the chair. Fabio let his hands rest on his lap until he moved them to cross his legs, after which he placed one hand on his knee with his other on top, fingers interweaved in between knuckles.

"Sorry. You're just seeing my frustration coming through."

"I understand—apology accepted."

"When we find out where they are, do we have a plan?"

"Not at the moment. A cautious approach is to be recommended."

"I thought we take a dozen of your men and we hit them hard and fast."

"That might work in Baltimore, but we operate differently in California."

"So what do you suggest instead?"

"Mary Lou, the aim will be to retrieve the kids before the shit hits the fan. Not create a fucking bloodbath. Your desire for revenge on the perpetrators of this heinous act is secondary to securing the release of the children."

"I know, but I don't want them to get away either."

"Have no fear: they won't."

"How can you be so certain?"

"Because this is my town. And if someone has come here and terrorized one of my people, then they must answer to me. I will hunt them down and kill them—whatever the outcome here."

Mary Lou found solace in those words and a comfort that was better than the warmth of Bobby's embrace. Revenge is a dish best served rather than thrown into the trash. She would taste that pleasure before all this was over. This knowledge sustained her over the next hour as the four men sat waiting for what she hoped would be a phone call from a stranger.

"I don't think I can sit around here any longer.

"And where do you propose you go?"

"I've been thinking. If it's been out-of-towners then the most obvious culprits who fit that description are the dudes we did for this morning. So I'm going back to their warehouse to see what's up. Better than wearing out the cover on this couch."

"You should stay exactly where you are. It is the best place for you to be —even if it doesn't feel like it is."

"I can't do this any longer. It's doing my melon in."

"Please reconsider. If there is any call from the kidnappers, we need them to know they can negotiate with you. They must feel secure so we get your babies back safe and sound. Unharmed. We need not give them any excuse to behave like the barbarians they are. To take children and kill a housekeeper. What's the world coming to?"

Pasquale was appealing to her maternal instincts and Mary Lou understood what he'd said: every word. But she also knew that too much time had passed and that if they were going to deal, they'd have contacted her by now. From Mary Lou's point of view, although her chest could not take the pain of saying this out loud, her babies were dead. All she had left was the certainty of wishing the guys who'd done it a slow and painful, tortured demise.

"I'm going back to the warehouse. Anyone care to join me?"

None of the men spoke and Pasquale shook his head. The three others understood his instructions and remained stationary. Mary Lou stood up and headed for the door.

"You all sure?"

Passive nodding from Roach and Bobby. Pasquale and Fabio stared blankly out, ignoring her question entirely. She checked her piece was in her waistband, walked out the house and into her car. Gunning the engine, she careered out the drive and off to the airport.

BACK NORTH TO Avant Way, Mary Lou slammed her car left and right until she reached two hundred feet of the warehouse. She hit the brakes like there was no tomorrow and dropped the vehicle into a legal parking space. She padded round the side of her automobile and lit a cigarette to give herself something to do while she checked out the scene before her.

Even though they'd shot off the head of the snake only a few hours earlier, there was a flurry of activity with at least three—no, count 'em—four thickset guys walking in and out as calm as day. Mary Lou noticed the truck pulled up near the entrance and the fact the dudes entered with nothing and came out with a cardboard box to dump in the rear of the pickup.

What she couldn't tell—not without getting back inside the building—was whether the children were being held there too. No one was behaving as though there was anything more than crap to shift, but these goons were so far down the totem pole, they were lucky not to be knee deep in soil.

Mary Lou flicked the butt of her cigarette onto the ground and leaned against the side of her car, hands in pockets. The warmth of her thighs drew the blood back to her fingertips, but she had no reason to be cold as the sun was still shining. Other than the chill of knowing Alice could be screaming as she was being tortured. Or worse. Without a moment's conscious thought,

Mary Lou's hand covered the area of her stomach where her tattooed rose lived.

Still the men waltzed in and out, boxes bulking out the back of that truck. She considered making her way to the rear of the building to find some less busy entry point. Mary Lou remembered there had been an outside door found this morning which they hadn't used because they didn't have much time for anything other than basic scavenging.

The row of warehouses were all separated and she saw there was a path running behind them. It was ten feet wide, which meant she'd walk down it with ease, but if anyone was out back, she'd be spotted in an instant. Mary Lou considered the odds, weighing up any other options open to her which didn't involve storming the front with her pistol and rifle. One against at least four? Not great.

Time seemed to drag and no better idea popped into her head. So she checked the position of her revolver and sauntered away from the warehouse so she could nip to the path without being too visible. Three warehouses along, she had a straight line of sight to the heroin hotel. Nothing. She crept forward, making sure she was never more than two feet away from a building wall: this minimized the angle for anyone stood on the rear step as she approached.

By the time she reached the corner of the warehouse, her breathing was in overdrive. She paused and hugged the wall with her back, fingers touching the brickwork. Five minutes rest to turn her lungfuls into silent gasps.

The door was painted dark green and a sign was attached, noting people should keep clear as it was a fire escape. Mary Lou edged nearer until she touched the handle. Then she bristled as she heard a crunch on the path. She looked around and saw Bobby ten feet away, approaching from the other side. Her quizzical expression spoke volumes.

"Wanted to make sure you were okay. Someone needed to watch you back."

"Get the fuck outta here!"

"No can do. You can't do everything by yourself. I can help."

Mary Lou became concerned their whispering might be heard inside and scurried over to stand by Bobby's ear. She flitted her eyes left, then right, and snorted out her words.

"Listen carefully. You are not welcome here. You are not needed here. Your time has long since gone and you are of no use to me."

"You don't want to hear this, but you are wrong. You need me more this minute than at any other point in your life. The guys in there are lowlife pond scum and, whatever they're up to, they'd drop you soon as look at you. And you know that, deep down."

Mary Lou blinked and carried on eyeballing the man. Bobby felt her exhalations hitting his cheek. Sensed how far on the edge she was standing.

On the precipice. The question was whether she'd see reason and back down, swallowed pride and all.

"I've got to know if they are in there. They could be on the other side of that wall for all I know."

Mary Lou waved a hand toward the brickwork a few feet away and Bobby's eyes followed the direction of her fingers and darted back to her face.

"If they are, we will find out together. There's five fellas in there minimum."

"I only counted four."

"Five to my certain knowledge. And there could be some who are staying indoors to supervise."

"You suggesting we should leave?"

"No, I'm saying we should think smart. Let's take it slow and find out what we need to—without getting caught."

"How?"

"Put your ear to the door and listen."

Truth was Mary Lou hadn't considered that even for an instant. She did as he suggested, craning into the wooden green slats to get better access to anything going on inside. Three, maybe four, minutes later and she removed her ear from the door.

"Well?"

"They'll be finished in a few minutes. After this morning's activity, they are cleaning the place out and I heard talk of lighting a fire."

"Any need for us to go in?"

"No, Bobby. Frank Jr and Alice aren't in there."

"Shall we go home then?"

Mary Lou nodded and they scurried away, down the path and back onto the road and the parking bays.

"Thank you."

Mary Lou pecked Bobby on the cheek and he smiled. She turned to fumble for her car keys and, before she looked up, Bobby had vanished into the dusk. Perhaps he had been an operator in his day. She got in the car and drove home with no greater knowledge about her kids than when she left. Sometimes men can be right, she sighed to herself.

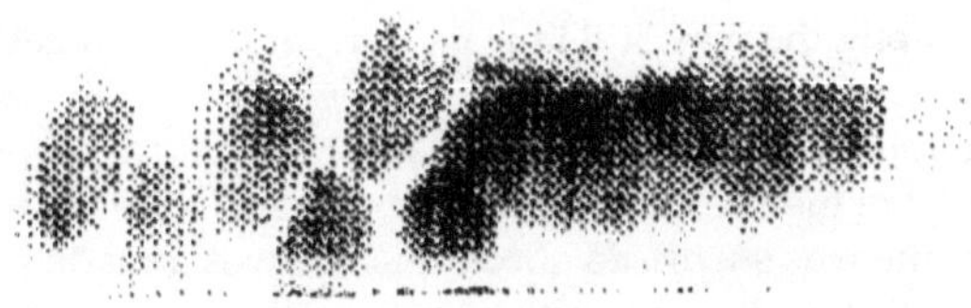

27

PASQUALE, FABIO AND Arnold were sat where she left them—no clear movement. There were coffee cups on the table to show they had made themselves at home. Mary Lou wondered how comfortable they had become and to what extent they'd taken advantage of her absence to check out the summerhouse or her panties drawer. Neither was positive.

"Any word?"

"Nothing yet. How did you guys get on?"

"They weren't there."

Bobby nodded confirmation but added no noise at all. He let attention remain on Mary Lou, who sat down and resumed her wait. He returned to her side and everyone remained precisely where they had originally landed earlier in the afternoon. She glanced at the clock on the mantlepiece and saw five to midnight. A long day with no sign of ending anytime soon.

Two minutes later, the phone rang. Mary Lou's hand darted over and grabbed the receiver. Bobby made out a muffled male voice, but couldn't discern a word that was said.

"For you."

She passed the phone over to Fabio.

"Yes?… Uh-huh."

More noises until Fabio put the receiver down—and smiled.

"We have a location and eyes on the building."

"How far? Who?"

"Let's talk along the way. It'll take us thirty minutes to get there. Who's coming?"

Pasquale explained he wouldn't be part of the rescue party. He was happy to offer more men if she needed it, but he no longer took part in any operations. No one was surprised about this. He was a made man and, despite Mary Lou's feelings, this was insufficiently big-league for Pasquale to be seen with a gun in his hand.

Roach stood up, removed guns from various holsters and checked the clips. He put them all back and announced he was in.

"Thanks, Arnold."

Fabio was next to bow out, but again there were no gasps of amazement. Men like Fabio do not get their hands dirty saving kidnapped children. That left Bobby and nobody thought he'd be coming along, not even as the chauffeur.

"You stay here, Bobby. You can relay messages to Fabio otherwise we'll be out there on our own."

"Sure thing."

"Where's Milton?"

Come to think of it, where the hell was that man? Mary Lou hadn't seen him since he went off with their score after lunch. Had he run off with the powder or had he gone to ground somewhere? Perhaps he'd been taken too.

"Anyone know how to get in touch with Albert Nardi? We could do with his skills right now, with or without Milton."

"You need any more muscle? A small group is better than an army but only three is not enough, surely?"

"Two more trusted souls would be great."

"Consider it done. I'll send them straight to the venue."

"And where is that, then?"

There was a simple reason nobody had discovered the kids in Palm Springs: they weren't there. If anyone had been sent north to Desert Hot Springs, on the other side of the freeway, they would have found a grassy space to the west near the corner of Pierson Boulevard and Golden Eagle Road. A two story white building in the shape of a cross stood opposite eight storage buildings. Gray concrete and monotone walls. Nothing to look at but plenty to find inside.

The time arrived to get back Mary Lou's babies.

Easter Sunday April 11, 1971

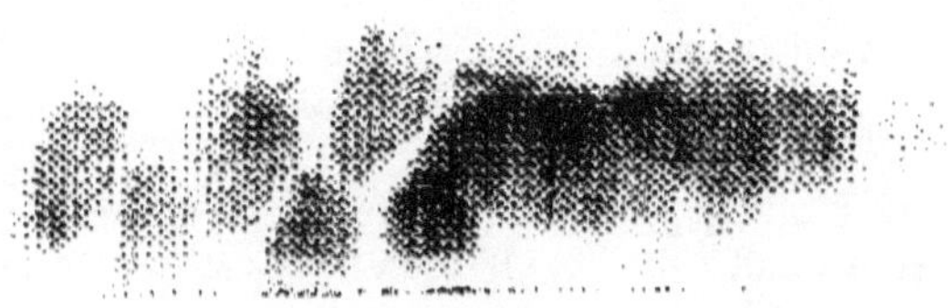

28

THEY CROUCHED BY the white wall of the building on the other side of the road. Mary Lou understood she had to wait for the cavalry to arrive in the form of men in dark suits: Anastasia Serafini and Naldo Pavone. Their introduction was a simple nod and a grunt, and they hunkered down along with the rest.

"We'll split up: Arnold and I will take the front and you two see if you can find an entrance round the back."

"We're looking for kids, right?"

"They are my children, yes. Try to keep people alive until Alice and Frank Jr are found and we are certain they are safe. After that, I don't care if any of them walk out or are carried out in a body bag."

The two newcomers didn't need to be given their instructions twice and vanished into the inky blackness. Roach and Mary Lou waited ten seconds and then headed to the corner of their building to peep round the wall and assess how they'd get to the front without being spotted.

One guy stood by the entrance, hands in pockets. Slouched against the brickwork, he was not expecting any trouble and had lulled himself to a point of distracted boredom. The door was shut behind him. Arnold and Mary Lou stared at the guy for seven, maybe eight, minutes. No one else came in or out: just the dude leaning against the wall waiting for problems to start.

Mary Lou checked her piece yet again, but this time kept it in her hand.

"You keep me covered and I'11 walk straight up to him."

"I could put a slug through his head from here."

"I don't doubt your professional ability, but we need him to land silently."

"Understood. Nothing personal. Use this if you get close enough."

He proffered a small knife he'd hidden up his sleeve. Mary Lou had definitely not noticed it before. Arnold was a consummate assassin. She slid the blade into her back pocket. It was only three inches long so fit snuggly with the handle sticking out, easy to reach.

She walked onto the sidewalk and crossed the street, careful to ensure she appeared from the corner of the road. The warehouse stood resolutely at the end of the row: nowhere to hide. She glanced up and down the street but there was no one visible. When she looked back at the white building, Arnold had blended into the night or he'd moved to a different vantage point. Either way, he was gone.

Her throat was dry and she swallowed to generate some spit. There was a twenty feet path from the sidewalk to the three steps leading to the guy and the entrance door. He had registered her existence and stopped his leaning, although both hands remained in his pockets. She pulled out a cigarette from her bag and pretended to fumble for a box of matches.

"Hey bud!"

She sauntered along the path to give the air of a lone girl needing help. Mary Lou couldn't believe anyone would buy that story, but it was all she had. She tried to squint at his hands to see if he was holding a piece, but the sole street light was behind her and she cast a shadow on the front door. Her outline reduced as she got nearer to the goon. Six feet... five, four, three...

"What you want, missy?"

"Have a light?"

"Wait there."

"Whatever you say, babe."

He scurried down the steps and put a hand into his pants pocket. The knife remained gripped in her palm and she was painfully aware of the beam shining over her shoulder. He squinted and she realized the street light was too bright for him.

"Here you go."

"Thanks, bud."

Mary Lou completed the two feet journey and he flicked the flint wheel of his lighter. It sparked into action and she looked into his dark brown eyes. He cupped the flame and she put a hand to his back. As she leaned in, bending her head sideways as though to take her cigarette to the fire, she plunged the knife into his chest. Mary Lou pushed the blade in as far as it would go using the force of her hand on his back. His eyes widened, shocked by what had just happened. Then she pulled the metal out and shoved it into his throat and tried to wiggle it side to side.

He slumped to the ground, gurgling and clutching his chest and larynx. She bent down and stabbed him in the heart in case the first two hits hadn't been enough to do him in. Then she looked up and down the street: no one had appeared. All was quiet.

Roach came out from out the darkness and they dragged the body along the wall of the warehouse, away from any windows. Before the blood crept over the entire corpse, he checked each pocket in every item of clothing. A wallet, two sets of keys and a packet of cigarettes made up his worldly possessions.

"The light is shining straight at him. We're gonna need to shift his carcass out of here."

"Moving him is more likely to garner unwanted attention than anything else."

Mary Lou thought for a second and nodded consent. Arnold rolled the guy over so he faced the wall and was half-perched between the gray brickwork and the black tarmac. His bleeding front was now hidden from sight and he presented darkened clothing to any casual passerby. Anyone walking up the path to enter the building would know they were staring at a corpse. But who'd be paying a visit at this time of night?

"This way."

Arnold padded up the steps and put an ear to the door. Nothing. He tried one key after another until the lock turned and he could push the door ajar. Mary Lou removed her pistol from her waistband and her stomach knotted. She clenched her piece and followed Roach inside.

THE ENTRANCE OF the warehouse comprised a large area with three doors leading off into the unknown. All remained quiet and Arnold chose one of the three, seemingly at random: left, right or straight ahead.

Once upon a time, this was a reception area but now there was a counter and space for a desk, filing cabinets and the makings of an office, but no furniture or any sign this was used nowadays or that they could expect anyone to appear either.

Back to the second door and Arnold tried the handle. Nothing. He and Mary Lou looked at each other, not understanding what was happening. How could it be locked? She shook her head and in the quietest voice she could muster:

"Let me try."

She gripped the handle until her knuckles were white, and twisted. The door opened just a hairline crack and Mary Lou glanced at Arnold and shrugged. She pushed at the door some more and one eye squinted into the light beyond. There was a staircase in the foreground leading both upstairs and down. Further away was a large room filled with boxes sitting on shelving.

Mary Lou just about made out the silhouette of a man grabbing a cardboard cube and then walking off out of sight. She waited to see if there was any more activity visible, but the guy didn't return. Nor did any of his friends appear. A beat and then they scurried to the stairs.

Arnold looked up and down, but saw jack.

"Where now?"

"Let's finish this floor and only then try somewhere else."

They scooted toward the shelving and found a labyrinth of aisles formed by the boxes. A small army would take at least an hour to check the whole area. There was only the two of them and they didn't have the time. Instead, they stood as still as mannequins and listened hard. If the guy she'd seen was on the floor, his footsteps were too far away to hear.

"Up or down?"

"Up?"

Mary Lou nodded consent and they padded back to the stairs and on to the second floor. The stairwell was industrial in size, so they arrived at the other end of the set of steps, guns pointing into the void. Near the stairs was an entrance comprising clear plastic strips hanging from the ceiling, each four inches wide. While the strips were technically transparent, you could see no detail looking through them. All Mary Lou and Arnold knew for sure was that no one stood immediately the other side. Beyond that was anyone's guess.

Arnold counted down with his fingers—three, two, one—and they both pushed through and stood the other side, arms aiming guns left to right in case trouble was standing, waiting for them. But, again, there was nobody there and nothing much to see. In the far distance, Mary Lou made out the sound of some machinery. She looked askance at Arnold.

"We'd better check it out."

She nodded and they edged their way through the gloom toward the metallic sounds. There were planks of wood and various lumps of debris scattered along their route, but eventually they reached an outside wall and realized they'd missed whatever machine they thought they'd been tracking. They stood a breath apart. Arnold craned his head and pointed to his right. Mary Lou thought for a second and knew he was correct.

Two minutes later, they found a partition wall and the sound was much louder now. Arnold ducked down below the solid lower half of the fake wall, padding along until they reached a swing door. With the most simple of hand gestures, Arnold indicated for Mary Lou to remain where she was.

He let the barrel of his gun peep through the other side, then allowed one eye and his nose to follow. His body vanished for a moment and then it reappeared.

"Nothing doing. It's a packaging plant, but I didn't get a chance to see what's being boxed up. Doesn't matter right now…"

"Because Alice and Frank Jr weren't there."

"Yep."

Back to the stairs and another decision: up again or back down? Up, but this time the floor was emptier than the last, so they returned to the first story and took a moment before hitting the basement. There had been no sign of Anastasia or Naldo. Either they were downstairs or they'd run away before the game got going. Another possibility was that they'd been caught and were spilling their guts as Mary Lou thought this through.

Come to think of it, they hadn't found any rear entrance. Had their men entered via the basement? There had been no shots fired—all was quiet apart from the low level hum emanating from the packing machine. The only thing to do was head to the floor below and everything would become clear.

"Let's get this done."

Like before, they each stood at the far end of a step to give best line of sight on anything about to appear. They edged down until they crouched at the bottom of the stairwell—a concrete floor comprising only a ten by ten feet space and two doors.

Before they could decide what to do, the left-hand door opened and a man walked straight into Arnold.

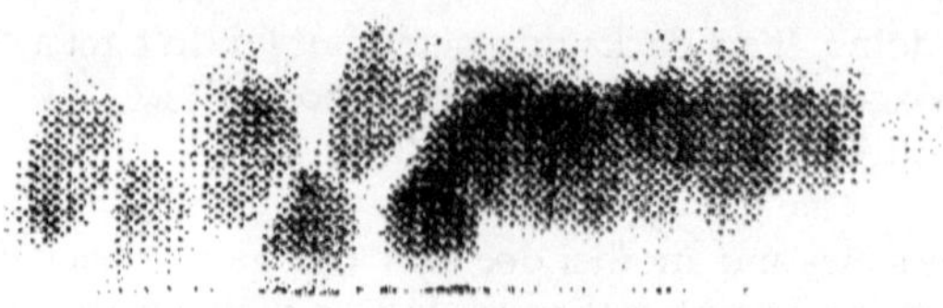

29

ARNOLD GRABBED THE guy by the throat and swung him round, slamming him into the nearest wall. He used one hand to wrap his fingers around the dude's wrist and smashed it twice against the brickwork until the man's gun fell to the floor. Arnold squeezed until the dude could only just breathe. He spluttered and wheezed, choked spittle landing on Arnold's first finger and thumb.

Mary Lou picked up the revolver from the ground and held it to the guy's temple as Arnold carried on squeezing the life out of his windpipe. His body went limp and he slumped down. Arnold checked his pockets and passed a snub nose over to her. Then a box of slugs appeared out of a jacket pocket. She filled the clip and stuffed it into her waistband—at the front though, as it was quite small and she didn't want to lose it.

"That answers the question which door to try first."

Arnold opened the left one just a crack to have a peep and closed it again, twisting round to face Mary Lou. A deep breath.

"Other side is a large room—more of a workspace, really. I spotted at least four guys hanging around either sat on chairs or leaning on a wall. They look bored like they've been there an eternity, but I couldn't see a reason for them to be huddled so close together. They can't be guarding the floor or they'd be more alert."

"Do you think we should leave them be for now and check out the other route?"

"Reckon so. It's a whole pile of trouble over there."

Arnold's thumb pointed through the left-hand door and they both imagined the first ten to twelve seconds after they popped their heads around to say hi. Instead, Arnold peeped round the right-hand door and reported all was safe. They went through into a corridor which stretched two hundred or more feet ahead. Both sides had office doors running every fifty feet; the top half of each was composed of glass, so they'd need to tread carefully as they made their way along.

Mary Lou was the first to scuttle down the aisle until she reached a door and then she flattened herself against the wall. Arnold stood two feet away from her. She heard his inhalations and imagined the stress he was feeling. A quick nod to acknowledge the next step and she swung round and rolled near the floor, swiftly followed by Arnold. They crouched facing each other to steady their nerves, aware how long the corridor felt.

Arnold pointed at himself to show he wanted to lead and Mary Lou remained stationary to let him pass. Roach stood upright and leaned his head right by the jamb of the next door. A few seconds of intense listening and he walked casually past. He turned round and winked at Mary Lou, who winked back and followed Roach until they arrived at the last door on the right.

This time, Arnold held a palm up to pause Mary Lou's progress. Once he was certain she would not blunder forwards, he placed a solitary finger to his lips. The universal hand gesture meaning 'shut up'. As they stood there, Mary Lou heard the mumbled sounds of a conversation, but she couldn't make out a single word.

Arnold kept his fingers on his lips as he continued to listen intently. His expression gave nothing away though. One long minute and he leaned into Mary Lou's ear.

"There's two, sat talking about all sorts. They are from the east coast and are bitching about being so far from home. No word on where the kids are but Sancho Mendoza is in the building."

"Huh?"

"You heard me right. He's got himself some hired hands."

"From New York? Baltimore? Boston?"

"I don't recognize them, so probably not from the Big Apple. Apart from that, no idea."

"But they didn't have time to come over this afternoon. They must be here on other business."

"And Mendoza has been using them as guards. That's why they aren't happy. Good news is that Alice and Frank Jr are here."

"We need to take them out."

"Leave it to me."

Before Mary Lou could pass any comment, Arnold vanished into the room. Ninety seconds later, he returned. She popped her head around the door and saw the two men lying on the ground, dead. But no sign of any knife wound and no sound from a revolver. Arnold had strangled them both. The most remarkable achievement was to kill the first guy without the other one noticing. Hats off to Arnold.

They scurried to the end of the corridor and held their breath as Mary Lou peeped past the door to see what they were up against. A square reception area with three doors leading off it. The biggest problem were the four fellas standing and sitting round. She had no idea at first glance who or what was behind any of the doors. Arnold pulled out his revolvers.

"Never bring a knife to a gun fight."

He winked and put his blade away into his belt. Mary Lou smiled back at him.

"How do we play this?"

"You take care of the two on the right. I'll handle the others. Anyone left standing: kill them wherever they are."

There was a curled smile around his mouth but Roach's eyes were fixed in a cold, hard glare. This was his business and he knew it well.

"But let's do this clean if we can. The quieter, the better."

She nodded understanding and Arnold pulled out a second gun from his jacket. He mouthed a countdown and slipped through the door without a sound. A solitary crack then a body crumpled to the floor. Mary Lou reached the other side of the door and put a slug in the chest of one of her targets. His body thumped the wall as it took the momentum of the shot and slithered down to the ground. Blood poured from his heart, forming a large puddle on the floor which seeped into the cracks of the tiled surface.

The other target sat at a table, holding playing cards. Must have been enjoying a game of solitaire. By the time he realized what was going down, Mary Lou had got one pace further toward him and aimed at his forehead. A squeeze of the trigger and his head pushed backwards with the force of the bullet that entered his left eye and exited the back of his skull. Red splatter spread across the wall behind him.

Arnold and Mary Lou crouched down and waited for a second. No one appeared from any of the rooms. They scurried over to the corpses and grabbed firearms and bullets aplenty. She was minutes away from finding her babies.

MARY LOU AND Arnold hugged the floor and took stock of their situation. Three rooms led off from the space they were in. Each had a shut door along with a wall comprising a long glass panel running from the ceiling to halfway up. From her position a few inches from the ground, Mary Lou saw heads bobbing in two of the rooms. The third had green Venetian blinds drawn.

Arnold wriggled his fingers to get her attention and showed which room they'd hit next. She blinked her agreement and they rolled over to the first door. Upright but flat against the wall, they could make out three guys inside talking. More hand gestures and nods, then a quick leap up and they were inside, snapping slugs into brains before the saps reacted. He pushed the door shut and they sorted out the corpses, taking more bullets but leaving the guns behind. He closed the blinds to give them a moment's respite.

"How you doing?"

"Just fine. You?"

"Cool bananas."

They put slugs into chambers and edged out the room and took out the second one much like the first. Mary Lou noticed little flecks of red on Arnold's cheeks and shirt. She figured she bore the marks of the blood letting too. The two hunkered over to outside the third room and waited. Arnold pressed an ear to the door while Mary Lou craned to hear any conversation through the glass half-partition. Nothing doing.

In her mind's eye, Mary Lou imagined Frank Jr and Alice sat on the floor playing, while two brutes stood over them. But she knew their situation was far worse than that—in ways she didn't want to consider. There would be only one way to find out and they were seconds from the truth. She breathed deeply twice and swallowed hard. A nod to Arnold, who threw the door open wide, and they shot at every adult they could see.

Four men stood at various locations and a handful of tables and chairs were scattered around. Made no sense: there was no order to the place. Mary Lou remained crouched and took out a black-haired dude who was fumbling for his piece in his jacket. Meanwhile, Arnold made mincemeat of one of the other's brains as pieces of flesh smacked against a far wall.

The other two hit the floor and flung the nearest table over as a barricade. To cause confusion, they hurled two chairs at the open doorway, but neither Arnold nor Mary Lou responded. They tried firing through the furniture but no joy. Arnold scurried into the room until he reached a square-based pillar. Mary Lou covered him during the manouevre with a spray of slugs all over the place. She searched for even a glimmer of the kids, but they didn't seem to be there, goddamnit.

Then all guns stopped firing and everyone took stock, trying to figure out their next move. Arnold and Mary Lou looked at each other and he beckoned her inside. She kept low and made her way to a table, flipping it over before another assault of bullets headed her direction. Then another eerie silence. She was ten feet from Arnold and the fellas were thirty feet behind their upturned table, now gouged with any number of bullet holes.

The wood surface was peppered to shit by the slugs, but it must have a metal base beneath or those guys would have met their maker by now.

There was a moment of calm and Mary Lou noticed a door at the other end of the room. In perfect synchrony, Arnold must have spotted the same thing as they both looked at each other, knowing. He slid away from the pillar to create a better line of sight to attack. Arnold turned his head back to Mary Lou and held three fingers up. How had they missed one guy? That wasn't important right now. Despite all his training and deep experience, Arnold blurted out two words.

"Sancho Mendoza."

Mary Lou's eyes widened as that single phrase unlocked all that had befallen her since lunchtime. This had nothing to do with the mob. This was all about the brown powder. If the deal hadn't gone south this morning, none of this would have happened. Mendoza wanted the sweet taste of revenge and the motherfucker who'd stolen her children was a few feet in front of her.

A red veil cast a shadow over her eyes and she ground her molars at the back of her jaw. She raised herself until she saw over her defenses and glimpsed the top of one head. Aimed slow and squeezed the trigger until the recoil sent her arm upwards and a bullet landed in the middle of the guy's skull. A quick duck-down as the survivors responded with their revolvers.

Before they knew what was going on, one of the two made a break for the door three feet behind him. Arnold and Mary Lou peppered the room with gunfire and the last dude behind the table splayed backwards with the force of Arnold's high caliber pistol. The other slammed the door behind him.

"Mendoza!"

They scrambled over to the other side of the room and Mary Lou flung open the door. She saw a leg disappear up a fire escape ladder and then she scanned the room.

"Leave Mendoza to me."

Arnold grabbed the fire escape and Mary Lou stood, guns in both hands, surveying an empty room with one cupboard against a wall and two bodies trussed up lying, one on top of the other, next to the solitary item of office furniture. She didn't need to give them a close inspection to know it was Serafini and Pavone.

Gunfire outside as Arnold gave chase. Complete nothing surrounded Mary Lou. Almost zilch: she noticed the ticking of a clock and swung round to see the circular dial and the blade markings near the edge, counting the seconds until her death.

Then a knocking. From the cupboard. A light tap and not much more than that, but enough to be audible. Mary Lou raised her revolver at the gray object and pulled open one door. Her eyes flitted across the top half as it was lined with empty shelves. The bottom section consumed half the space inside. On the floor sat a bundle of ropes and a gag in each mouth. Their hands and feet were tied, but Mary Lou had found her loves.

Taking the knife from her jeans, she cut through the fibers and undid the knots on the handkerchief gags. Then she held them both as they hugged her back and all three sobbed with happiness.

WHEN THEY ARRIVED home, Bobby opened the door and everyone tumbled inside. The family stood in the hallway in an enormous embrace for a full five minutes. Mary Lou picked up Alice in her arms and Bobby took Frank Jr as they entered the living room. Arnold followed them in, hands deep in pockets.

Once they sat down on the couches, she allowed another tear to roll down her cheek as she pressed Alice against her body. There was a moment when Arnold thought she would never let go, but eventually she scampered off and checked on her brother before returning to her mother and forcing Mary Lou's legs apart so she could loll over one knee.

Ten minutes later, they took the kids off to bed, leaving Arnold to forage for some Scotch and soda. It had been a long night—and an even longer day before. Mary Lou kissed them both as Bobby returned downstairs, but she didn't follow. Instead, she waited until they were both asleep before she dared to leave them.

Back in the living room, the two men had spread themselves out. Each nursed a tumbler containing a yellow-brown liquid and ice. A third glass rested on a coffee table. She picked it up and sat next to Bobby, but she kept her head pointed at Roach.

"Thank you again."

"De nada."

"No, really. You saved my children's lives tonight."

Arnold nodded and smiled in recognition of her words, but he was not comfortable with this kind of attention.

"Let's move on. Mendoza is still out there. We cut off the tail of the worm but the head is alive and well."

"For Mendoza to have acted so quickly, he must have had help."

"East Coast help?"

"That's what it sounded like."

Mary Lou took a sip of her drink and swallowed hard. This wasn't over yet. Not by a long way. If her family was ever to be safe then she would need to finish off Sancho Mendoza but also there had to be a day of reckoning with the men who supported him from New York. The same mob who'd killed her husband and driven her away from the only place she had called home: a dingy one-bedroom apartment in the crappy end of Baltimore.

Monday April 12, 1971

30

MARY LOU AWOKE alone in bed, much as she had done ever since Frank
lay dying in her arms a lifetime ago. She sat bolt upright and allowed herself
a fleeting moment of panic before she remembered where she was and that
her babies were safe. Just to make certain, she tiptoed into their room to see
them sleeping soundly. A smile and she closed the door behind her.

Bobby was in the spare room and Arnold was downstairs on the couch.
The man had quite a snore on him to be so audible from this distance. Proof
he lived alone. She returned to her own bedroom and got dressed. Then
down to make breakfast.

Eggs, bacon and toast smells roused Arnold and he slunk off the couch,
rubbed his eyes of sleep and joined her in the kitchen. Five minutes later,
Bobby appeared—the aroma of cooked food had seeped up the stairs but
wasn't strong enough to wake the kids, not on this morning. The three sat
around the table, quietly chewing and swallowing, lost in their own worlds.

Mary Lou had placed a pot of coffee in the middle of the table and once
they had mopped up their crumbs with the crusts of their toast, they filled
up their mugs and felt able to talk to each other.

"I'll call the agency and get a housekeeper in fast. This business isn't
over."

"First speak with Fabio: if you want Alice and Frank Jr to remain safe,
we'll need their help. Two guys in the front, two in the rear and two inside. If
Mendoza tries to attack, he'll bring a fucking army."

"Do you think he will?"

"I dunno the fella so I have no clue how hot-tempered he is. Me? I'd exit stage left and come back once the dust had settled. But I'm content serving my revenge stone cold. Others prefer a warmer dish."

At that moment, a scampering of feet and the twins descended on the kitchen. Mary Lou prepared breakfast while Bobby kept them occupied. Arnold remained separate from all this hubbub, somehow able to stay in the room, sat on his chair, while all around domestic normality oozed out of every corner of the surrounding people.

He took a swig of coffee and took a tour of the estate. Out of respect to Mary Lou, he kept his piece in its holster until he was out of sight of the kids. They'd seen enough guns and blood to last them forever and a day.

Forty-five minutes later, a knock on the door and the family's new housekeeper appeared. She looked at least ten years older than Cindy, but had warm eyes. Truth was Mary Lou had explained she was having security issues, so the agency found her somebody who could handle themselves in times of trouble. Within a few days, she could be swapped out for a more playful youngster, if the kids didn't like her. The woman's name was Irma and that was all that mattered.

Alice was especially nervous of this stranger, but Frank Jr warmed to her almost as soon as she'd stepped into the room. He was so much like a puppy dog.

They talked in the kitchen and let Alice see that Irma was part of the extended family. Then Mary Lou suggested they go upstairs to get dressed. The two women and the children left and hit the kids' bedroom. Mary Lou stayed long enough for Irma to take command of the twins and then she made her excuses and returned downstairs.

"All good?"

"Yeah. They'll be fine."

"I'm gonna stick around here today. If you're off taking care of Mendoza, I'll mind the twins."

"Thanks. They need someone they know and can trust. If they are to stay alive, I have to leave them and finish what I started."

Mary Lou popped up to the children and played with them a short while. A simple look in Irma's direction gave all the explanation that was needed. Alice and Frank Jr were excited when their mom told them she was going out for some ice-cream but it might take a while to find. A long hug for each of them and a hushed word with Irma. Mary Lou turned her back on her precious family and left the room.

Arnold had finished his first sweep of the estate when she found him in the summerhouse.

"You ready to hook up with Fabio?"

"I've been waiting all my life for this moment."

They smiled at each other and filled up their pieces with bullets from last night's adventure and from the hidden room's stash. She squeezed

Bobby's hand and pecked him on the cheek. Then she and Arnold hopped into her car and sped off to have a private conversation with Fabio.

MARY LOU SAT in Fabio's garden while Arnold stood indoors. She had stopped counting the supporting cast when Fabio started introducing them to her. Each wore the same clothes—white shirt and pants to match the jacket, which contained a concealed weapon. A tie was optional.

A pleasant enough patio area and a gazebo had been erected halfway down the expansive lawn. Fabio's men stood a respectful distance away from him, facing outward in case of trouble. Mary Lou sipped at her coffee and languished in the warm air. To his credit, Fabio was in no hurry and she experienced a peace she thought she'd never know again. He let her completely drain the cup before he got down to business.

"I am glad the unpleasantness with your children has been positively resolved."

"Thank you. May I send a token of appreciation to the widows of your men, who died last night?"

"There is no need, but your respect is well noted."

"To work then: Mendoza is alive and those who backed him remain in operation."

"What are your plans?"

"Roach and I will dispose of Mendoza. There is no question in my mind that mook must die."

"We agree. He crossed a line—no matter what decision you make in business, your family should not bear the physical consequences of your difficulties. Taking your children was an ill-thought through act of a coward."

"But he didn't act alone."

"Very perceptive. No, we don't believe so either."

"You know where the help came from?"

"The east, I'd say."

"Anywhere in particular?"

Fabio's lips curled upward as he witnessed her trying to tease the information out of him. Some things dare not bear uttering.

"Are you aware of the issues faced by the Bassani family these past few years?"

Mary Lou shrugged as she was fairly ignorant of all the goings on. She only knew what she'd picked up from conversations in the Country Club. And there was a lot of rumor masquerading as fact at the nineteenth hole.

"For quite some time, interests back east have conflicted with those on this side of the country. The situation has not been helped by local law enforcement issues."

In the most coded way possible, Fabio affirmed what Mary Lou had heard before: when underboss, Joe Dippolito went down in '69, Bassani took over his rackets. Trouble was that the New York mob needed to extend its tentacles just at the time when Joe Dip was at his weakest. This meant the Pentangelo clan had been nipping at their heels ever since.

That name sent a shudder down Mary Lou's spine. These were the people who'd had the Feds in their pockets and had gunned down Frank.

"Who would have given the order and supplied Mendoza with financing?"

"Charles Pentangelo. Charlie. Leave him to us. Do not go after him."

"He's been trouble to you for three years to my knowledge and you have done nothing about him. You won't change your mind in the next twenty-four hours."

She stared into Fabio's eyes, seeking to instill in him the absolute certainty and clarity that Pentangelo would soon meet his maker.

"He's a made guy and he cannot be touched."

"Even if it frees us from unwarranted attention in the east and delivers us the heroin trade across South LA and Watts?"

"If anything were to befall him, it must not be traced back here. Were that to happen, the kidnapping of Alice and Frank Jr would be the least of your worries. Capiche?"

Mary Lou nodded and checked her cup for coffee but it was long since empty. Only a trickle of dregs at the bottom. The thought of Charlie Pentangelo sucking the barrel of her gun made her smile inside. This was mirrored on her expression as she imagined his gray matter leaving the back of his skull and hitting a wall.

"So we are clear?"

"Like my nail polish."

Fabio frowned in confusion at her words, then looked down at her fingers and understood.

"I have business to attend out of town."

"Just remember you have deliveries to make in California before you go anywhere else."

"I know. And thank you for providing the men to keep my house secure."

"No one should live in fear in their home, should they?"

His comments seemed more labored than Mary Lou might have expected and she stored that thought away for later. She got up and they shook hands. Fabio walked her back to the house and acknowledged Roach with a look. Arnold's reputation stood before him and no words were necessary for this artist.

As they drove back to Bobby and the kids, Arnold refrained from asking a single question about her private conversation. Classy guy.

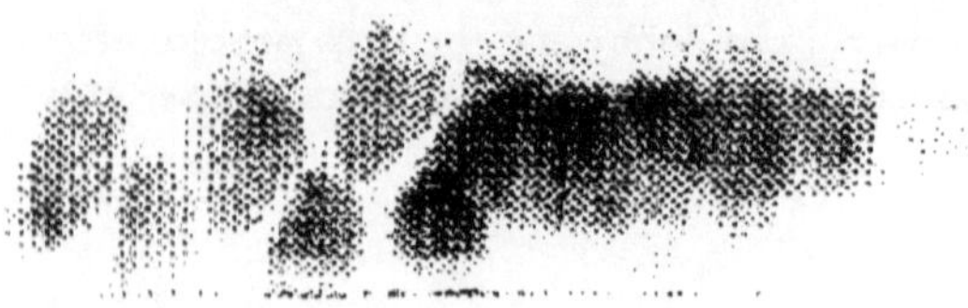

31

IRMA HAD TAKEN the kids out for an early pizza, so Bobby was resting by the pool. They all sat down and soaked in the late morning rays knowing this moment would surely pass too soon. And they were right.

"First, we take out Mendoza and then Pentangelo."

"Charlie is no an easy hit but at least we know where he is. Mendoza has flown in the wind."

"He won't have gone far. My guess is he's in hiding in LA. And I'd like the opportunity to do more than watch the kids."

"It is an important job."

"Yes, Arnold. But it isn't man's work."

Mary Lou laughed and the two men looked at her.

"Listen to you two. You're assuming a man will do the killing of Sancho Mendoza."

"We are both professionals. Or we were."

Arnold cast a withering eye at Bobby and resumed.

"You've come rather late to this game and are a robber at heart. That's said with all respect due to you. If you don't mind me saying, the Bank of Baltimore heist was nothing short of brilliant."

"Damn straight."

"It is one thing to fire a gun from a hundred feet and hit your mark. That is a world apart from walking up to somebody and putting a bullet in their skull when you can taste the fear in their breath. And do it in such a way you get out of the venue alive."

"Arnold, you're right, but this is a job for a local guy—someone who knows the dives in Watts and can ferret out a dealer who's hit the mattresses."

"Not so fast, old man. You don't need to know every local bar to find a dirty rat. You forget, that's how I earn my crust. I traveled four thousand miles to find Mary Lou. Some sleazebag smack merchant a few miles down the road will be no bother to me at all."

They glared at each other while Mary Lou stared both down. This was not the time for petty squabbles.

"You boys want a drink?"

Shake of heads from both and she continued sipping her coffee.

"The question isn't who will pull the trigger on the mook, but when."

"Today."

Arnold's response began almost before she finished her last syllable. Bobby nodded agreement but remained silent. For a man who wanted to do more then look after the kids, he was doing a great impersonation of chopped liver.

"Can you get the job done by tonight?"

"Yes."

"Good. Bobby, you stay here. As much as you wish to kill someone for me, you are the person I am trusting with my children. I trust Arnold with a slug, but I entrust you with my flesh and blood. And I don't want either of you to let me down."

"I'm here for you."

"I know you are."

She reached out an arm and Bobby took her hand to squeeze it for three long seconds. Then Mary Lou withdrew the limb and he grabbed a gulp from his mug. The seriousness of his situation engulfed him for a moment and he lost focus on the conversation between Mary Lou and Arnold.

CHARLIE PENTANGELO WAS a capo in the New York mob and would have plenty of protection surrounding him every minute of each hour. The trick was to find a crack in this seemingly impenetrable armor. If anyone could figure it out, Arnold Roach was at the top of most people's lists. He held his mug in both hands, repeatedly sipping and swallowing. All the while, staring into the empty pool. The memory of Cindy's corpse floating in the pink sea was just that: a piece of the past. History.

"During the day, there is enough security you'd need either someone on a suicide mission or a Molotov cocktail. Neither option has a great survival rate."

"Especially suicide."

"Most people who throw Molotovs dowse themselves in burning gas."

"Like a Buddhist monk on a 'Nam protest."

"So we should avoid the day, then?"

"Unless you're sitting on a mighty clever idea."

"Only my ass."

"And what about evening?"

"I think we'd have more options. There're the times when his guards change shift. They stand in the hallway, outside his apartment, and get bored. Better still, in the middle of the night, they fall asleep. Protecting Charlie is a dull job. You work your way up as an enforcer to show you can handle yourself in a crisis, but then you hang around doing nothing for weeks at a time, because no one is stupid enough to attack Charlie Pentangelo. Present company excepted. No offense, you understand."

"None taken. Right, Bobby?"

"For sure. Too stupid to care, me."

Arnold blushed, but the grin on Bobby's face belied how he actually felt. Roach was more concerned about Mary Lou's response, because Bobby was just the nurse. Her wink to him gave Arnold the comfort of knowing all was well in the Lagotti household.

"So down the fire escape and hit him while he's asleep?"

"If you've taken out the guys on the roof and have padded down the metal stairs so quietly you haven't woken up the whole neighborhood."

Mary Lou stared at the water in the pool. Arnold sure wasn't making this easy. She'd been certain he'd have had a plan up his sleeve, but they had bupkis.

"What about blowing the place up? Plant a bomb under his bed and be long gone out of town by the time his brains are mixing with the ceiling."

Sigh.

"If we could get inside without being suspicious, then there's just killing his wife at the same time. Neither you nor I care if she lives or dies, but the Pentangelo family will judge it an unnecessarily cruel act to take her out. And then they would come after us. If we can make this a pure business hit, then we might get away with the assault on the capo as a piece of justifiable revenge. He funded an attack on Mary Lou's children, which was so out of line."

"Sounds like you don't think there's a way to get to him."

"I didn't say that, but it won't be easy."

"And we do it, how?"

"Dunno. Blowing him up or shooting him on the sidewalk are not solutions. That I know."

"What's wrong with where he works?"

"It's a mob stronghold. He's not sat in an office dictating memos to some big-tittied secretary, sitting on his knee massaging his… ego."

Mary Lou stiffened on her sunbed and Arnold realized he had gone a pinch too far.

"Sorry."

"De nada. How are we going to kill this motherfucker?"

Everyone remained silent as they mulled over ideas too foolish or insane to voice out loud. Mary Lou went inside after ten minutes to brew more Java. Sitting around was not good for her mental state. She needed action and the closest proxy was the coffee pot.

The problem wasn't how to kill Pentangelo—they would use a bullet or two. The difficulty was getting in and out without being caught. This was a situation more akin to guerilla warfare than an assassination. With this notion as a backdrop, Mary Lou saw she needed to stop thinking like Arnold and Bobby. What would her Frank have done?

He would have got her to turn up in a short skirt and heels and let the goons check her clutch bag. Then when she was alone with Pentangalo, she'd have pulled a piece from beneath her panties and plugged him full of holes. Gun in her bag, she'd walk out, ask the mooks for a light and make sure she pressed herself close just to take their minds off guarding the boss long enough for her to get out of Dodge.

When Mary Lou described the plan to the other two, they nodded, pondered and nodded again. All they had to figure out was where Charlie would be on his own so she could pay him a visit. At home in the evening, at lunch if he didn't go to a restaurant. Even in the mob's headquarters if they came up with a a satisfactory enough excuse for her to be there. The good news was that none of the New York contingent had any idea what Mary Lou looked like. And only a handful, who'd been in the game two years before, had any clue about her past connection to Charlie Pentangelo.

"Let me make a few calls."

Arnold stepped inside to speak to his contacts back east. Fifteen minutes later, he returned with a smile on his face and a fleshed-out plan in his pocket. They ran through it twice, trying to find any holes and to check it out from every angle. Two minor amendments and Mary Lou knew exactly what to do and when to do it.

"Once I've spoken to Milton about the China white, I'll be on my way."

"You need a hand?"

"No thank you. Arnold: you attend to Mendoza. Bobby: keep my babies safe."

They stood up and each hugged the other two. However the dice rolled, nothing would be the same again.

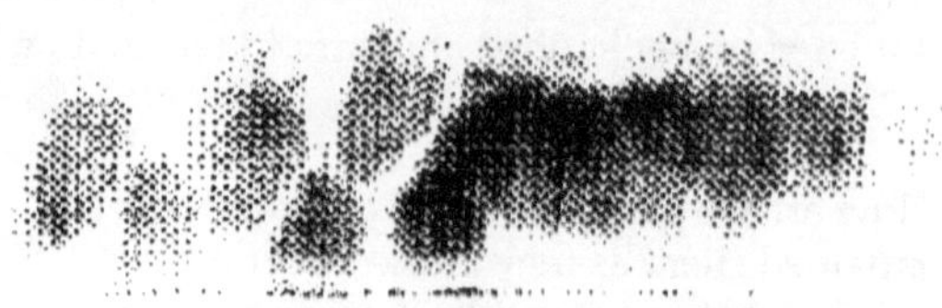

32

MARY LOU DROVE over to the Country Club to find Milton. He'd been missing since he scooted off with her powder, but this was the first opportunity for she to do anything about it. Despite all that had gone down with the twins, she knew deep in her heart she needed to pay her tribute to Pasquale on Friday. So she had to generate some income during the week otherwise Irma would find her employer floating in her own swimming pool, which was not a good look.

Her concern right now wasn't the appreciation, so much as Milton's absence. In the darkest recesses of her mind, a worm burrowed through with the thought he'd absconded with the white—or cut a deal behind her back.

The Country Club was empty—or rather, it was full of people imbibing an early cocktail, but none of them was Milton. The blond hairs at the nape of her neck froze and an icy chill shuddered through her body at the thought of losing all that smack.

Next stop was Milton's house. Janet answered the door in her dressing gown. Mary Lou glanced at her watch and saw it was nearly eleven.

"How are you?"

The woman was frosty—had been ever since Mary Lou talked business with her husband—but there was an extra edge to her voice this morning.

"Just fine, thanks. How's Milton?"

"Fine too."

Terse. Janet's eyes flitted away from the door and to the stairs. Something was amiss in the state of California.

"Am I keeping you from anything?"

"What? No!"

She wrapped her dressing gown tighter round her body, pulling at the belt. Arms folded.

"How's Paulie?"

"Good. At a sleep over with a friend. We should organize a play date with him and the twins."

"He's twice their age…"

"What? Oh yes. Silly me."

Janet wasn't thinking straight and spouting crap.

"Can I come in? I need to talk to Milton about some business."

"Come in? Huh? He's not… It's not convenient."

"Convenient?"

Janet's eyes glanced upstairs again. She gripped the edge of the door firmer than before. Mary Lou noticed the throbbing of a blood vessel on her right temple.

"Is Milton there?"

More discomfort as Janet tied her dressing gown again, only this time she revealed she was naked underneath the silky bed coat. Then Mary Lou woke up and smelled the coffee. Janet had a house guest in her bedroom, no clothes on and Milton wasn't home. When the cat's away…

"No, he's not."

Another furtive glance up the stairs and a shuffling of dressing gown cords.

"Sorry Janet. I didn't realize. Let Milton know I'm looking for him next time you see him."

With a single wink and a dirty grin, Mary Lou turned round and headed back to the car, leaving Janet to slam the door shut and return to her paramour. For a second, Mary Lou wondered who she was fucking. Then she realized she didn't care—unless it interfered with her business interests with Milton.

This left open the question of where the man had gone. Apart from the possibility of having missed him at the clubhouse, she thought she'd try the lab where he should have taken the heroin for processing.

To call the place a laboratory was stretching the meaning of the word—it was a disused factory on the edge of nowhere surrounded by the memory of a Palm Springs long since faded and died. On the corner of Belardo and East Ramon Road, east of the city, the place looked like every other building on the block. Each one was run down to the point of senility and comprised a rusty gate, once imposing doors and brickwork that contained more pockmarks than a teenager's face.

Mary Lou parked round the back and watched as a young dude eyed her vehicle and placed a hand on his concealed weapon. She got out the car and, open palmed, walked toward him. He stared at her as though she was the woman who'd slashed his mother's face.

"Hi. I'm Mary Lou. Is Milton in?"

A flicker of recognition and a terrible quandary: how to figure out if she was telling the truth? His mouth opened, but no words emerged.

"Well boy?"

He stared and caught flies. Mary Lou brushed past him and through the door. What a waste of space. Up some stairs and into the main area. There was a glass room in the middle where the drugs were processed. Scales, bunsen burners, the works. Looked like the biggest science experiment in the world. Mary Lou spotted Milton on the far side and raised an arm to grab his attention.

He smiled and waved back. She held her ground and waited for him to do the right thing and come over. Thirty seconds later and he got the message.

"Good to see you."

"Yeah. Working hard, I see."

"Just trying to make my quota."

"Been here all the time since we split up?"

"More or less. I mean I popped out to get some smokes and a bite to eat. But I slept on a chair in the corner of the office upstairs."

He appeared genuinely confused, unsure of the meaning behind her question. She stared at his expression, trying to read his face and decide whether he'd helped Mendoza at all. There was nothing to suggest he'd double crossed her so she told him about the twins and Cindy.

Milton was devastated and sat down to collect his thoughts. Mary Lou gave him some time to pull his shit back together and briefed him on what she needed over the next couple of days. Bottom line: he must generate and distribute a large quantity of brown sugar by the end of the week.

"Anything else I can do?"

"Just keep these wagons rolling."

"Okay."

"Actually, there's one thing."

"Name it."

"Get rid of the boy on the back door. I never want to see him again. Find someone with some cajones who'll protect my investment."

"You won't see that kid again. Promise."

With business taken care of, she was now free to pursue Charlie Pentangelo to the gates of hell.

MARY LOU PARKED her car around the corner so she wouldn't be seen. She walked to the rear of the house, past the pool and into the summerhouse. As much as she wanted to see the twins she knew there needed to be no witnesses. The last thing she required was Irma to walk in unannounced.

To the back of the hidden room to get her hands on the right snub nose to do the job: as small as possible—given where she'd be hiding it—but with enough punch to take Pentangelo out with one shot. A silencer would make the whole thing quieter, but there was only so much space below her rose.

While she was pondering the matter, the summerhouse door creaked open. She froze. Irma? The kids?

"Is that you, Mary Lou?"

Bobby's voice caused the tension in her shoulders to ebb away. She popped her head out and winked.

"Just grabbing some provisions."

"Make sure the safety's on. That's my best advice."

"Any idea how to muffle the sound?"

Bobby was silent while he thought. He scrunched up his face as he struggled to come up with an answer.

"Not right now. Sorry. Arnold might know, but I'm out of ideas."

"Where's he got to?"

"Already left for his destiny with Mendoza's death."

"Goddamn."

"You'll come up of something. You always do."

"Thanks for the vote of confidence, but this is real serious. I am about to take out a high roller in the New York mob."

Bobby eyed her in silence and nodded. She was right: rubbing out a local heroin dealer wasn't in the same ballpark as whacking Charlie Pentangelo. He walked over and put his arms around her. She responded to the hug allowing her head to lean on his chest for a moment. Then a squeeze and she turned her back to him and rummaged for the perfect killing machine.

Mary Lou heard the door close behind Bobby as he returned to minding her brood. She stared at a .38 and a .22 with no idea how to choose between them. The former would pack more of a punch, but it was a bigger object to shove down her front. Even with the .22, a skimpy G-string was not on the cards as the piece would fall down to her ankles as soon as she moved.

A moment's more thought told her to pick the .38 because she'd need to wear a sanitary napkin to hold the damn thing up no matter what time of the month it was. Did that mean she could afford to bring a silencer too? Mary Lou considered that still a step too far. Where was Roach when you needed him?

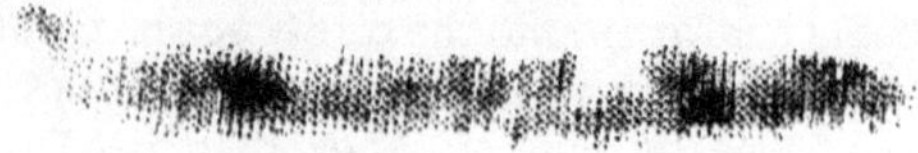

ARNOLD REGRETTED HIS decision to save money when he rented his car when he first arrived in California. For five bucks a day more, he could have been sitting in a cooling breeze. Instead, his journey to LA felt like a sauna on wheels. He was roasting and there was still over four hours to go—even if he kept his foot on the gas all the way there. Already he was looking forward to the first stopover.

He wound down his window, but that just let the warm air into the car. Twenty minutes into the journey and his back was sticking to his seat. And there wasn't even any money at the end of this rainbow. Doing a worthy thing was sweaty work. Might be okay for priests but this hired gun wasn't smiling. A bead of salty perspiration dripped over his right eyelid and dropped onto his cheek. This would be a quite a day.

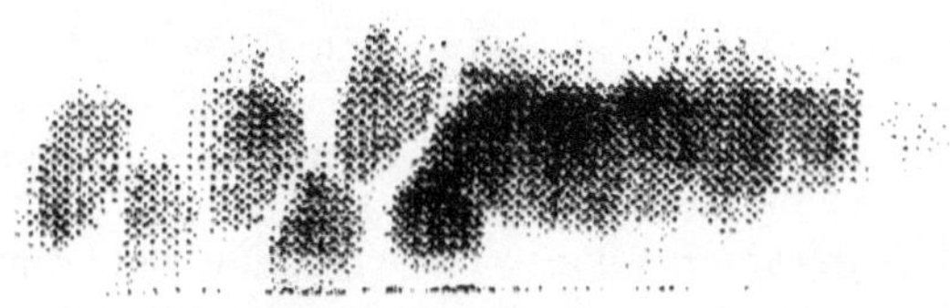

33

MARY LOU DROVE over to Sunrise Way and Park Canyon Drive. Even though the trip lasted a few minutes, the car temperature got comfortable real fast. So by the time she was in a cab heading for the airport, she was cool, calm and collected.

A simple plan: a short hop to LAX and then try to fly nonstop to New York. She brought a fake ID so's she'd have an alibi if one were needed, but tracing her movements across country would be hard as she paid cash all the way.

At Palm Springs Airport, Mary Lou waited in line at the sales desk. She hadn't expected the place to be so busy. Five people stood in front of her and each wanted to tell their life story to the hapless rep on the other side of the counter. Two of the group formed a couple although you couldn't see by their body language. He was the same height as her with matching brown hair. That was all they had in common as their ensuing argument revealed.

They were heading for Miami and he was happy to have a layover in San Francisco, but she was not. Traveling via Los Angeles was her highest priority. As if by magic, Mary Lou hoped he won because she couldn't face another minute of their bickering—especially if she was trapped in a tin can with them.

Ten minutes later and Mary Lou was at the counter discussing options to get to the City of Angels.

"You can catch the 11:10 if you hurry…"

"Or?"

"Or there's the 11:55 nonstop, gets you into LA by 13:05."

The woman watched Mary Lou all the time she stood and considered the choices. She knew what the rep was deciding: does she represent a security risk or does this lone girl simply want a ticket to ride?

"I need to see my boyfriend real soon, you know, but I can't arrive with tousled hair. We haven't seen each other in ages, if ya get me?"

Mary Lou tried to appear embarrassed about the implication of fucking her fictional fella. Her life story revealed, she ducked her eyes downward to show there was more to her relationship with this man than she'd express at a sales counter.

"So what'll it be?"

She popped a finger to the corner of her mouth as if still perplexed by the conundrum.

"I'd better wait. The amount this hairdo cost me, I can't afford to ruin it."

The rep's eyes lifted to the heavens in despair or to glance at the nest on top of Mary Lou's head. Either way, she issued the ticket and Mary Lou jiggled her tush toward the departure gates.

With time to kill, she bought a coffee and sat down at a formica table. After she placed her holdall by her feet, she hugged her drink while keeping her clutch bag on her shoulder. The minute hand on her watch made its way round the dial like a hopped-out hippy. The first announcement from the public address broke Mary Lou's ennui.

She showed her boarding pass to anyone in a uniform who cared to look at it. Despite the hijackings that had taken place the past year or two, American airports had a relaxed attitude to who sat on their planes—even though US aircraft had been attacked. Mary Lou did not complain. This made her life so much easier. To take a pistol on board would be a nightmare if the x-ray security machines were used on everyone and not just with the men who looked like PLO members.

Once she had taken her seat, the plane taxied to the runway within five minutes of her getting comfy. The pilot had a plane to catch. Up in the air, a flick through four pages of the in-house magazine and the descent began.

An uneventful wait at LAX and soon she stood in line to board her LaGuardia flight. Mary Lou had bought two magazines at the news kiosk by the gate and hoped she could use the rest of her time stuck in the plane to relax and to focus her thoughts on any details in her plan she'd missed. The lack of a silencer was near the top of the list—and how to pick the right moment to tackle Pentangelo on his own.

Instead Mary Lou found her choice of a window seat was a poor one. A guy sat next to her who barely fit within the confines of his allotted space and felt the overwhelming urge to express his views to the world, using as loud a voice as humanly possible. She considered elbowing him in the larynx to shut him up, but realized she'd have to mount him to reach past the bulbous fat of his torso.

An hour into the flight and silence reigned—or rather there were silent moments in between his incessant snoring. At least his opinions remained inside him.

Mary Lou allowed her head to relax onto the back rest and she soaked in the calm. With her eyes closed, she contemplated Charlie Pentangelo's last day on Earth. Then darkness engulfed her, and she woke up with a judder and a start two hours later. Jack Blowhard was complaining about the food and his drink. The stewardess did her level best to stay cool under pressure, but Mary Lou could see the woman was about to lose it big time.

The waitress in an airline uniform called over the chief steward and Blowhard heard how his feedback was valued, and as it had been provided, they would take a note for future reference. For now, he needed to shut the fuck up and stop bothering them as they tried to get on with their jobs. Mary Lou paraphrased because, even if Jack wasn't listening, all the other passengers knew exactly what was being said.

As if proof were required that shouting loudly gets yourself heard, Blowhard was offered an upgrade to business class. With more reluctance than you might expect, he accepted the offer with the utmost disregard to anyone's feelings and comfort but his own. Five minutes later, he departed Mary Lou's life forever. She eyed the man sat on the other side of Blowhard, who appeared as relieved as she was to see the whale go.

Three hours later and the wheels touched down at LaGuardia. If Mary Lou had a plan, it was as well laid out as it would ever be.

NEW YORK'S DOMESTIC airport was as dirty and disgusting as Mary Lou remembered. LaGuardia held the unique accolade of being the most ugly monstrosity the Brutalist Movement could create. Like so many air transport facilities around the world, the filth and noise of the establishment attracted the worst elements of society—like flies to a midden.

She had spent too many years living in such surroundings to pay much attention to the lowlife scum swarming around her as she waited for a cab to take her into the city. Pan-handlers, smack-heads and winos vied for the money held by the recently disembarked. They were ignored or shouted at: this was New York City.

"To Wall Street and South."

Manhattan looked beautiful in the moonlight: the lights of the buildings twinkled as the taxi hurled itself over Queensboro Bridge. Mary Lou marveled at the skyscrapers, punching their way into the inky blackness above the Big Apple. Her first sight of the city of her childhood hopes. When she left home, she'd planned to head straight here, but one curve ball after anther sent her on a different path. Now she had arrived in the land of her dreams and it felt good.

The cab reached Manhattan and turned south onto Second Avenue, just past 59th Street. Every block felt as though the taxi moved from one world to another. The ghettos existed cheek by jowl with barely a sheet of cigarette paper between them. Down into single digit streets on the edge of the East Village and over Houston to Chrystie.

"Right on Delancey and left on Varick."

Mary Lou barked out her instruction because Little Italy loomed and she didn't want to take any risks. Better to spend an extra buck or two than get stuck in traffic and while away the minutes staring at Pentangelo's goons. Arnold's detailed mental map of the city was serving her well.

"Head to Liberty and then right onto Pearl. After that, you can go straight there."

"It's your dime, lady."

These were the first words the driver uttered since Mary Lou got in the cab. She was grateful he hadn't told her his life story or shared his world view on aliens or indigents.

When he pulled up at Water and South, Mary Lou rounded the fare up to the next dollar and exited the vehicle. She pretended to search in her clutch bag until the taxi drove off: she didn't want anyone to piece together her movements from airport to her lodgings. She sucked in gas fumes and then turned down Cuylers Alley to reach a quiet unobtrusive hotel.

The Roxboro was a family-owned affair, where decades old grandeur had made room to faded wallpaper, crumbling plasterwork and a musty aroma reminiscent of decay. A place where nobody cared what you did or who you were—provided you didn't trash the joint more than it was already trashed. Mary Lou would do well there.

She paid cash in advance to facilitate a rapid exit the next day and trudged up the stairs to reach her bedroom—that way she had time to check out her emergency exits, although she wasn't worried about hotel fires.

Up in her one room, Mary Lou closed the drapes so no one could see in. She locked the door and placed her pistol on the desk. Two minutes later, the revolver lay in pieces on the guest furniture and was reconstituted back into a deadly weapon in a matter of seconds. Mary Lou knew better than to check it more than once. If everything was fine, messing with the gun would do no good.

She removed her possessions from her bag and hung them up onto one of the two hangers supplied inside the flimsy wardrobe. Then a brief trip out to grab a slice of pizza and a soda then back to her room and a quick shower. Off to sleep with no bed clothes—perhaps she'd packed a bit too lightly. Within a minute, Mary Lou's snoring kicked off, but only the guy next door could hear her heavy breathing as he jerked himself off to what he thought was going on in her chamber.

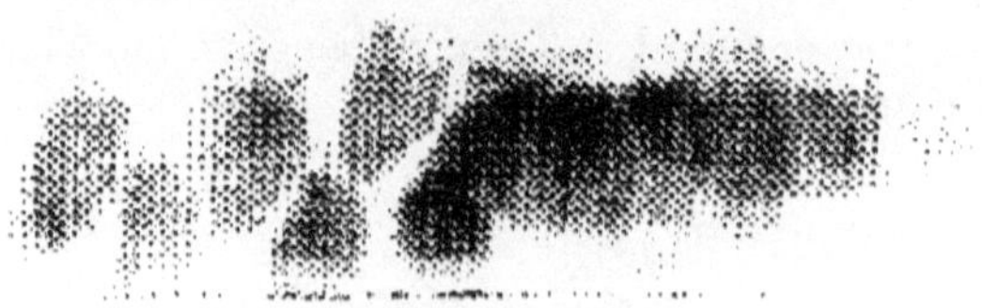

34

WHEN SHE WOKE up, Mary Lou rolled yesterday's clothes into a ball and shoved them into her carry bag. She considered wrapping the piece in the blouse, but decided against it. Life would be hard enough today without having to wrestle a revolver from the armhole of her top. She gritted her teeth and placed the cold steel inside the largest panties she owned, underpinned by a sanitary napkin. Then she slipped on a miniskirt and checked herself in the mirror. For the briefest of moments she convinced herself nobody would see the bulge protruding between her legs. She practiced walking from one side of the room to the other—a John Wayne impersonation playing in her head.

Finally, an uplift bra and a white blouse which was too tight. She had meant to throw it out, but had never got around to doing so. Good job: part of her plan rested on the goons staring more at her legs and boobs than at anything in between.

Down the stairs and out the door. Left out the alley entrance and back onto Wall Street. Everyone was too busy to spot a woman place an item of clothing in every trashcan she passed. May Lou's final deposit: the carry-on bag itself. She had no further use for it and besides, the damn thing would end up being a liability.

Once free of her refuse, Mary Lou headed uptown in case anyone followed her. When she reached William and Pine, she stopped and hailed a cab to Broadway and Broome. Then a walk five blocks east to arrive at the north side of Little Italy. Somewhere south lay her prey.

FIVE BLOCKS WIDE and three down, Little Italy had become the most intense and Sicilian location outside of Europe. Many people had emigrated from the Old Country, but the Sicilian dons were in charge. They were leaders back home and they had brought their power with them in their suitcases. Some were natural-born Americans, but they remained a breed apart: Italianamericans.

When Mary Lou sauntered south of Broome, she entered this foreign land with no passport, no experience of the place before and no knowledge of the local language. Armed with high heels, a short skirt and cleavage, she made her way down Mott Street and endured the catcalls and whistles from the neighborhood chimpanzees. When hands pinched her ass—or worse— she did her best to flick the fingers away with a hand as if they were annoying insects, even though all her instincts told her to stop and knee the fuckers in the balls.

But Mary Lou was not in this ghetto to fight for female emancipation: she was here to free Charlie Pentangelo from his mortal bonds. Instead she walked by the kerb as that meant the men could only attack her from one side—a cute ass wasn't worth getting run over for. Not even hers.

She crossed over Grande and turned right, back a block, until she reached Mulberry, the epicenter of the ghetto. Mary Lou knew that at the other end of this block was Charlie Pentangelo. Or rather, Arnold had told her Pentangelo's business was on the corner of Mulberry and Hester and that was one block away.

When she got within spit of Hester, she ducked into a cafe and ordered a coffee. The waiter leered at her and returned with the drink, using his reappearance as another excuse to stare at her cleavage. Mary Lou ignored his gaze and focused on the job at hand. She positioned herself at a table next to the glass frontage. This gave her an excellent vantage point to survey the street.

For an hour she sat and let the world go by. Couples holding hands wishing their lives away, businessmen pounding the sidewalk as they rushed to make more green. Housewives scooping brown bags in their arms, brimming with provisions. They all hustled past, but no one appeared of any interest to her.

On the other side of the street stood a restaurant and out front were four tables. Three were occupied and she saw a small upside down V-shaped notice at the empty setting. People came and went, but that table remained untouched. This absence was only a happy accident when Mary Lou first sat down, but now the lunch trade began to arrive and there was no obvious reason to hang onto prime real-estate unless it was reserved for someone special.

He arrived at twelve thirty along with two associates. How could she tell? One guy rested his haunches and the others stood, looking away just like guards do. The other clue was that these three fellas wore gray suits with a vest. The only dudes on the street sporting such attire: mob through and through.

She put her coffee back on its saucer and stared. Twenty seconds later and the waiter came forward and leered again.

"Is everything okay?"

Mary Lou nodded and let him beam down at her cleavage some more. His gaze was less important to her at this point than her keeping complete command of the vista before her. She rested her eyes on the main man as he placed his order and a glass of red wine was presented shortly after. Five minutes later and he tucked into what looked like a bowl of fettuccine.

While she froze in her seat, Mary Lou failed to notice a simple fact about the man chowing down on his pasta: his blond mane. Now she stared for an extended period, her attention drifted from his actions to the environment. Something was amiss, but she couldn't say what. Then it struck her—he was far too young to be a capo. And then the hair.

Her eyes flitted from one part of the street to the next as she realized she'd wasted so much time on the wrong person. Pentangelo might have gone straight past her and she wouldn't have seen. Damn. Goddam it!

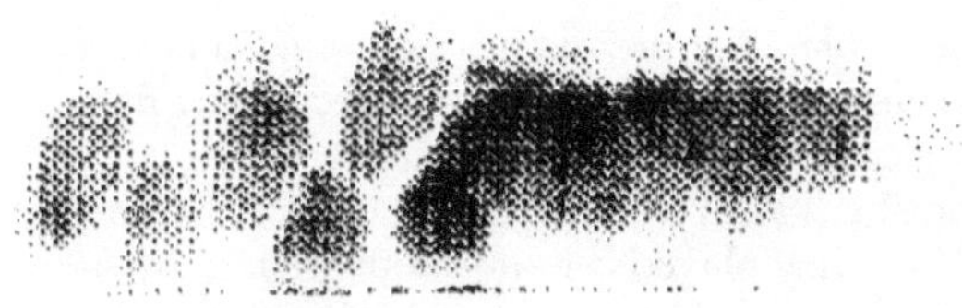

35

THE GRIM REALITY of her ruined time fell on Mary Lou's back and her shoulders slumped.

"You all right? You're looking mighty pale. Sure I can't get you something? Another coffee or a small grappa?"

"Huh? No, I'm fine, thanks. All I need is the check when you have a chance."

Calmness personified, Mary Lou left a five spot and walked out the cafe with one thing on her mind: to find Charlie Pentangelo. She waggled her tush along the sidewalk, hoping her presence as a stranger would be ignored in favor of her physical assets. And she wasn't wrong. The women looked straight through her and the men kept their minds on anything apart from her face—just how she wanted it.

Four storefronts further on Hester, Mary Lou stopped, opened her purse and pulled out a compact mirror and lipstick. For no obvious reason, she stared at her forehead, eyes, cheeks, lips and chin in the circular reflection. Then she put the objects back in her bag and removed a pack of cigarettes and a box of matches. After six, no seven, attempts, she kept the flame alight long enough to ignite the end of her smoke. A deep inhalation and she continued down Hester.

Anyone who knew her in Manhattan would have known what she was really up to. Mary Lou was certain Pentangelo was based within one or two buildings from the corner of Hester and Mulberry—unless Arnold was misinformed. As she'd gone so far west, she reckoned Pentangelo must have been behind her. The mirror proved her right. Like all great capos, he was flanked by two well-dressed goons and sported a gray flannel suit with the jacket nuzzling defiantly around his shoulders.

By messing about with her cigarette, she gave him enough time to overtake her. Then they played cat-and-mouse along the sidewalk as he crossed there and back, grabbing an orange off a stall and talking with a storekeeper a little further on. All the while, his two gorillas stood only three feet away from him.

As she and Arnold thought: there was no way to plug him and flee the scene without getting a slug from one or both heavies. When they walked past, she noticed the bulge in their jacket pockets, reflecting the exact position of their revolvers. They'd be high caliber—massive power to be unleashed with a thunderous clap.

They continued along Hester until Pentangelo headed south onto Baxter. Mary Lou kept walking in case the goons were getting twitchy. When she reached the far side, she turned south remaining on the opposite sidewalk for two hundred feet. The three men stopped and Pentangelo spoke in hushed tones. His mouth was inches from their ears: nobody would hear his instructions other than the intended recipient.

They nodded and one walked back north. The other stayed with Pentangelo as he disappeared into a doorway. Mary Lou wanted to follow straight inside, but she knew she had to deal with the pinstripe gorilla first. There was no point entering the lion's den if an army was about to be brought in behind her.

Instead, she leaned against a building window as if she was feeling faint, but this was New York so nobody came to help. She watched Pinstripe retrace his steps back to the corner and then he stopped, planted his feet into the paving slabs and waited.

He made everybody walk round him—he plain didn't care. And he was sufficiently well known by most locals that they shifted away from him before they needed to. The man's reputation preceded him.

What was he doing? Who was he waiting for? Two minutes later and the mystery was resolved: a woman appeared holding a bunch of flowers—white, purple and an unusual shade of brown. The goon put his hand in his pocket and pulled out a roll of green. Far too big an amount to be carrying on the New York streets but that didn't seem to be bother him. Cash handed over, he took ownership of the blooms and headed into Pentangelo's building.

Mary Lou waited a short while before making any move. The last thing she needed was to go through the front door only to be met by Pentangelo and his gorillas coming straight out. So doing nothing was the best option, but this wasn't one of Mary Lou's strengths. Her desire to get the job done gnawed at her stomach, but she held firm and made sure her feet remained glued to the sidewalk.

She tried counting slowly to ten, but that took only a few seconds. Another cigarette and she let it burn through without one inhalation. That was five minutes clear and she could wait no longer. A uniform cop walked his beat past her and she waited some more for him to make his way down the street. When he was four hundred feet away, she jaywalked over to Pentangelo's entrance.

Now the first decision of significance for the assassination of Charlie Pentangelo. To go in the front or take a different route inside? Every instinct told her to follow the plan and walk straight in, but part of her wanted sneak round the back and get in some other way.

Arnold's words echoed in her head: they won't suspect a pretty broad with a sob story. Anyone else will be met with a hail of bullets. That sealed Mary Lou's fate as she strode to the front door and pushed it aside, entering the foyer in one swift motion. No matter what happened later, there was no turning back.

MARY LOU SQUINTED in the half-light, trying to get a feel for the first floor interior. To her right, immediately next to the entrance, were a row of mailboxes. The lobby was unassuming and small: only twenty feet by twenty. An elevator door, paired brown to match the walls, stood facing her and to the right was a sign showing the stairs.

The elevator system was modeled on an art déco design with a dial containing numbers from one to six and a needle pointing at the digit representing each floor. As Mary Lou examined the dial, she witnessed the arrow leave number four and start its return to one. She braced herself and sprinted for the stairs. No sooner was she hidden behind the stairwell door than the elevator opened to reveal… nobody.

The cockroach by her feet heard Mary Lou exhale and she returned to the lobby. The insect scurried back into a dark hole in the skirting. She stood in front of the open bronze door, sighed and stepped inside. A finger pressed 'four' and the doors slid shut. Several deep gulps of air and she clutched the strap of her bag. The next minute would dictate the shape of the rest of her life.

A whir and a clunk as the machinery weaved its magic spell and hauled Mary Lou up to the fourth floor as she undid another button on her blouse. The box juddered to a halt and screamed open to reveal an ordinary corridor with small apartments scattered behind the row of doors before her. The two gorillas stood either side of a particular doorway and Mary Lou knew she'd found her quarry.

She shimmied over to the nearest gorilla and looked up at him. As she approached, his eyes bore down on her breasts and upper legs and—against her will—a warmth spread across her cheeks. While she was annoyed with herself for reacting that way, she understood how it played well for her conversation with him.

"Excuse me, but I need to speak with Mr. Pentangelo."

"Do you, missy?"

"Yessir. It's on a mighty delicate matter."

Mary Lou sent her eyes downwards and she placed her free hand on her belly, immediately over her rose tattoo. She stroked it twice and left it on her stomach, implying there was something beneath her palm she needed to keep safe.

Now it was the gorilla's turn to change to a shade of red and he looked at his colleague, who'd been stood on the other side of the doorway and had observed everything, but without moving one iota of his body.

"Is he expecting you?"

Mary Lou sashayed over to the other guy and ensured she straightened her back when she halted within two feet of him to afford him the maximum opportunity to eye up her cleavage. The strategy worked because the next four seconds he said nothing and just stared. During this enormous gulf of time, the first gorilla ogled from the side. His gaze burned the sides of her breasts and the point on her thigh where her miniskirt ended. All part of the plan, but it still made her feel dirty, used and then angry—very much not part of the plan. To succeed, she must play the game cool. Cool as an ice cube.

She shifted weight from one foot to the other and that gave both gorillas another opportunity to enjoy the view some more. Mary Lou picked off some imaginary fluff from the gorilla's jacket and smiled at him, feigning nerves.

"Do you think I can see him?"

"You haven't answered our question."

"Huh? What's a girl to do? I'm so confused."

"An appointment. Do you have one?"

Mary Lou detected an edge to his voice, like suspicions were growing inside his pea-sized brain. Stay calm. Stay cold.

"I'm afraid not. You see, I've just received some shocking news and I came straight round to seek help. And justice."

As she uttered the last two words, she put her hand back on her stomach and implied a connection between the baby in her belly and some wrongdoing. Had she drawn enough dots for this lunk to see the implicit picture she painted?

Perhaps her nervousness was conspiring against her, but at that precise moment, Mary Lou noticed a shifting of the steel touching her groin. If that snub nose moved any more then it would land on the floor and she'd be dead in less than three seconds.

Good news was that her genuine anxiety played right into her hand. The two goons huddled and whispered to each other for half a minute.

"Wait here."

The one she had first spoken to took her shoulder and pushed her back to the other side of the corridor. A firm but gentle move. No aggression or anger: she wasn't a perceived threat. The pistol shifted again and some piece of metal cut into her flesh. Mary Lou gritted her teeth and hoped this would all end soon. Like real fast.

The other goon opened the apartment door and slithered inside. She leaned against the wall and pushed one knee in front of the other to appear coquettish and to change position and shift the revolver to a more comfortable location. Mary Lou made sure she didn't make eye contact with the dude. A woman in her state would be too embarrassed to look this guy directly at him.

A painful minute stretched to eternity as they waited in silence for a decision from the high priest inside. Finally, the door opened and the goon slithered back out.

"You're in luck. He'll listen to what you have to say."

"Oh thanks."

"I done nothing, lady. It is the big man eating his lunch, you should thank."

"Now we gotta search you. It's the rules, see?"

A lascivious grin took over the first gorilla's expression as he stepped one pace toward her. Mary Lou knew this moment would come and braced herself for its passing.

Plump fingers fumbled over her sides and lingered on her breasts far too long, but she said and did nothing. Much worse had happened to her in the past and if she survived being frisked, then she'd get to Pentangelo. Those sweaty hands stopped mauling her chest and continued on their journey to her stomach and then made their way to her back. This meant he stepped inches from her face so he could reach and she inhaled his stale breath.

Last, he kneeled down with his head by her groin and patted down her legs. Right one first, working from her foot up past the hem of her skirt. Her muscles tensed slightly and his grin appeared to tighten on his face some more. Five inches further and she knew he'd touch the steel of her piece.

Then the fingers swapped legs and he stroked the inside of her thighs before heading to her left foot. All the while, she said nothing and let him find what little pleasure he could in what Mary Lou hoped would be the final minutes of his life.

"She's clean."

"Not that clean or she wouldn't be seeking a meet with Charlie."

Both men laughed and, for a second, acted as though she wasn't there. Then one opened the door for her and Mary Lou entered the lion's den.

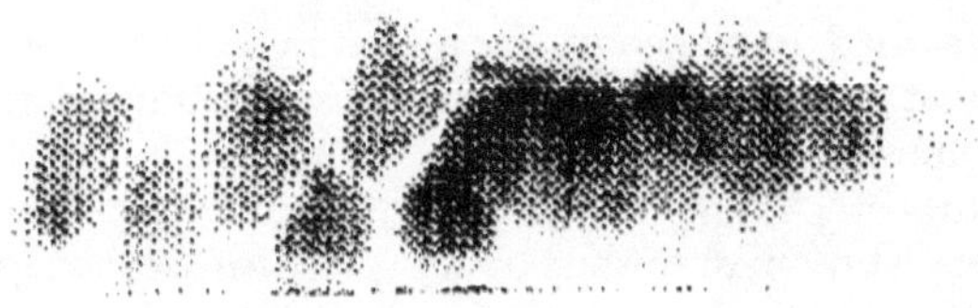

36

ARNOLD STRAPPED HIMSELF into that sweatbox of a car for four more hours. He convinced himself that taking too many breaks would just delay the arrival time, but halfway through and the sweltering heat became too much to bear and he forced the vehicle to park outside a nondescript diner.

There was little to speak of inside either, but Arnold selected a booth underneath a ceiling fan and ordered a jug of water with a glass of ice—and a bite to eat. When the steak and fries arrived, he asked for a coffee too. No matter how hot he felt on the outside, he knew the brew would refresh him. There was nothing like a steaming cup of Java.

He hit the head and walked back to his car, wiped the sweat off the driver's seat and stepped inside. Within seconds he was as drenched as before he entered Dexy's Diner.

"Fucking Californian highways."

Arnold's foot hit the gas and he carried on towards his least favorite city in America. Why LA? It had no heart—there was nowhere you could be in the middle. Just an endless series of ghettos interspersed by nothing. And if that wasn't bad enough: there was Hollywood. The immense wealth surrounded by an ocean of poverty. He was no Communist, but he didn't think people should earn that much money without breaking into a sweat— like he did.

Twenty years before, he'd have been a member of Murder Inc, the mob outfit that resolved all family conflict. They were paid a good wage, but nothing too crazy. As a gun for hire, he commanded an A-list fee for his services—and earned every penny. The reason his clientele kept coming back for more was that he knew how to handle himself in times of trouble and he was a ruthless murderer.

The outskirts of LA came into view and Arnold stopped at a diner. Straight to the washroom to freshen up and a change of shirt from the trunk. Next he headed off to the Watts district in the south and into the center of Mendoza's territory.

He parked in the first lot he came to—the advantage of using a false name on a car rental. If he never saw the damn thing would be a day too soon. Arnold vowed to himself an empty promise: to not be so cheap the next time he drove cross country.

A walk around the nearby blocks revealed the hopelessness of the local youth. They had few options: leave to find their American dream away from their friends or join a gang. Most chose the latter and any who took the first route were long gone.

Inside a dive bar, Arnold hugged a beer and waited. He knew he'd promised Mary Lou to get the job done today, but his vast experience told him it might take several days to find Mendoza. He kept his ears open and his mouth shut, allowing everyone to ignore this stranger in town. The trick was to choose a table near the counter but not to sit on a highchair, because you were bound to steal the silently reserved seat of a local barfly.

Arnold sat, sipped and waited. His patience was rewarded in less than three hours when two dudes grabbed a brew each and talked. As the height of the beer reduced in their glasses, conversation moved onto the day's affairs—instead of pissing and moaning about their women.

"Sancho's got a bee up his ass."

"Any reason?"

"Trouble in Palm Springs."

"What went down?"

"Murder and mayhem from what I've heard. He's on the warpath—demanding heads on plates."

While most would think this chance encounter was way too unlikely to happen within Arnold's earshot, he hadn't picked the venue at random. Roach was well aware the Crew Inn was the Mendoza gang's bar of choice for a late lunchtime drink: he'd dropped a dime when he first reached town. The only thing left to do was to figure out the man's location. Arnold sipped and waited for the golden nugget.

Sure enough, less than one beer later, the men had spilled Mendoza's hole in the ground. Although he was planning to hit the mattresses as soon as he could, he'd done the rounds of his main labs before sending out his goons to wreak merry revenge on Mary Lou and Milton.

Arnold remained in his seat even though he needed no more from the men. He'd learned not to make himself visible when doing nothing could help him vanish into the ether. If no one saw him leave, then chances were that he was never drinking at the Crew Inn at all. Roach spent his life ensuring he had no witnesses to report on his whereabouts to the cops or to the mob. This helped him stay alive despite his vocation.

Fifteen minutes after the two men left, he stood up and exited the bar. It was time to pay Mendoza a little visit.

ARNOLD CHECKED THE address twice and stared at the house in front of him. The right place for sure. He continued past the corner plot to see how many guys were protecting the joint. Two on each side and an unknown number in the backyard. Plus an even bigger quantity inside—they were processing heroin and Mendoza was not a one-man band.

He carried on walking up a block until he figured the goons stopped looking at him. Then he leaned against a tree and took stock of the situation. The chances of Mendoza being indoors were very high. The probability of Roach getting in the building, killing Mendoza and exiting safely was exceedingly low. So he needed to not think about how to get in, but should concentrate on what to do until Mendoza came out.

From his vantage point, Arnold had a good view of the exit routes from the house, so he could react quickly whenever Mendoza appeared. The issue he had now was that an ordinary Joe doesn't hang near a tree for hours in the Watts district of South LA. No civilian would dream of doing something that stupid. He'd need some camouflage if he didn't want to be spotted.

Squatting in a bush was not Arnold's style and he looked round the vicinity for inspiration. While the street was residential, not every house was occupied if the boarded-up windows were anything to go by. Arnold counted buildings and walked away from his tree and went to the back of the houses on the other side of the road to Mendoza's.

A property diagonally opposite the target had windows made of either broken glass or wooden beams. The chances of any legitimate occupiers was low, but he was still careful as he jimmied open the back door using a piece of metal lying in the backyard.

Inside was dark due to the boarded-up windows and Arnold wasn't stupid enough to flip a switch. The art of surveillance was to see but not be seen. To watch and not be noticed. Ideally, you should be able to take a clean shot at a target and get away, but Arnold was less sure this was the right location for the hit itself. He might be completely hidden, but there were a lot of fellas on the other side of the street. All way too close for comfort.

He stumbled his way to the front of the house and struggled to view the staircase well enough to know the upstairs floorboards were safe. Not wishing to take any unnecessary risks, Arnold found his way to a front room with two rectangular windows. One was filled with wood and nails and the other was a gaping hole where glass once lived.

Arnold hunkered down so his head was at the height of the base of the window: his eyes could see out but almost all of his body was hidden by the brick wall. A perfect spot. He glanced at his watch and saw it was nearly two. Chances were Mendoza wouldn't show until evening. Arnold wished he'd eaten something before coming over here. He felt ill-prepared for the afternoon's wait. He cupped his hands and lit a smoke, just as soldiers did in the trenches back in the day.

The second hour was always the easiest, he found. Arnold took a while to get comfortable and not notice the conditions surrounding him. Only then did he occupy the right headspace to last a tedious amount of time.

He twisted his wrist so he could view the face of his watch. Nearly four and nada. Another stare out the window. The goons out front had swapped with fellas from inside about thirty minutes before and that was the only excitement since Arnold had sat down. If this was a normal day's business then Arnold would have contained his impatience. Almost all his working life was spent sitting and doing nothing.

This time things were different: there was no payoff, only revenge. But this wasn't his vengeance—he was merely the agent of death. Arnold knew the real difference was that now he cared. Mendoza deserved to die for kidnapping the twins. Just not right to steal children because a drug meet didn't go his way.

Times were changing—for the worse. He couldn't decide if it was the immense profit that came from the white powder which caused bad decisions or if the caliber of fella was going downhill, anyway. Probably a mix of the two: easy money can be made if you're able to get bankrolled. And a fast buck attracts the wrong dude to the business. It spirals from there, he mused.

As these ideas permeated his thoughts, Arnold continued to stare out the window. The front door opened a crack and three men appeared. Two were dressed like locals but the one in the middle had a three piece suit and wore an air of superiority: Sancho Mendoza—kiddy kidnapper.

Arnold stayed put until he was certain which route they intended to take. Then he slithered out the back and caught up with them, remaining a safe four hundred feet behind at all times. He lost count how many blocks they walked down but he had to catch himself because they stopped. Looked like a restaurant and Mendoza went in, leaving one guy at the front entrance. Arnold guessed the other went to the rear to secure the venue without having to cramp Mendoza's appetite while he ate.

He lit another cigarette and eyeballed the joint before making his move. He walked up to the place and entered, careful not to brush past the goon waiting for Mendoza. For someone whose job was to keep Mendoza out of harm's way, the guy failed at his first opportunity to earn his wages for the day.

Roach, professional assassin, took a table ten feet from him and ordered a steak. He was hungry and after he murdered Mendoza, he'd have no time for food until he had left the city. And he wasn't prepared to wait that long.

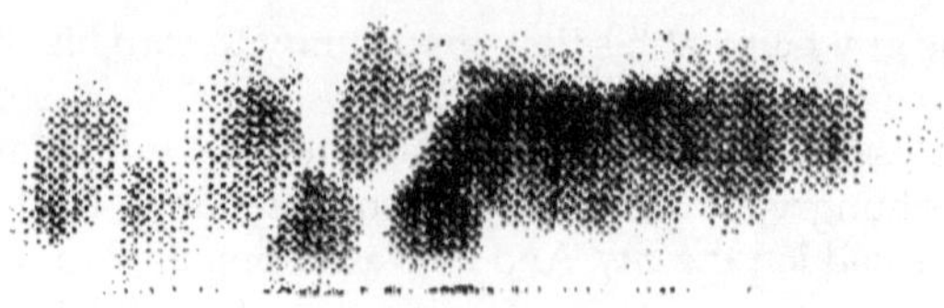

37

LINGUINE, POSSIBLY WITH clams, was plonked in front of Mendoza. He tucked his napkin into his shirt collar and stuffed pasta into his mouth. Before Arnold had time to chew more than a handful of bites, Mendoza's bowl was empty and he mopped up any remaining sauce with pieces of bread. He almost looked Italian.

Arnold glared at his steak and raised his gaze to keep watch on Mendoza. A bus boy removed the dish and two minutes later, a waiter delivered a dessert menu, which his prey perused and threw down. He couldn't tell if he would have time to finish his meal or rush out the door with his stomach more or less empty and Mendoza very much alive and back surrounded by his protection detail.

The answer came from a moment's conversation with the waiter and the subsequent delivery of a cup of coffee and some cutlery. Arnold breathed easy and set about attacking the meat waiting under his nose. It was on the chewy side and if he hadn't been working, he'd have sent it back. The fries were okay and the ketchup helped him swallow the gristle served alongside them.

A portion of apple pie with a miniature jug of cream was delivered to Mendoza, who drowned the pastry with the white liquid. Here was a man who did not eat for pleasure, just for fuel. Arnold finished picking at his steak and asked for a coffee and the check. That way he could leave whenever he needed without making a scene or having to rush.

Powder

As he sipped the hot colored water, Roach saw Mendoza for what he was: a street punk made good, funded by the mob, but with no style to call his own—another goon in an ill-fitting suit, selling dreams down the river in small packets containing a little brown powder.

The three-piece stood and headed to the back of the restaurant. For a second, Arnold panicked because he thought Mendoza was leaving. A glance at the table showed a bill with no payment. Either he was pulling a fast one —unlikely—or he was about to hit the head.

Arnold got up, making sure he'd left a big enough tip—not so generous for him to be remembered and not so tight to be recalled when the cops came calling. Twenty per cent and not a penny more. He wended his way around and past all the tables until he faced a corridor with a pair of signs: men and women. He opened the right-hand door and stepped inside.

The cramped room comprised a urinal, sinks and a pair of cubicles. Mendoza stood next to another guy at the urinal and both doors to the cubicles were ajar. Arnold waited as though a cubicle was an inappropriate place to take a piss. When the civilian finished, Arnold stepped up, barely two feet away from his target.

He ensured his head remained pointing at the wall in front, but Arnold kept his eyes fixed on Mendoza all the time. The man's hands stayed by his groin until the trickling sound abated, the usual jiggling and Arnold heard the zip go up.

Like every man before him, Mendoza turned his back on Arnold as he vacated his position at the urinal. And that was when Arnold Roach struck.

He used one hand to punch Mendoza in a kidney and the other to grab his mouth and yank the head backward. Mendoza lost his footing for a moment, due to the surprise of the attack, but had the presence of mind—or pure instinct—to reach up and cling onto Roach's arm as it reduced his supply of oxygen.

In response, Roach gave him another punch—this time in the small of his back—before moving the fist to Mendoza's face and pinching his nose. He scrambled with both arms flailing, hoping to catch Arnold out or get some purchase on a limb. Roach held firm and pushed his feet into the tiled floor. Then he raised both hands two inches so Mendoza was forced to go on tiptoe to breathe.

That was Roach's mistake, because Mendoza used the opportunity to kick back with a heel into his leg. Despite himself, Roach released him and Mendoza spun round, fists punching. One thump landed on the side of Roach's head, right by the ear, and he stumbled before regaining his balance. Mendoza ran for the door, aware that help was only a few feet away.

Roach slammed his arm into the back of Mendoza's skull, causing it to ricochet into a cubicle door. The three-piece turned round, blood dripping from his forehead and left cheek. He lunged at Roach, who sidestepped and let him crash to the floor. A swift boot to the groin and Roach picked up

Mendoza by the lapels, punched him in the mouth and dragged him to the sinks. With one hand grasping a bunch of hair, Roach pummeled Mendoza's face into a faucet. He screamed briefly but Roach continued until the body fell limp.

He dropped the corpse on the floor, bent down to check the pulse and listened hawk-like for any movement outside. Nothing apart from the clatter of plates and customer conversation.

Roach dragged Mendoza's body into a cubicle, forcing limbs and torso into the narrow confines. He closed the door, allowing the body to fall forward, preventing anyone from discovering the cubicle's dark secret. Roach kicked a hand back under, which was sticking out from the front. He grabbed some towels and attempted to clean up the red mess he'd generated. He checked himself in the bathroom mirror, straightened his tie and tucked his shirt into his pants.

As he made his way through the restaurant, Arnold stopped by Mendoza's table and threw some green down. That way, staff would be even less inclined to go searching as they'd assume he'd paid and went. Or they would hold that belief until someone wanted to have a shit.

He pushed open the front door just as Mendoza's gorilla walked inside. Perhaps his boss had spent longer than normal. Maybe Arnold was paranoid. Either way, he turned left and sauntered down the block, knowing that Sancho Mendoza slept with the fishes.

DOWN THE STREET and Arnold only heard his own footsteps. The echoes engulfed him as he focused on concentrating on not being noticed. Although he had yet to see behind him, Arnold sensed there was something wrong in the state of California.

He pricked up his ears and thought he discerned the clip-clop of leather shoes. Arnold paused, bent down to pretend to tie a shoelace and took a quick look at what was happening. The footsteps had just been a businessman, hot on his heels.

About a block away, Arnold spotted one gorilla hurrying toward him. A second glance revealed the other gorilla four hundred feet behind his colleague. He swallowed hard and picked up the pace, hanging left to cross the street. His jaywalking did nothing and the two fellas kept on coming.

Walking, walking and almost forming a trot, Arnold hurried along the sidewalk, ducking and diving, left and right, hoping to shake his tail. But they remained on his six.

Up ahead, an alleyway and Arnold strode into it and hid behind a municipal dumpster. He squatted and waited, still able to see people passing by the end of the alley. First one gorilla, then ten seconds later, the other fella. He stayed a further twenty seconds, but he had to know if he was free and clear.

Arnold peeked round the corner, gun in hand, but all he saw was a sea formed from the backs of heads. He stood up to get a better view and realized he'd been spotted. The two guys were waiting for him half a block ahead. He reversed into the alley, back pressed against the wall. Think. Think goddamn it!

The alley made an L-shape and the entrance contained the dumpster, some boxes and general waste along with some wooden pallets. He had no idea what was around the corner. Arnold had a handful of seconds to decide and threw himself under the pallets, covering himself with whatever crap he could grab. He lay under there, inhaling the stink, for a lifetime.

After a minute he saw a pair of shoes between the ground and the lowest slat of the pallet lying on top of him. They remained there for four, maybe five, seconds and carried on deeper into the alley. Arnold held his breath and tried to break the laws of Physics by remaining as still as a corpse, while moving his arm to get a clear shot. No can do. By the time his hand was in position, the footwear had gone left and taken their owner further down the alley.

Another minute and no one new had appeared and the first fella hadn't returned. Arnold tried to wait longer, but his overwhelming desire for survival drove him to act. He slithered out from under the pallets. No-show on his man, so he padded over to the corner to see what the dude was up to. Answer: pissing against a wall. Unfortunately for Arnold, he couldn't make it two-for-two as the fella finished before he had a chance to shoot him in the back of the head.

Instead a slug to the heart did the job and the guy crumpled to the ground. He checked the entrance to the alley, but no one was coming. No one had even heard the shot ring out with the din of the traffic. He scurried over to the body, two fingers on the carotid to verify it was a corpse, then he pulled out the wallet and grabbed the green.

Arnold didn't waste time hiding the fella because he wasn't visible from the street anyway. Would take days before even a hobo found the carcass— and by then everyone would know about the hit on Mendoza and do the math.

Back on the main drag, Arnold peered as far ahead as he could, but the other fella was nowhere. Part of him wanted to find and kill the dude and the rest yearned to run away. The chances of the goon remembering his face was low, but non-zero: a decision made. He had to get to the guy before the gorilla got to him—or a payphone.

Arnold figured the best he could do was keep going in the last direction the fella was walking and take it from there—knowing all the while, the guy might jump him at any moment. There's a skill to walking along a sidewalk with the utmost caution while appearing not to have a care in the world. Arnold was a pro.

Three blocks later and the crowd thinned out, giving him a chance to see further ahead. One block up, he recognized the hairstyle of his prey. An increase in pace and he was only two hundred feet behind.

The fella stopped and lit a smoke. Had he made Arnold? Difficult to say. It was a classic move—he'd done it himself that same morning—but the dude might just be a smoker. He pretended to stare at a storefront for five seconds and carried on walking. Without breaking his pace for a moment, he blinked hard because the guy had vanished. Out the blue. Gone. Nada.

He placed a hand on his gun, which he'd put in his pants pocket and took off the safety. He knew the feel of every inch of that piece and achieved the task without blowing his balls clean off. Arnold slowed as he reached the next corner. He headed to the kerb to have the maximum angle as he turned left past the building.

As the new street appeared in his field of vision, so did the fella, who was standing feet apart, gun in hand, aiming directly at him. They both fired at each other at exactly the same time and the guy crashed to his knees. Arnold felt the zing of a bullet and a burning heat in his chest. Then blackout.

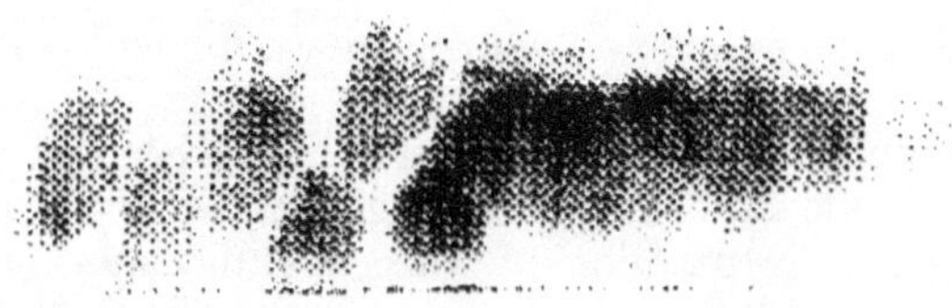

38

AS MARY LOU entered the hallway, she noticed it was festooned with family photographs, young and old, groups and solos. She ignored the blood ties connecting Charles Pentangelo. She didn't care.

A glass door in front of her revealed a mix of colors beyond, but no discernable shapes. She hesitated for a second and pushed it open. The living room contained an array of couches, easy chairs and coffee tables. The red-patterned wallpaper dragged the space down to the size of a postage stamp. At the far end was an eight seat dining table. A man sat with his back to her while the slurping noise of pasta sauce echoed round the apartment. The sound of washing up emanated from a kitchen to the left.

As soundlessly as possible, Mary Lou bent her knees and shoved her hand past her rose and into her panties. Three seconds later, she held her snub nose and had thrown the sanitary napkin to the floor. She flipped off the safety with her thumb. Two hands gripped the gun, arms straight in front as she prepared to take the kill shot.

Pentangelo turned his head ten degrees to the right and she threw both hands behind her back, one finger remaining on the trigger. Without a word, he beckoned her nearer with first and second fingers waving in her direction. The clattering of pans continued in the kitchen and she discerned the sound of running water. A woman's voice hummed to herself.

Keeping her head bowed, she stepped forward until she was ten feet away from the man who ordered the death of her husband and sanctioned her children's kidnapping. Although her overwhelming urge was to fill his brains full of lead, the second part of the plan was for her to escape in one piece.

Mary Lou needed to assess the danger in the kitchen and plug the guy so the gorillas outside didn't suspect a thing. That way, she could walk right past them and vanish on the wide sidewalks of Little Italy.

SHE WAITED TO see what he would do. Without turning his head any further, Pentangelo continued slurping his linguini.

"Come nearer, my dear, so you can tell me your story. My associate tells me you have traveled on a sad path to arrive at my home."

"This is true, Signor Pentangelo."

She let out a tiny sob and ceremonially stepped up a pace, one foot after the other, heels returning next to each other. Second step, then the third. Pentangelo sensed her approach and held out a hand, limp, for her to kiss it —out of respect.

Mary Lou touched the fingers and planted her lips on his cygnet ring. A blood-red ruby set in gold. She thought she would throw up, but she resumed her position, averting her gaze lest the mighty capo incurred any displeasure. The bubbly slurps showed he was relaxed and hungry.

"I met this boy."

"There is always a boy. What is his name and how old is he?"

"Frankie and he's only a few years older than me."

Pentangelo raised an eye to her to gauge her age. This was the first time he'd taken a proper look at her since she'd entered his home. Mary Lou watched his eyes rest on her breasts. This beast of a man was the same as all the others. His brains lived in his dick. He breathed deep gasps of air, and then he resumed his chewing.

"And what happened with this Frankie?"

"We fell in love and he wanted more."

"More?"

"More than I was prepared to give him, at least before we were married."

Pentangelo dropped his fork and spoon into his bowl. Mary Lou tensed, shifting her weight onto the balls of her feet, ready to pounce.

"He dishonored you?"

She let out another sob for an answer to his old-fashioned question. His body was in America but his soul stayed in Sicily.

"Motherfucker."

This word was whispered by one of them, but Mary Lou was unsure if it had been her or him. She could take no chances and knew he had sensed a change in her body language. He swiveled round in his chair just as she took the butt of the pistol and slammed it into the back of his head.

His face hit the pasta bowl, which broke into pieces, and he pushed himself off to snatch at her. Bits of ceramic stuck to his forehead and cheek as he lunged at her, trying to grab at her throat but finding only air. She put the barrel of the snub nose onto Pentangelo's lips, causing him to stop in his tracks. She hissed at him, sulfurous words spat at him, a living embodiment of pure hate.

"My name is Mary Lou Lagotti and you will never forget it. So. Long. As. You. Live."

His eyes remained quizzical and fearful. Then a flicker of recognition and the same orbits widened in understanding and acknowledgement. She pushed the barrel between his teeth and into his mouth. Now he could only breathe through his nose. Small bubbles appeared at his nostrils and she enjoyed hearing him pant his short gasps.

"You finished yet, Charlie?"

A muffled voice from the kitchen. Mary Lou assumed the woman had been a cook, but the familiarity of the question meant she must be his wife.

"Will she come in here?"

Mary Lou's spittle landed on an eyelid, but Pentangelo's expression showed he had no clue. He glanced at the door and back to Mary Lou.

"Don't…"

"I don't care about your wife. If she stays out of my business, I'll stay out of hers."

His widened eyes relaxed slightly and a tear departed his right eye. He gulped. They both heard the squeak of the doorknob as Mary Lou squeezed the trigger. With all the stress of getting into the apartment, she had forgotten about not having a silencer.

Charlie Pentangelo's body flung itself onto the floor, blood splatter landed on the ground before the corpse arrived, and also hit the dining room table and the red wallpaper behind. There was no need for a second shot and Mary Lou knew this before the capo hit the deck. She moved her arm a quarter turn to face the kitchen.

A woman's hand reached out the door and Charlie's wife stood there, staring at his carcass. She pissed herself immediately and remained still, whimpering.

"Go into that kitchen and stay there for ten minutes. If you come out before then, I'll fucking kill you too. Capiche?"

The frightened mass nodded and slunk back, shutting the door behind her and began sobbing as soon as the door shut. She hurried to the hallway and listened for the gorillas. Despite the retort of the revolver, they hadn't moved from their positions. She peeked out the fish eye to make certain: nothing. For the first time since she entered the apartment, Mary Lou heard the radio blasting an opera. How had she not noticed? It didn't matter. What counted was getting out here alive. She checked herself in the mirror and opened the front door.

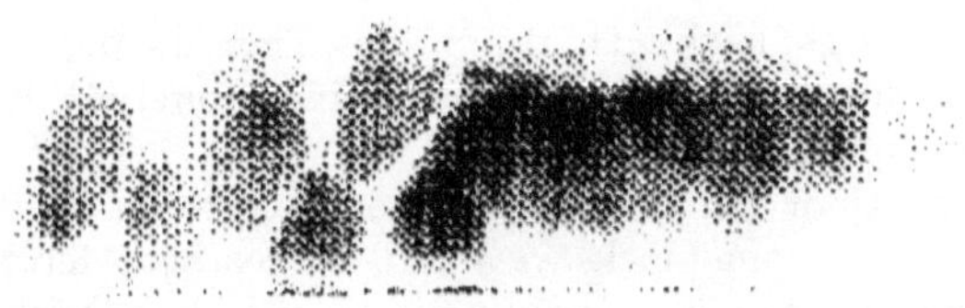

39

WITH THE REVOLVER in her clutch bag, Mary Lou smiled at the two men, both of whom had their arms crossed and stared at her, eyes darting between her cleavage and thighs. She couldn't help feeling as though they were comparing her skirt before and after, but she convinced herself this was paranoia on her part.

"Everything sorted, little lady?"

Mary Lou glanced downwards as if embarrassed by what had transpired in the apartment.

"Yes, thank you. I'll be able to sleep easy tonight."

"Pentangelo is a miracle worker."

"He sure has set my mind at ease. The man knows how to make a girl smile inside."

"Certainly does."

The speaking gorilla winked at his silent partner, who replied with a dirty grin. Mary Lou stepped over to the elevator and pressed the down button. While she waited, she moved sideways so she could continue to hypnotize the man with her breasts. It worked and the longer she stood there, the more engrossed they became. When the doors eventually opened, the nearest gorilla popped his head inside and selected the lobby for her. He seized the opportunity to place a hand on her ass before removing himself from the elevator.

Using all her self-control, Mary Lou smiled at him as the doors shut and she felt the jolt of the descending mechanism. She stood in the lobby to check it wasn't going straight back up to the gorillas. Then she popped round to the stairwell to listen for footsteps. Silence—apart from the tiny scuttling of cockroaches and other bugs.

Out the front door and a flick of her head backwards. On the street, Mary Lou strode four long blocks west until she reached Mercer and Grand. Then she hopped a cab to Fifth Avenue and scurried into the first women's boutique she found. She grabbed a pair of black slacks and a cream blouse. Brown jacket. All paid with cash.

To not draw attention to herself, she walked north half a block and went into a different shop to try on any random garment. When she left the changing rooms, her old clothes were in the shopping bag. The purchased items were draped on her body. Mary Lou sauntered along one of New York's most famous roads until she reached a trashcan. She threw in her skirt and kept on going. Each trashcan she came across ended up containing an additional object from her bags. After five blocks, the bags were empty and, at the next trashcan, Mary Lou dumped them too.

Another taxi ride took her to Wall Street and she disposed of some pieces of her gun. Two more blocks trudged and Mary Lou got rid of the rest of the revolver. Over Broadway and waited at the corner of Trinity and Rector for a cab to take her to LaGuardia.

She kept her eyes on the road in the hope of willing a taxi to appear, but this was New York and not Hicksville, Tennessee. Before long, the periphery of her vision filled with possible goons. Even though she had been extraordinarily careful, the fear of getting caught hung over her imagination.

"I hope Arnold is doing okay."

A shiver ran down her spine as she imagined Sancho Mendoza still breathing. She twisted her head right, then left. A suit on the other side of the street was looking at her funny. Had he made her? Did she recognize him, even? Don't think so and no—in that order. A woman brushed past her and crossed the road to meet him. Paranoia. Focus on getting a cab.

Half a block south, on her side of the street, a man sauntered toward her. Mary Lou thought something was hickey, but couldn't be sure. As he approached, she noticed a lump in his jacket breast pocket. Four hundred feet… three hundred. He raised his arm and shoved his hand into the bulge. Mary Lou couldn't take the chance and turned around to walk away. Headed west and picked up the pace, ducking into the entrance of an apartment building. He was still behind her. Nearer now, so he'd increased speed too.

She'd been so careful. Where had this fella come from? No time for that. She ran west until she reached the end of the block. Why had she been so stupid to jettison her only gun? As she sprinted round the corner, he was a mere hundred feet behind. Man, that guy can cover the ground.

A taxi was kerb side and an elderly woman closed the door. It flipped its hire light on and Mary Lou leaped inside.

"Drive, goddamn it!"

The cabbie needed no further instructions: this was downtown Manhattan. As they sped away, she watched out of the rear window and saw the guy stop to catch his breath. She blinked and he was gone.

"LaGuardia. Pronto."

The battered vehicle bumped up a gear, snapped into a pothole, and bounced its way to the airport. In the back of the cab, Mary Lou checked herself and applied some lipstick. This part of the journey should be simple, she had thought, but now they could get to her anywhere in the city. They'd acted so fast. Perhaps the wife had rushed out before her time was up.

As soon as she clutched the plane ticket in her hand, Mary Lou ran to the bathroom and hid in a cubicle until the final minute before boarding. When the announcement for the last call came over the public address, she left the safety of her cubicle and joined the throng—careful to remain on the edge of the crowd. Always checking out every face, every person, who looked like they might be on her flight.

Her stress only abated when the pilot instructed the stewardesses to set the doors to automatic. Even then, she clung to the inflight magazine, but didn't read a single word. Twenty minutes in and the only way to gain any peace of mind was to walk up and down the aisles and assess all the passengers. Everyone seemed clean, so she relaxed and tried to get some rest until Palm Springs.

TUESDAY APRIL 13, 1971

40

MARY LOU TURNED the key in the lock and stepped into the hallway. There was an eerie silence and she feared the worst. She glanced at her watch and saw it was nearly midnight. Up the stairs and a check on the twins: both asleep, Frank snored like a state trooper and Alice unconscious while her butt stuck up in the air.

A skip down the stairs and into the living room to find Bobby. No one there. And where was the new housekeeper? Mary Lou couldn't even remember her name. Did that make her a bad parent? Or a busy assassin? Both. The fine distinction was irrelevant, because the woman was nowhere to be found.

Into the conservatory and a view of the pool. Still nothing. She walked out onto the patio and saw Bobby asleep on a chair. She bent down, touched his shoulder and planted a gentle kiss on his forehead. He stirred and, before he got the chance to rearrange himself, Mary Lou blew in his ear and he woke up with a start.

"What the f…"

"All's good. Only me. The kids are crashed out upstairs."

"Jeez. How long you been back?"

"A minute. No more. Everything go okay here? No trouble?"

"No, it's been quiet. Like my conscience."

"Did what's-her-name workout?"

"Irma? Sure. I sent her up for the night once the kids were in bed."

"And they were safe, right?"

"I told you I would look after them."

"But they are my babies."

Bobby laughed.

"Getting older now. Especially Alice. She's middle-aged before her time."

Now it was Mary Lou's turn to smile.

"Yeah, but Frank Jr is still a little boy."

"Little monkey."

Mary Lou chuckled again.

"And he has your laugh. Was good to spend the day with them though. How was your trip?"

"In, shot, out."

"Trouble?"

"Thought I might have been followed to the airport, but all was fine. Well, I was, but I shook my tail."

Bobby nodded in approval.

"Any word from Arnold?"

"Nothing from him, but Fabio called to say Mendoza was confirmed whacked a few hours ago."

"Did he not have anything on Arnold?"

"Nope. So it doesn't look good."

Mary Lou and Bobby were silent, both contained within their own thoughts. Arnold was dead in all but name. She slumped on a chair of her own and let the unspoken truth settle in their stomachs. The ripples in the water picked up as a breeze increased.

Bobby might not have gone out and killed one of her enemies—like Arnold, but he'd done the single thing no other person had ever accomplished: protected her children with the potential to lose his life. Mary Lou opened her eyes and gazed at the man, lying there in front of her. The creases either side of his eyelids and the folds of his pants near his crotch.

She stood up and took him by the hand and led him indoors.

SANCHO MENDOZA'S WIFE, Constanza waited at home for her husband's return. This regular wait was normal as she never knew when, or if, he would show. He never told her the details of his business affairs, but she was smart enough to never ask. Constanza understood her role was to take care of their children and to prepare food for her beloved Sancho.

When one of his underlings came to the door to inform her that Sancho had been gunned down in a restaurant, the best thing for her to do was don black and find a long veil to cover her face.

While he might have been an average lover and rotten husband and father, Sancho had been a great provider and she was a scrupulous saver. There was a sadness welling up her insides, but her eyes flashed dollars. With the amount of green she'd stashed away over the years, her family would be fine for the rest of her life—or so she hoped.

IN CONTRAST, MRS. Pentangelo knew her husband was dead almost before he hit the floor. The noises from the living room were threatening and vicious. The sound of the gun shot still echoed round her skull. She wanted to remember the face of her husband's killer but she had already repressed the shock of the experience out of her mind. An inevitable end given the life Charlie had chosen. By the time she cowered in the kitchen and tried to hang on ten minutes—as instructed by Mary Lou—tears of grief overwhelmed her. Two minutes into the wait, the front door closed and she knew it'd be safe to come out.

As soon as she saw Mary Lou leave the floor using the fish eye, she burst open the door to reveal the carnage inside. Then she sat in an easy chair whimpering while men zoomed in and rushed out again. What happened for the rest of that afternoon didn't matter to her. Everything was as clear as morning: she was the widow of a capo in a New York mob family and she would want for nothing from now until the day she died.

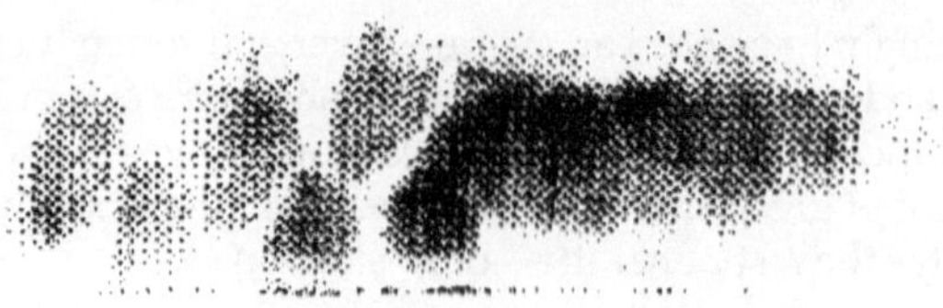

41

MARY LOU STOOD facing Bobby with her back to the bed. She had her family safe, enough money to live out the rest of her days, a man she was prepared to be naked with again. And power that came from the brown powder. She wrapped her hands around Bobby's neck and head. And they kissed. His tongue tasted sweet, and she closed her eyes to capture the moment in her mind.

Then she separated her body from his, unbuttoned her blouse and pulled down her pants. Without a word, she let herself fall back onto the mattress with a coquettish giggle. Bobby smiled, took off his own pants and ripped off his shirt.

He lay on top of her and they kissed some more. Mary Lou's cheeks were warm to the touch, and she thought she might have noticed a tingle at the base of her spine. She placed both hands on Bobby's head and pushed, encouraged and cajoled him downward until his lips were inches below her belly button: right by her rose tattoo. The sensation of his fingers on the inside of her thighs made the tingles shoot up to the nape of her neck.

Images flashed though her mind. Her sweaty body entwined with Frank's until dawn in Miami. Carter tied to her bed in their love nest in Baltimore. Frank lying, head on her lap, as his blood soaked into her skirt by the lockers in Burbank Airport.

Then she snapped open her eyes: Mary Lou told herself to stop living in the past. As that thought flickered in her mind, tingles flowed from her ass to her neck and she allowed herself the luxury of existing in the moment. Of forgetting the pain she'd caused Alice and Frank Jr. Of ignoring the very real possibility the East Coast mob had a hit out on her while she lay on her Palm Springs bed. And pushed away the worries of being part of the mob's heroin trade.

Mary Lou closed her eyes and savored the wet sensation of Bobby's tongue as it followed the path of her rose stem and she gave into the anticipation of pleasure. She giggled again. Mary Lou Lagotti had found peace and her libido was screaming for some action. In a matter of seconds, those tingles of hers became intense. She sucked in a mouthful of air. Let the good times roll.

THE END

THANK YOU FOR READING!

Get a free novella

Building a relationship with my readers is the very best thing about writing. I send weekly newsletters with details of new releases, special offers and other bits of news relating to the Lagotti Family and Alex Cohen series, as well as information about my stand-alone novels.

And if you sign up to the mailing list I'll send you a copy of the Lagotti Family prequel, The Stickup. Just go to www.leopoldborstinski.com/newsletter-signup-book and we'll take it from there.

Enjoy this book? You can make a difference

Reviews are the most powerful tools in my arsenal when it comes to getting attention for my books. Much as I'd like to, I don't have the financial muscle of a New York publisher. I can't take out full page ads or put posters on the subway.

(Not yet, anyway).

But I do have something much more powerful and effective than that, and it's something that those publishers would kill to get their hands on.

A committed and loyal bunch of readers.

Honest reviews of my books help bring them to the attention of other readers.

If you've enjoyed this book I shall be very grateful if you would spend just five minutes leaving a review (it can be as short as you like) on the book's page. You can jump right to the page by clicking www.books2read.com/powder

Thank you very much.

Leo

SNEAK PREVIEW

In the next instalment…

Zing. Alice first heard a whizzing noise and then felt a sharp movement of air - way before she saw anything. And then it was all too late. She turned to her Mama sat to her left and watched as the woman's head hurtled backward. The red circular mess where an eye once was. The blast of brain and skull that hit the wall. Bobby threw himself on top of Mary Lou to protect her from the assault, but he was far too late.

He lay on his dead wife and Alice hit the deck. Nikolay drew his revolver almost before the bullet flew through her Mama, or so Alice thought. His two colleagues dragged him down to the floor. No one in the room was above window height and there had been no second shot.

"Anyone else hurt?"

One shot, one dead. A professional hit for sure. Worthy of the great Arnold Roach, may he rest in peace. Alice held her piece ready for action and Bobby cradled Mary Lou in his arms, rocking them side-to-side in the first moments of his grief.

Alice glanced at Bobby and looked at Nikolay. Had his gun been out before she heard the zing? Couldn't be certain of anything right now. Events unfolded around her and she felt completely estranged from the world surrounding her. Despite the body lying near feet, Alice didn't believe Mama was dead. She saw it was true but it meant nothing to her. Like the world stopped still and she carried on breathing - only she continued to watch events unfold.

Nikolay's bodyguards edged to a window each and cautiously inched their heads to spot the sniper. Nothing. She watched Nikolay speak to her but heard no words - still trapped in her time-slipped bubble. His mouth moved again but his expression became more aggressive. Angry.

"What just happened?"

"We know nothing of this. My mother's been killed. You think I'd do that? To my Mama?"

Alice found a pistol lying in her hand, which she must have taken out of her handbag. An unconscious action. She glanced round and noticed Bobby had let go of Mama and also held a revolver. Someone would pay for killing her Mama…

Grab your copy NOW at www.leob.ws/mamasgone.

OTHER BOOKS BY THE AUTHOR

The Lagotti Family

The Stickup (Free Prequel Novella)
The Heist (Book 1)
The Getaway (Book 2)
Powder (Book 3)
Mama's Gone (Book 4)
The Girl in the Striped Bikini (Sequel Short Story)

Other Releases

The Case
The Death and Life of Penny Pitstop

Alex Cohen

The Bowery Slugger (Book 1)
East Side Hustler (Book 2)
Midtown Huckster (Book 3 - Due 2020)

ABOUT THE AUTHOR

Leopold Borstinski is an independent author whose past careers have included financial journalism, business management of financial software companies, consulting and product sales and marketing, as well as teaching.

There is nothing he likes better so he does as much nothing as he possibly can. He has travelled extensively in Europe and the US and has visited Asia on several occasions. Leopold holds a Philosophy degree and tries not to drop it too often.

He lives near London and is married with one wife, one child and no pets.

Find out more at LeopoldBorstinski.com.